Danube Delivery

Best wishes from the
Coppers For Kids.

Jan Allan

Danube Delivery

Published by The Conrad Press in the United Kingdom 2021

Tel: +44(0)1227 472 874
www.theconradpress.com
info@theconradpress.com

ISBN 978-1-913567-93-4

Typesetting and Cover Design by: Charlotte Mouncey, www.bookstyle.co.uk
The Conrad Press logo was designed by Maria Priestley.

Printed and bound in Great Britain by Clays Ltd, Elcograf S.p.A.

Danube Delivery

Ian Allan

1

April in Moscow means a little more sunshine and a little less frost, welcome samples of impending spring; but Muscovites are not fooled by watery sunshine, so the fur hats and heavy coats stay on.

Alexei Golovkin shivered and tucked his chin into the woollen scarf spilling out from his fur-collared coat and set a brisk pace towards the Metro station. Striding alongside him was a man with the build of a wrestler and the face of a peasant, but his shrewd little eyes belied the yokel facade.

Keeping his pace, Alexei looked towards his companion and said, 'Peter, it's very good of you to look after me, but I'm a big boy now and I think that I can make a fifteen-minute journey on the Metro by myself. It isn't even dark yet. Why don't you go on home? I'll be fine.'

'Professor, it is a great honour to accompany a distinguished scientist like you. We would be very upset if anything happened to you in our beautiful city. The city fathers would never forgive themselves. I still don't know why you insist on using the Metro during your stay, when we have an excellent Mercedes at your disposal.'

Alexei thought, City fathers? Is that what the KGB are calling themselves now? I wonder how many people swallow that line?

However, he smiled at Peter, 'You know, Peter, I spend most of my time at a research facility beyond Sverdlovsk and the weather there makes conditions difficult, most of the year. It's such a pleasure to walk the city streets and ride on the Metro. I'm only here for a few weeks, so I'll make the most of it. Even professors can enjoy simple pleasures. Don't you enjoy walking, Peter?'

His companion grunted, then said flatly, 'It's not a novelty for me, and we city people prefer travelling in comfort.'

Alexei kept smiling, 'Well we are nearly at the station where you can enjoy the comfort of your beautiful city's beautiful Metro. Will that please you?'

Peter's face broke into a sly grimace, not quite a smile. 'Professor, I think you are making fun of me, but you should appreciate what we are trying to do. Now that Gorbachev and his *glasnost* are destroying the old standards of the Soviet Union, there has been an increase in crime in the city and we must do all we can to protect important guests.'

Protect me from what? thought Alexei. Protect me from talking to real people.

Protect me from telling the world what my real work is - what nonsense!

To Peter he replied, 'Don't take it so personally, Peter. It's spring and I'm in Moscow and I'm happy. Tomorrow night we are going to the ballet, and the following night to a concert. We are making the most of our visit. So, come on, be happy for me, I'm just a country cousin seeing the bright lights.'

Peter glanced shrewdly at Alexei, but said, 'We are all happy that you are enjoying your visit, Professor.'

'Look' said Alexei, 'Tomorrow night we can use your comfortable Mercedes to go to the ballet, if it is available. Do you think that will be possible?'

'Of course, Professor. And if you and your wife agree, we could show you some of the sights on the way.'

'That is an excellent idea, Peter. Katya and I would like that.'

Peter had a triumphant smirk on his face. He was in control of the situation. Alexei maintained his facile smile.

The Metro journey was a genuine pleasure for Alexei. The stations impressed him with their gleaming walls in various attractive types of natural stone and they were always clean and warm after the outdoor chill. He felt like a little boy as he counted the stations: four stops from university on Line One then change at Culture Park to the Circle Line and one hop to Smolenskaya.

Coming out of the station onto Arbat Street, Alexei stepped back into reality. There were still some finely-proportioned buildings here from the days of the Tsars, but further east, towards Arbat Square, the tasteless concrete and glass monuments to Socialist mediocrity increasingly dominated the street.

Alexei and his 'shadow' turned left opposite the Bely House Museum then right into Karmanitskiy Lane, stopping halfway along the pleasant little street at a four-storey house dating from the previous century.

A black Mercedes was parked outside with two bulky clones of Peter sitting inside. They nodded to Peter who turned to Alexei and said, 'You see how we look after your safety, Professor. You and Madame Golovkin have nothing to worry about. Just enjoy your visit.'

'Thank you, Peter.' said Alexei, 'No doubt I will see you in the morning.'

'You can rely on me, Professor.'

I'll bet I can, thought Alexei.

He let himself into the house and climbed the staircase to the second-floor apartment which he and Katya had been allocated for their stay.

The apartment was comfortable in a utilitarian way, furnished with relatively basic Soviet fittings. There were some concessions to progress, like the Japanese-made mini hi-fi system playing Delibes whilst Katya improvised her own interpretation of the Coppelia dance movements.

Alexei watched her admiringly. She was a constant delight to the eye, he thought. A blond western Russian, contrasting with his dark southern roots, she circled the room in fluid motion interpreting the music beautifully. He noted with pleasure how her slightly full body was not the classic ballerina's, but thought, Thank God, I have a real woman, not a bony clothes horse.

Katya laughed with genuine pleasure as she twirled, then came to a halt in front of him. Alexei wrapped his arms around her and they hugged warmly.

They broke apart, and Katya asked, 'How did your lectures go today? Were there many students attending? Did all the girls fall in love with you?', she laughed as she teased him.

Alexei laughed with her, 'The lecture hall was nearly full, and the girls were all half my age and very respectful.'

She put on a soothing look, 'Poor old man; thirty-nine years old and too old to look at the girls anymore.'

Alexei started undoing his tie and looked menacingly at her. 'Let's see if I'm too old for my favourite girl.' He started towards her, slowly and deliberately.

Katya brought her hands to her face in mock horror, 'Help. Who will save me from a terrible fate? I'm too young to suffer.'

8

Then she burst out laughing again, threw her arms around his neck and kissed him full on the mouth. 'I love you, my beautiful old man.'

'Not so much emphasis on the *old*, if you don't mind. I am only seven years older than you, which I don't think is a lot.'

They sat down on the lumpy sofa, and Katya poured coffee from a pot she had prepared for his arrival home.

He looked at her and said, 'What about some Tchaikowsky? We have a tape of his music, don't we?'

Katya understood his meaning. The Delibes tape had ended and she changed it for another. She turned the volume up a little, not so much that it would attract attention, but sufficient for the 1812 Overture to cover any conversation in the room.

As the music gathered pace and volume, she looked at him with a question in her eyes.

Alexei looked serious. He spoke quietly so that the microphones they had discovered in the light fitting and on the curtain rail would not pick up their conversation.

'Things are now moving since our last trip to Moscow. The Canadian girl at the university is my go-between. She has told me that the Americans are serious about our wish to get out. I know that they want my knowledge of the chemical and biological program of the Kamera laboratories, but that doesn't matter to me any more. The future is what matters now, our future and the world's. I will tell them all I know. I want us to have a life where we are free; free from secret police and free to live as we choose. Perhaps even free enough to think about having children.' He smiled at her and raised his eyebrows.

Katya gripped his arm and looked at him, 'Oh Alexei, I dream of that, and I want it to happen soon. But do you know where we will go, and will we be safe? And, more important, will any children we have be safe?'

'My darling Katya, the signs are good. The Americans know all about me. So much for Soviet secrecy. The only people who don't know anything about me are my own Russians. They are talking about protecting us and giving us new identities and ensuring that we have a good life.'

'But Alex, how are we realistically going to get out of Russia? You are always escorted by people like Peter and his thugs. I usually have someone hovering around when we come to Moscow or Leningrad. What will happen to us?'

'I think we will have to trust the Americans. They have considerable experience of these operations. I have given them our plans for the next month and we will see what they can make from them. Tomorrow night, someone may contact me at the ballet. That's the message from the Canadian girl. We must be patient.'

'And we must be careful Alex. The KGB know that you are a valuable prize to the West and will be watching. They might even try a double-cross on you to test your loyalty. I am afraid.'

'I know that and I am afraid too, but I think that will help us to be careful. The Canadian may have some more news for me tomorrow and then we will see what happens. We must be positive and think of the future that lies ahead, the future we have dreamt of.' He smiled at her reassuringly, 'I will do my utmost to ensure that you face no danger. We must wait to hear what the plan will be.'

Katya looked doubtful and distant until Alexei kissed her cheek and said, 'How about some supper for a hungry man.'

Katya brightened and stood up. 'Come on then, let's have some bread and dripping, or would you prefer the goulash I have made?'

'You know what I'd prefer,' he said as he reached out to her.

She twisted away smoothly and laughed, 'After dinner, if you eat it all up.'

2

Alexei kissed Katya and she held on to him a little longer than usual as she whispered in his ear, 'Be careful, my darling.'

He hugged her, then stepped back and smiled before starting downstairs. As he expected, Peter was waiting in the hall.

'Good morning, Peter,' he called cheerily, 'Have you slept well?'

Peter betrayed no emotion as he grunted, 'It's not something I think about, Professor, I just do it.'

Alexei kept up the cheery manner and said, 'Come on then. Let's face the world.'

They stepped outside into sunshine and Alexei stopped and looked around. At the far end of the lane he could see the beginning of a tree-lined area.

'What's along there, Peter?' he asked.

'That's Spasopeskovskiy Lane which widens into a large square, with a fine garden and a statue of Alexander Pushkin.'

'That all sounds interesting, Peter. I think Katya would like to walk round there. You know, Peter, you sounded like a tourist guide, just now,' Alexei teased.

'Professor you are making fun of me again.' But the faint traces of a smile chased across the solemn face.

The Metro journey proceeded like clockwork, with Alexei enjoying the hubbub of urban travel and Peter sitting silent and watchful. They alighted at University Station and walked to the campus. On such a sunny morning, they enjoyed the panoramic view of the city.

Peter left Alexei at the entrance where the ubiquitous Mercedes was waiting with its two bulky occupants. Alexei smiled and waved, but evoked no response. He turned to Peter. 'I should be finished by early afternoon today. Will I see you again, Peter?'

'But of course, Professor, I shall wait for you and we are escorting you and Madame to the ballet tonight, in the Mercedes.'

'Ah yes. We are looking forward to the ballet. Katya loves ballet and music, which I suppose you might expect from a teacher of music and dance. Right, Peter, I'll see you later.'

'Of course you will, Professor,' Peter nodded.

Alexei walked up to the staff room in the Medical Faculty, where he intended to review the notes for his lecture. He should have done this last night, he told himself, but after dinner the lovely Katya completely took his mind away from work. He smiled to himself at the memory and applied himself to the task.

His talk would be on some aspects of virology, a subject he was well grounded in. When he talked of smallpox and anthrax, he could not mention the stockpiles of these pathogens which he had helped develop and produce on the far side of the Urals, nor the more deadly Novichok nerve agents which he felt should never have been developed. There were many things the proletariat did not need to know. The Party knew best.

Suddenly aware of his train of thought, Alexei slowly looked around the room to see if his face had betrayed his thoughts. Two elderly professors were engrossed in a game of chess by a window, and another was scribbling furiously in green ink on what appeared to be a student's essay. Nobody was paying him any attention.

Stay calm, he told himself, Don't spoil everything. Act normal.

Just then the telephone rang at his elbow. He started, then took a deep breath and reached for the phone.

'Golovkin,' he said.

'Hi Professor. It's Anna here,' the girl's voice said in unusually-accented Russian. 'I was reading my notes on your lecture yesterday, and there's a diagram I want to ask you about. I think I may have drawn it wrong. Can I possibly see you before the lecture starts?'

Even with her accent, Alexei thought her Russian was very good for someone from the Canadian prairies.

'Of course Anna, I'll meet you outside the lecture hall in five minutes and we will see what you got wrong.'

'Thanks Professor, I'm sorry to be a nuisance.'

'No problem, Anna.'

Alexei felt his heart beat a little faster. What news might Anna have for him? Controlling his excitement - or was it fear? - he affected a calm demeanour and pretended to have a last look over his notes before slowly gathering his papers together. He walked slowly across the room, stopping to look at the chess game in progress. He smiled to one of the contestants, who nodded back to him, and walked out of the room.

Outside the lecture hall, Anna Vernigora was walking towards him as he arrived.

14

'Good morning, Professor. Can I show you this diagram from yesterday?' Anna smiled as she reached into a folder whilst casually glancing around her. There were a few students passing. She produced a sheet of paper and stood closely alongside Alexei while they both looked at it.

'Someone will speak to you tonight at the ballet,' she whispered, while waving a pencil over the paper as though demonstrating something.

'The code-word will be 'Boxer'. That's all I've been told. And keep smiling,' she added.

His mind in a whirl, he smiled and pointed to the diagram on the paper. 'Is that all you have for me?' he muttered.

Still smiling, Anna replied, 'You must stick to the plan. Remember the code-word "Boxer". That's all I have to tell you. I don't know any more than that.' Then she turned to him and said in a normal voice, 'Now I understand the diagram. I must have missed that detail while I was listening to you yesterday. Thanks Professor.'

She turned and walked into the lecture hall which was starting to fill.

Trying to gather his thoughts into some semblance of order, Alexei followed.

The lecture went without a hitch, though Alexei felt somewhat detached from everything. The words on his notes, the bright young faces in front of him, seemed unconnected with the carousel in his own mind. When he had finished, several of the students approached him, as usual, to pursue points he had made. He was forced to focus his thoughts on their questions and after a few minutes of this found himself surprisingly calm.

He felt reassured that he would cope with whatever lay ahead. He knew that he had to succeed.

Katya had prepared a meal, earlier than normal, in anticipation of their outing to the ballet. As usual, the music was turned up a fraction to counter the microphones listening to their daily lives. As they ate, Alexei quietly told Katya of his conversation with the Canadian girl.

Katya looked worried. 'Can we really trust her? I mean, what do we know of her?'

Alexei spoke softly, 'She is as genuine as I can confirm. There were some queries when she applied for her year in Moscow, especially with a Ukrainian surname. Some of the staff though it might be a practical joke, but she is fourth or fifth genera-tion Canadian, descended from the thousands of Ukrainian migrants who went to make a new life on the Canadian prairies around 1890. I read that they still praise Queen Victoria for allowing them to migrate there, which amused me. She will be our link to a new life. I trust her, and I hope you will trust my judgement, my darling.'

'Alexei, you know that I never doubt you, but you must agree that the future is very worrying.'

'Katya, we must think of the future as very exciting.'

He took her hand and said, 'Yes, it is a bit worrying, I know, and you are right that we must take every care. I recognise your worries about the Canadian girl and that is good. We must be alert to danger and remember that in the Soviet Union of the KGB there are real dangers.'

Katya looked a picture of loveliness in a simple blue dress which complimented her blond hair. Alexei felt like an ugly duckling in his dark suit and red tie - it felt like a uniform.

When they got downstairs, Peter and one of his team were waiting with the Mercedes. Peter forced his face into a smile which softened into something natural when Katya smiled warmly at him and thanked him for opening the car door.

The trip to the theatre should have been interesting, with Peter giving a good commentary on the sights, but Alexei felt fairly tense and had to force himself to take notice.

Their destination, the Bolshoi Theatre in Teatralnaya Square, was a boost to their spirits. The statue of Apollo in the Chariot of the Sun above the entrance was impressive and the white marble staircases up to the spacious first floor foyer gave a feeling of luxury and timelessness.

They took their seats in the beautiful auditorium, and perused their programmes. Alexei couldn't help having a furtive look around, but had the sense to keep a smile on his face to disguise the turmoil he felt. He saw nothing untoward then thought,

What do you expect to see, you fool, someone in an Uncle Sam outfit?

Katya stayed calm and gave him a brief rundown on the impending performance of La Bayadere.

'It's based on some Indian classics. The music is by Ludwig Minkus and the choreography was originally set by Marius Petipa. It was first performed at the Maryinsky Theatre in Leningrad.' She then dropped her voice to a whisper and said, 'When the Kirov performed this ballet in London thirty years ago, Rudolf Nuryev defected to the West. Is that a good omen?'

Alexei looked at her in surprise then leaned over and kissed

17

her gently on the cheek. 'I don't care about omens or lucky talismans. With you beside me, everything is possible,' he whispered.

Katya patted his arm and smiled. Just then the lights went down and the performance started. The magic of the music and dance enthralled them both. When the interval came, they walked out to the bar which was crowded and eventually got drinks.

As they stood chatting quietly and looking around, a group of six people alongside them included them in their discussion about the performance so far. They exchanged pleasantries and the three women in the group engaged Katya in a conversation which ranged over fashion as well as music.

The men's conversation veered from music to the current Gulf War activities then to sport. One of the men, who explained that though he was Russian-born he now lived in Israel, manoeuvred Alexei slightly apart from the others whilst talking about the immediate surroundings.

The man held out his hand, 'I'm David Krawitz. We moved to Israel ten years ago. This is the first return trip for Rachel and me. This bar gets really crowded. I'd forgotten how popular the old theatre is. Did you have to wait a long time for a drink?'

Alexei smiled, 'Not too long, but I did need a drink. It was quite warm in the auditorium.'

'Yes' said David, 'Me too. I looked at the crowd and managed to get my way through quite quickly. 'He smiled and leaned closer,' A bit of fancy footwork; took me back to my days as a boxer.'

Alexei looked at him. The word boxer had leapt out at him. David was looking him straight in the eye.

'Rachel and I are seeing some of the sights tomorrow. There aren't too many Jewish places left, so we are visiting everything that takes our fancy.'

He waved his hand in the direction of his companions and said, 'They have given me a list of places they think are worth seeing. They even gave me some churches to visit. Can you imagine a good Jewish boy like me in a church? I said I'd give them a try because I'm on holiday.'

He leaned closer with a grin as though he were telling a joke and muttered, 'We will be in the Church of the Saviour in Spasopeskovskiy Lane, near your place, about eleven tomorrow morning. Maybe you will be having a look at it too.'

He turned towards the others with a big grin on his face as though he had just told a good story.

The warning sounded for the audience to return to their seats and Katya and Alexei said goodbye to their erstwhile companions.

Alexei said nothing to Katya who was entranced with the music and dance.

When they came out of the theatre, Peter was waiting in the foyer. Alexei wondered where he had been during the performance and what he might have seen. Peter appeared his impassive self, though his expression softened noticeably when Katya smiled at him. She asked if he had seen the performance, but he smiled and shook his head.

She said, 'Oh shame on you Peter. And this was a Russian ballet too. Whatever are we going to do with you?'

Alexei noticed how Peter became almost normal when he reacted to Katya's teasing.

The Mercedes was waiting and they were whisked back to

the flat very quickly.

Once indoors, Alexei put on some music while Katya made coffee. They sat down and she looked at him.

'Tell me,' she said quietly, 'I got the feeling that something was said to you in the bar.'

He repeated the conversation in the bar and said, 'It's very odd. The church he mentioned is just along the street, and it is near to the place Peter was describing to me this morning. Is it coincidence or am I being set up?'

'What did Peter say this morning? You didn't tell me.' Alexei repeated the chat he had with Peter.

Katya thought for a few moments then said, 'You told Peter that I would probably like to see that area, so let's go and do that tomorrow. If this church looks like an interesting place to visit, then that's what we will do. We'll make everything look as natural as possible and play it all by ear. We should watch Peter and see if he acts out of character, because that might give a clue as to whether it's a set-up or not; and just be careful!'

Alexei looked into his coffee for a moment then said, 'I think you're right. That makes sense. We'll play the tourists and see the sights, but try to watch our backs at the same time.'

3

Peter appeared flattered when he was asked to show them Spasopeskovskiy Lane next morning. Katya and Alexei were well wrapped up for the cold weather, and thankful that it wasn't yet raining.

They commented on some of the older houses and when they turned into the square, Katya stopped to admire the impressive old mansion on the far side.

'Peter,' she said, 'Is that beautiful building a museum of some kind?'

Peter wrinkled his nose as though a bad smell had hit him. 'A museum to capitalism, perhaps, madame. That is the American Ambassador's house. They have been there since the 1930s. Too long, I think.'

Katya said disdainfully, 'That house is far too good for them.'

Peter nodded in smiling agreement. Alexei was impressed by Katya's quick and apt response.

She said, 'Come on Peter, tell us what is along this way.'

They entered the garden with the statue to Alexander Pushkin, and a discussion developed on his life and the merits of his work, with which all of them were acquainted. Peter pointed out that the Pushkin Museum was nearby, in Arbat Street.

Katya pointed and said 'What's that building?'

Peter looked and said, dismissively, 'It's a church. The Church

21

of the Saviour I believe it's called.'

'I think we should have a look while we are here,' said Katya. 'How about you, Alexei?'

'It's an attractive building. Do you know how old it is Peter?' he asked.

'I think it is eighteenth century, Professor.' Peter showed a distinct lack of enthusiasm for the church.

Katya grinned at Peter. 'Come on, Peter, it is Russian, but you must promise not to chant any prayers when we go in.'

Her infectious humour forced a lopsided grin from Peter. 'You can count on that, madame.'

The church was not very large, but well preserved with ornate Orthodox decoration. There were a few other people inside. Alexei noticed David Krawitz and his wife, Rachel, nearby. They appeared to be referring to a guide book.

Alexei asked Peter, 'What can you tell us about this place?'

Peter shrugged, 'I am not a believer, so I don't visit these places.'

Katya was looking round and had worked out who David Krawitz might be.

'I wonder if these people would mind me asking for a look at their guide book?' she said, inclining her head in that direction.

Alexei said, 'I'm sure you could charm them, even if they did mind.'

She walked over to them, and after a few words, David Krawitz smiled towards Alexei and Peter and waved them over.

Katya and Rachel had the book between them and engaged Peter in helping them by pretending they did not understand the ground plan of the church. Peter was charmed by the combined attention of the ladies.

David and Alexei had drifted a short distance away and out of earshot. They pretended to be looking at the decor while David quietly spoke.

'Your plans show you are going to Lvov in Ukraine soon.'

'Yes', said Alexei, 'I'm giving a guest lecture to the medical faculty on virology. An old colleague is in charge there and he organised the invitation. The Party approved.'

'Get him to organise another invitation to speak to the medical school in Uzhgorod. Tell him you want to visit the Cemetery of Heroes there. Your father's eldest brother was buried there during the war, and you want to visit his grave.'

Alexei was taken aback but tried to maintain a relaxed expression. 'How did you know about my uncle? My father spoke of him often, and that he died fighting in the Ukraine. I have thought about visiting that cemetery for years.'

David smiled and pointed towards a window admiringly, 'Just listen. Be in Uzhgorod before 8th May, and book into the Verkhovina Hotel. Don't be late, you'll be contacted there and you move on 8th May. Have you got that?'

Still smiling, though his mouth felt dry, Alexei nodded. 'What about Katya, she was not intending to visit Lvov with me.'

'I know. We think Katya would love to re-visit the Hermitage Museum in Leningrad. She will book into the Hotel Neva, remember that, and she will insist on a room on the fourth floor, because her friends have recommended that floor for its views. She will be contacted there, and she will leave simultaneously with you, but obviously by another route. Have you got that?'

Alexei was now in a turmoil. The dream was becoming

reality, and the reality could turn into a nightmare. He turned to face away from Peter in case his face betrayed him and tried to moisten his dry mouth. David Krawitz was looking closely at an icon.

Alexei also looked closely and quietly repeated the bare facts as he remembered them. 'Uzhgorod before 8th May; Verkhovina Hotel. Hotel Neva, Leningrad, fourth floor; visit Hermitage. Is that right?'

David smiled, 'Yes. You've got it. Don't forget any of it. Any hiccups and you can come back to us through the Canadian.'

Alexei looked straight ahead. 'Whatever you do, make sure Katya is safe.'

Krawitz smiled as he continued to scrutinise the icon, 'Follow your instructions and we will all be fine. Tell our Canadian friend when you have made your arrangements.'

They strolled over to Peter and the ladies and joined in the discussion on church decoration.

After a few minutes, Katya and Alexei thanked Rachel and David for sharing their guide book and wished them a pleasant visit to Moscow, then strolled out into the square. Peter did not appear to have noticed anything untoward. Katya had sensed Alexei's tension and took control.

'Right Peter, that was interesting; now where is the Pushkin Museum you talked of. Is it very far, or should we leave it for another day?'

'It's only a few hundred metres madame, in Arbat Street. Even I could walk that far.'

He seemed to be infected with Katya's light-heartedness and was actually smiling.

'Then let's go there, and fill ourselves with culture before we fill ourselves with lunch,' she said, and took Alexei's arm.

Alexei realised what she was doing and forced a smile.

They all enjoyed their visit to the museum; Katya and Alexei because they had not been there before, and Peter who had assumed a rather paternal manner, which they encouraged with their questions, and he genuinely seemed to get pleasure from their enthusiasm.

Back in the apartment, and without Peter, Alexei was able to relax at last. Katya put on the music and prepared some food and coffee, while Alexei slumped back on the sofa with eyes closed and mind whirling.

'Come and have lunch,' she called, 'you look like you need something. It was quite cold out there today.' Alexei nodded and sat at the table where the appetising food soon occupied his attention. Afterwards, he recounted his conversation in the church to Katya, in a low voice whilst the music played. She was very quiet for some time.

'My first reaction is that I had thought we were going together and this plan separates us. However, if we think it through, it might be better this way because you won't be fussing around worrying about me and I won't be there worrying about you. We will have the professionals doing all the worrying for us. Don't you think?' She smiled.

'Katya, you are always the practical one. I think that we will worry about each other anyway, but it might be less of a worry this way. It will still be a really serious concern until it is all over and we are safe.'

'Have courage, my love,' she smiled. 'And we have the concert to look forward to tonight.'

'Of course we have. I was forgetting. What are we going to hear tonight?'

'Tchaikowsky, Shostakovitch and Moussorgsky. Does that appeal to you?'

He smiled, 'Ah, all Russian composers for a change, and one of my favourite nationalists, Moussorgsky.'

'I thought you might approve,' she said.

Alexei smiled at her pleasure, though he still felt troubled. They went over their instructions several times until everything was clear in their heads.

The trip to the concert was similar to Peter's guided tour of the previous evening, and there was no doubt of the Mercedes' comfort. Their destination was the Arts Theatre in Kamergerskiy Lane. Performances here were usually plays - it was famous for Chekhov's 'Seagull' - but tonight was a special performance by a youth orchestra which had been recommended to Katya by one of her teaching colleagues.

They were both dressed less stylishly and more sensibly for the cold evening, in jumpers and trousers, as well as warm coats.

In the interval, after collecting drinks for themselves, they stood slightly apart from the others in the bar.

Katya said, 'Alexei, you must think about your expression. It is so obvious that you have something on your mind. You are going to give the game away.'

'Does it show?' he said, 'I wasn't aware that my worries were so obvious. I keep imagining what perils and obstacles we may face, and it scares me. We are not spies or spetznaz, I hope we can succeed.'

'Look Alexei, we both agreed to go on this path. The new

26

life we have hoped for will be the reward; a reward that I think is worth taking risks for. So we are not special agents? What does that matter? Think of this. You have just enjoyed listening to Moussorgsky's Bare Mountain. That beautiful music was written by a man who was not a professional musician. He was an army officer. If he had followed your argument, he would not even have tried to write music, would he? But he had the courage to see his ambition become reality. I know the circumstances we face are more serious than writing music, but you are a brave man Alexei. To even think about the course we have chosen takes bravery, and I know we will see it through.'

Alexei nodded, 'You are right, as usual. You have bravery enough for both of us. It is silly of me, but my main worry is about how you will cope with the coming difficulties; and it is obvious that you will cope splendidly, as you always do. I care very much about what happens to you, and will worry until the troubles are past and we are together again.' He was smiling now as he looked at her lovely face.

'I know that, Alexei, and it's one of the reasons I love you so much. If you stopped caring, then I would really worry. Let's stop talking about worry. Give me a hug.'

He put his arm around her shoulders and hugged her close.

She giggled and said, 'Hey, I just wanted a hug, not a full scale seduction,' then she laughed up at him teasingly, 'Later, maybe.'

Her laughter was infectious and they wandered back into the auditorium hand in hand and grinning like mischievous children.

The next few days kept Alexei and Katya busy; she by arranging her visit to Leningrad, and he by confirming travel arrangements for his visit to Lvov and, after dropping heavy hints over the telephone to his old colleague at the University there about his long-cherished wish to visit Uzhgorod, he got an invitation, approved by the Party, to speak to the medical faculty at that city's university.

After a long discussion, he and Katya agreed that they should speak openly and as naturally as possible to Peter about their respective travel plans in an effort to offset any suspicions he might have. They felt confident that they had not betrayed themselves, so far. They were equally sure that Peter would be reporting regularly on them to the Second Chief Directorate, so they had to maintain an air of apparent frankness.

Alexei was also involved with his series of lectures at the University of Moscow which had to be completed before the Ukrainian trip. The Canadian girl had made no overt contact since she gave him the 'boxer' password message. He had managed to briefly inform her that the travel arrangements for him and Katya were completed. He felt that she might have more to tell him, but common sense dictated that he must not make any more approaches to her on the matter. That might look like he was panicking, and though he frequently felt his stomach churning at the thought of what they might face, he was determined to try to assess everything logically and keep it all in perspective.

'Fine words,' he said to himself, 'but the butterflies are still spinning around my stomach.'

4

On Thursday morning, two days before his departure for Lvov, he gave his final talk at the University before his projected trip to Ukraine. In winding up his series of lectures, this session was in the form of a review of his previous lectures and an opportunity for the students to query any misunderstandings they might have. The lecture did not last long, and he wished them well before closing.

Most of the students tarried long enough to thank him. The Canadian girl, Anna Vernigora, was the last to speak to him and, after thanking him in a normal tone of voice like the others, quietly said, 'Everything's in place, I've been told, for both of you.'

Then in her Canadian accent, 'Stay cool, Dad,' and laughed.

He laughed too and said in slow careful English, 'I understand enough English to know you are joking with me, young lady.'

She smiled, 'Hey Professor, your English is pretty good, and I guess you ain't so old as your title suggests.'

Alexei laughed and shook his head, 'I think I understand you and I think that was a compliment. Good luck with your studies.'

Some students drifted into the room and Anna said, in Russian, 'Thanks again, Professor, and maybe I'll see you next year if you lecture here again.'

Alexei responded formally, 'That is possible. Good luck Miss, and work hard.' Then he gathered up his briefcase and left.

Peter and the Mercedes crew were waiting for him. He was counting on them being available today, since he had an important call to make.

'Hallo Peter. I'm glad to see you. There seems to be a lot to fit in before I go to Lvov, and your Mercedes beats the Metro today.'

Peter shrugged but did not smile as he said, 'I think the Mercedes beats the Metro every day, Professor.'

Alexei smiled and said, 'No, I'm not letting you win. It's only today, when I need some speed, that your car is best. Any other time I find the Metro quite soothing and therapeutic.'

Peter burst out laughing, 'Professor, you can be so funny sometimes. I don't know of any Muscovite who would describe the Metro as soothing and therapeutic. If I didn't know better I would think you were a country peasant on his first visit to the big city.'

Alexei also laughed and said, 'Well this country peasant, if that's what I seem, knows what he likes. Now we had better get going if I am to keep that appointment.'

Peter nodded and they both got into the car.

As they moved off, Alexei asked, 'How long will the journey take, Peter?'

In a slightly boastful manner Peter said, 'With us driving you Professor, we'll be at the Institute in fifteen minutes.'

Alexei soon realised the truth in Peter's boast. The car sped along the empty central lane of the boulevards, reserved for the Party vehicles, and after fifteen minutes they entered the State Scientific Research Institute of Organic Chemistry and

Technology, sometimes referred to as *Biopreparat*, where some of the most advanced biological warfare programmes in the world were undertaken.

Once his identification had been examined, Alexei was welcomed by a smartly dressed young lady who introduced herself as Valentina without explaining her position in the establishment. She welcomed him on behalf of General Kuntsevich, the director, who was away on Party business, then conducted him to a small conference room where five men were already seated. She introduced him then left.

He nodded towards Mirzov whom he had met the previous year and to Fyodorov whom he recognised and knew by reputation.

The discussion began, but a pattern developed where Mirzov and Fyodorov did most of the talking. The main thrust of the discussion was on limiting peripheral pollution of the atmosphere and countryside around the various establishments involved in the *Biopreparat* programmes.

Alexei noted the diplomacy of the main speakers in their delivery. They did not castigate their Party masters openly, but stressed the responsibility which they themselves as scientists should accept in attempting to contain collateral pollution.

In his briefcase Alexei had a list of readings he had taken at his establishment after Mirzov had privately requested him so to do. He passed the data to him at the close of the discussion. Mirzov thanked him and asked how his visit to Moscow was going. Alexei chatted for a few moments whilst Mirzov discreetly looked around them.

When there was nobody in earshot, Mirzov whispered, 'Is the *Novichok* production going ahead; the nerve agents?'

Alexei drew in a sharp breath and looked at his companion. 'You are asking an impossible question. You know I cannot answer it.' he muttered softly.

Mirzov smiled slightly and whispered, 'I think you just answered me.'

For Alexei the meeting did not really break any new scientific ground. What it did achieve was to confirm that he was not alone in his concerns about the long-term effects of the work they were all involved in. It was obvious that, outside the monolithic confines of the Party, consideration for humanity still existed amongst real Russians. Unfortunately, that consideration still could not be openly expressed.

His brief conversation with Mirzov had unsettled him. Knowledge of the Novichok production was kept so secret that most of the Politburo had been kept in the dark. Where had Mirzov's information come from? Was it a test question? Just how much did he know?

The United States Embassy occupied the western side of Grosvenor Square in London, overlooking the pleasant central garden with its memorial to President Franklin D. Roosevelt.

Regional Security Officer Jack Bergen looked across the desk at Harvey Fletcher who had been seconded to the embassy as Jack's deputy for the operation.

'All the invitations to the party have been accepted, Harvey. This time next week we'll know if it's been a success. Our man flies down to Lvov and his wife to Leningrad on Saturday. Our teams are waiting to slot into position at the right time, to brief them and to help them out.'

Harvey grinned at Jack, 'You know, you really come alive

when you're involved in one of these operations. You look like you're really enjoying yourself.'

Jack shook his head. 'Wait till next Thursday, and I'll tell you if I'm enjoying myself. When the right messages come in, then I'll enjoy myself.'

Jack looked at his watch, 'Come on and I'll buy you a coffee and a doughnut,' he said.

He and Harvey made their way to the lift and went down to the basement restaurant, which was buzzing with staff, as usual.

As they walked in, a voice called to Jack. He turned to see the Marine Guard Sergeant, Paul Rook, beckon him over. Paul was sitting with another two marines in uniform and two men in suits.

'Jack,' said Paul. 'You still do a bit of cycling, don't you?'

'Whenever I can,' agreed Jack.

Paul pointed to the men at his table, 'Meet Sergeant Jock Marshall and Constable Paddy O'Malley of the Metropolitan Police. They and some of the other cops at Westminster are taking off this weekend to cycle from Big Ben to Budapest for charity. We agreed to give them some sponsorship money. You're a cyclist and probably want to join in.'

'Big Ben to Budapest?' asked Jack in disbelief. 'You must be crazy. How long will that take you?'

'Ten days if all goes to plan. Here's a copy of our route and timetable for you,' Jock replied. 'We are trying to help children suffering from cerebral palsy by raising money for an extended treatment facility in Birmingham, based on the practices and experience of the Peto Clinic in Budapest. How would you like to contribute? We all know from the movies that you Americans are very rich.' He rolled his eyes.

Jack laughed and took the proffered information. 'I surely would. That's a hell of a ride,' he said, taking out his wallet and offering a note.

He sat at the table and asked a bit more about the ride and the bikes and equipment involved, and about their timetable, until eventually, Jock and Paddy excused themselves and left, with good wishes following them.

Jack asked Paul what he knew about Jock and his team. Paul told him that Jock was a friend of their contact at Saville Row Police Station, and had proved helpful in arranging trips around Parliament for the families of the FBI staff and for the marines. He and Paddy had apparently been involved in a number of fund-raising trips for sick kids over the years and seemed to be well regarded amongst their colleagues.

Jack shook his head at the thought of riding thirteen hundred miles across Europe in ten days, and felt slightly envious. He would be saddled to his desk and telephone for the coming week. He mused about the sights to be seen on such a ride.

5

On Friday evening, Alexei and Katya finished their packing then had dinner indoors. They both felt that a meal in a restaurant would not have been a good idea with their emotions boiling just under the surface. In the flat they could be more expressive and honest with each other - always provided the music was muting their voices.

Each quietly tested the other about the relatively sparse details they had been given for their travel. The travel plans had been occupying their minds for days and they could recite the details backwards by this time. They were satisfied that each knew what to do, and vainly tried to take some comfort from that knowledge. The thought of the danger involved kept resurfacing.

Katya appeared the more optimistic, 'Alexei, we must look at this sensibly. You are a real prize to the West, and we must assume that they will be doing their best to make sure the plans are foolproof.'

Alexei was grateful for her efforts to reassure him, 'I know what you mean, Katya, but all their efforts this year so far have been on their Iraq war. Most of their resources must still be committed there. We might be dealing with the reserve team.'

'Don't be silly,' she said, 'Their resources must be as big as Russia's, and our forces can be in several places at once. Anyway, when they want something as badly as they probably want you, they will do things properly. I am certain of it.'

'Once again, you are probably right.' he said. 'But how about you, how do you feel about the dangers you may face?'

She pouted at him. 'Dangers indeed! I will follow my instructions like an actress in a play, and I am sure you will join me to take a curtain call.'

He smiled and hugged her and whispered to her. 'I will be with you to take that curtain call, and maybe our rescuers can arrange an Oscar for your acting.'

She drew back from him slightly, 'Oscar my foot,' she whispered, 'what I want is to go on to a bigger and better production, one where we both star and the cast will be bigger too - if we work at it.' She looked into his eyes with a sensual smile on her face. 'Maybe we should put in some practice before we part, even though it's only for a few days.'

'I can't think of a better rehearsal' said Alexei, and pulled her towards him.

6

In the morning, Alexei was amazed at how calmly everything seemed to happen. They enjoyed breakfast then he had to hurry to make sure he had everything for the Lvov lecture. Peter and his merry men would drive him to Vnukovo airport to the south-west of Moscow where a Party plane would fly him south to Lvov.

His parting with Katya was warm, but there were no tears. She was being excessively cheerful, chattering about the delights of the Hermitage Museum she would soon see. He thought this was an act for the benefit of the listeners on the hidden microphones, and went along with it, talking about his uncle's grave in the Heroes Cemetery in Uzhgorod.

Eventually the time came round to say goodbye. They clung to each other then she pushed him away and said, 'Go on, you will miss that plane. I'll see you when you get back. Take care of yourself and stay away from those Ukrainian girls.'

He laughed, 'The Ukrainian girls like tractor drivers, not university types. I know what I like, and it looks good from where I'm standing.'

She waved him away, 'Come on you old charmer, I know where you are heading and there is no time for any of that. Goodbye.'

They kissed and he went downstairs with his bags. Peter and the driver were waiting by the car.

'Good morning, Peter. Am I going to have good weather for my flight today?'

Peter grimaced, 'I don't know why anyone would want to fly to the Ukraine; nothing but wheatfields. But since you must fly, I think your journey will be fine. The weather report is good for Lvov at the moment, so you should get some sunshine.'

'Well, if it does rain, I can always think of the sunshine of your smile, Peter,' he laughed.

Peter shook his head, 'Professor, I am going to miss your leg-pulling while you are away. I look forward to meeting you at the airport when you return.'

'Thanks.' He said. 'I will be back in a week, but we'll only have a few days in Moscow after that, before we return home. I'm sure there will be a lot of shopping for Katya to do. You will make sure that Katya gets to the airport for the Leningrad plane, won't you?'

Peter straightened up and puffed out his chest slightly.

'Don't worry Professor. Just you enjoy your views of the wheatfields and tractors. We will make sure that madame is safely delivered to the airport and we will collect her when she returns.'

The journey to the airport took about forty-five minutes. Alexei was guided to the plane, a domestic Ilyushin, and found that it was only half full for the journey. He settled down in his seat by a window. The plane took off and he relaxed and opened his copy of Pravda.

There was the daily criticism of 'foreign meddling' in Soviet affairs with sweeping generalisations like *the people will not stand for this!*

Alexei knew this was propaganda spin designed to justify the

38

repression of democrats and dissenters, like the bloody attacks in Vilnius and Riga in January by the KGB *spetsnaz* Group A-7.

He eventually tired of the newspaper and, as he looked out over the unfolding landscape of Russia and Belarus before the steppes of Ukraine, he thought of how the last few months had brought him and Katya to their present knife-edge situation.

Listening to Mirzoyanov's arguments last September in Moscow had helped clear his mind of the growing doubts he had then harboured regarding the Soviet biochemical warfare programmes and his participation in them. He and Katya had talked long and hard about what their future would or could be. She had ventured, several times in recent months, to tentatively voice her misgivings on the long-term outcome of his work for *Biopreparat* and the *Kamera*. What kind of world would the programmes create? What could the children she taught look forward to?

Alexei was well aware of what their future might be, should he take a moral stand and speak out against the biological time-bomb he was helping create. At best he would be sacked, vilified and denied any opportunity to work, and sentenced to internal exile. At worst he would be tried, or pronounced insane, and locked away until his death from natural causes would be announced. Meanwhile the giant juggernaut of *Biopreparat* and its doomsday concoctions would trundle on unhindered, perhaps to blight humanity for ever.

He and Katya came to the decision that, much as they loved their Russian heritage, the Russia they lived in was not a fit place to have a family. They had never thought of themselves as having excessively high morals, but even their tolerant and flexible standards were at odds with the society they lived in.

They agreed to think the unthinkable; they would leave Russia.

Alexei remembered the sense of shock they shared when they arrived at this decision. The next decision was where they might go, and how, and when.

They were intelligent enough to evaluate the possible options, coolly and dispassionately, and reasoned that their best and safest option would probably lie with the USA. The next step, if they dared to take it, would be their most adventurous, or devastating, depending on how they went about it.

That September they had stayed in a small flat on the University campus whilst he gave his programme of lectures. It was a cramped little place for the two weeks they were there and they tended to go out most evenings and weekends, sometimes socialising with the students, but always with a KGB minder lurking in the vicinity.

It was at one social evening in a restaurant that they encountered Anna Vernigorna amongst the group, while their minder waited outside. After a few beers, Alexei had been trying out his English on her. She complimented him and said that if he felt like visiting her family in Canada some time he would have little difficulty with the language.

She went on to ask if he had ever been to Canada or the USA.

He gulped at the memory of it. He told her, quietly, that he and his wife would like to visit the USA and Canada, but that to do this officially would be very difficult.

She suggested that he might be interested in unofficial channels, and that she had some friends who could prove useful.

Did he want her to ask them?

Alexei had felt small beads of sweat on his brow. He and Katya had held a whispered and necessarily short conversation with her. Anna nodded her understanding and held his gaze as she asked him once again if he wanted her help.

He had swigged his beer before muttering, 'Yes. Do it.'

His next visit to *Biopreparat* in Moscow in January had been brief and he had travelled without Katya. A very brief conversation with Anna confirmed that wheels had started turning and that his scheduled lecture visit in April and May would be when he and Katya took the irrevocable step, if they still had the nerve.

So here we are, he thought. Are we being fools, I wonder? No, we'd be fools to stay here and allow our lives to wither away like the mice in my laboratory.

He was suddenly aware of someone speaking to him.

A stewardess was saying, 'Would you like coffee, Professor?' He nodded and said, 'I'm sorry, had I nodded off?'

She laughed, 'No, but you seemed miles away.'

He smiled back at her, 'Yes, I was thinking of my wife back in Moscow, and hoping she will manage without me.'

'How sweet; you are a considerate man,' she smiled, handing him his coffee before moving along the aisle.

The flight continued, uneventfully, and after landing at Lvov, he was met and welcomed by his old university colleague, Sasha Kivshik, who was a deputy director in the medical faculty of the university. A car and driver were waiting for them. The KGB tentacles stretched a long way.

He and Sasha had not met for a number of years and were occupied on the car trip into the city bringing each other up to date on their respective professional and domestic situations.

Alexei explained how he came to be on the lecture circuit. He did not explain that it was part of the propaganda exercise which most state enterprises undertook to try to make their activities appear respectable and attractive, in the hope of recruiting suitable personnel for their activities. Sasha understood him to be a senior microbiologist in a research establishment. Alexei did not elaborate on his duties, especially whilst travelling in the KGB car..

Sasha and his wife Irina were both doctors; Irina working in the State Hospital attached to the University. Since 1986, she had been involved in monitoring the effects of the Chernobyl nuclear disaster on health patterns in their region.

The State University, Sasha explained, was founded during the period when Lvov became part of Austria after four hundred years under Polish rule.

During this time the city was known as Lviv. It was annexed by Poland again in 1919, then ceded to the USSR in 1945 when its name was changed to Lvov.

Alexei was to stay in a student flat at the University for his short visit, but Sasha made it clear that he and Irina would be entertaining him.

Alexei found the University's setting, overlooking the Ivan Franko Park, very pleasant, and the classically columned front of the building added to the illusion of being back in the days of the Austro-Hungarian regime.

As he unpacked his case, Alexei was conscious that Katya would be flying out at that time from Moscow to Leningrad. The thought of praying was not a natural action for him as a product of the Soviet system, but he no longer considered himself Soviet. He was a Russian, he thought to himself, and his ancestors were not ashamed to pray. Nevertheless, he felt strangely self-conscious about his silent prayer for Katya's safety.

He had dinner that evening with Sasha and Irina in their apartment, after a quick tour of some of the city sights. They pointed out High Castle Hill, which no longer had a castle but an unsightly television tower. Freedom Boulevard was an interesting series of contrasts, where modern shops with tasteless socialist decor were housed in the ground floors of old Polish buildings which again evoked memories of bygone ages.

Rynok Square was the heart of the old city, he was told, and was the traditional market place. The old merchant houses with their beautiful decoration dated from the sixteenth to eighteenth centuries. He was captivated, and said so.

'I must own up, he said, 'I expected only wheatfields and tractors, here. This is a very fine city.'

His friends laughed. Sasha said, 'Wait until you go to Uzhgorod. It is closer to the old Hapsburg world and is very well preserved, especially along the river area. The modern area is like any other town, unfortunately.'

Alexei kept a straight face, as he said, 'Do I detect an artist's disdain for the wonderful work of the Soviet Union?'

Sasha shook his head. He casually glanced round to check that Alexei's minder was out of earshot, then said, 'I find that as I grow older my tastes are changing, and my perception of beauty is veering away from the functional structures I admired in my youth to buildings and paintings, where the vision or character of the artist or designer shines through and lends individuality to the end product. I hope that does not sound like disloyalty to the efforts of our predecessors, or too pompous,

43

but I feel, more and more, that individuality is important.'

He stopped and looked around him, slightly embarrassed and wary. Irina watched Alexei carefully.

Alexei patted Sasha on the shoulder and said, 'I could not have said it as well as you. I agree with your sentiment, and I hope it is not just our age that is causing us to change our views. The world is becoming smaller, as a result of communications and transport, and we can see the beauty that is out there and the benefits that the freedom of expression by individuals gives to their society. I don't consider that disloyalty either, merely constructive criticism.'

Then he grinned and said, 'But I'm not making my views public.'

Irina clapped her hands, and said, 'Bravo to our two brave speechmakers.' Then she lowered her voice. 'I don't think it will be too long before we might be able to express some of those opinions. Certainly in the Ukraine; I can envisage us following the Czechs, the Hungarians and the East Germans. I doubt whether we will be allowed to dispense with the KGB so quickly, as those countries did. Ukraine has been a close part of Russia for a long time.'

'As a doctor,' she laughed cynically, 'I would estimate that the separation operation would be a success, but the underlying infection might never be cleared up. But remember the first line of Ukraine's national anthem - 'Ukraine is not dead yet'.'

The men nodded and each of them was silent with his thoughts.

Sasha and Irina's apartment was in a building very much redolent of the Hapsburg era, with high ceilings and a feeling

44

of grander times. The dinner was excellent, with traditional Ukrainian dishes to the fore, like borsch, then galushky dumplings. They talked of old times and drank wine, not vodka like the Muscovites, until late.

A Party car was waiting to take Alexei back to his University flat. On the journey, the driver addressed him as Professor and showed the same patronising self-confidence as Peter had in Moscow. He would just have to keep his guard up.

As he lay in bed that night, he wondered how Katya was coping. He could not escape feelings of guilt that she would be facing hazards alone. He had no idea what these imaginary hazards could be, but somehow felt that spiriting Katya out of a large city like Leningrad with its millions of people might be less of a problem than his journey from a provincial city like Uzhgorod. He took some comfort from that, and eventually the soporific effect of Sasha's generous glasses of wine carried him into sleep.

The Palace of Westminster sits like a huge aircraft carrier on the west bank of the River Thames as it loops northwards. At the northern end of the building, under the clock tower of Big Ben, the Speaker's House looks over Speaker's Court.

This area is normally busy with government vehicles when Parliament is sitting, but on this Saturday morning the only vehicle present was a Renault minibus plastered with sponsors' slogans and Coppers For Kids - Big Ben to Budapest in large letters along each side.

A group of cyclists, all police officers who worked in the building, was assembled; ready for their ground-breaking ride across Europe. Jock Marshall and Pat O'Malley had launched

the project and had been joined by fellow cyclists Tommy
Evans, Roy Kitchen and Inspector Dave Hastings in organising
the route. Ron Meadows, a veteran of previous trips, would
drive the support minibus.

The months of preparation and fund-raising were coming to
fruition and they were all optimistic about the success of the
ride and the donations to the children.

Their send-off was being televised by ITN, and a group of
well-wishers, including Molly Sugden, the television actress,
had come along to cheer them on their way. Police colleagues
from Birmingham, where the chosen charity was based, had
cycled down to London the previous day and would cycle with
them as far as Dover.

Just before nine o'clock, Mr Speaker himself, Bernard
Wetherill MP, came out of the Speaker's House to shake hands
and wish them a safe journey.

As Big Ben started its chorus to announce the hour, the
Speaker's cavalry background resurfaced.

'Mount up, gentlemen,' he ordered, 'And God speed.'

The group headed out into Parliament Square where police
motor cyclists were waiting to assist them through the traffic
of Westminster and Waterloo and down the Old Kent Road.

After clearing Deptford and climbing up to Blackheath, their
motorcycle escort left them and the cyclists settled in for the
haul to Dover. With the Birmingham officers, the group made
an enjoyable journey, coaxing and teasing each other to keep
up the momentum along the A2 and they arrived comfortably
in Dover at 1.30p.m.

The Birmingham lads went off with the Dover Harbour
Police who had arranged a billet for them for the night, and

no doubt a few beers.

The Coppers for Kids team headed to the Western Docks and grabbed a quick bite at a cafe while waiting for their time to board the hovercraft. Hoverspeed was one of their sponsors again, as they had been on the Great Ormond Street Hospital cycle ride three years earlier. The coppers felt they were travelling with friends.

The hovercraft crossing was very bumpy that afternoon, so bumpy that Jock lost his chicken sandwich into a sick bag, and consequently was teased for the rest of the day. He also had the mini boxing glove tied to his bike seat, indicating that he was 'twit of the day'. He didn't mind, it kept the fun factor alive.

They had a fast run from Calais, just as the light was starting to fade, across the flat farmlands, into St Omer where they enjoyed a comfortable night and a few beers at the Ibis Hotel; pleased to have completed the first day without mishap. They hoped the following days would be equally enjoyable.

Peter was like a genial and caring uncle when he called for Katya that afternoon. She played the part of the helpless female to perfection, asking Peter how long the car trip would take, and would he take the keys for the flat or should she hang on to them since she would only be away five days.

She gave him a bag of perishable groceries to share with his colleagues since they would not keep fresh whilst she was away.

The smile never left Peter's face, and his chest seemed to grow as he dispensed information and advice in a patronising, yet kindly, way.

In the car she chattered about how long it had been since she visited Leningrad, and how much she liked the Hermitage.

She hoped to get a ticket for the Mussorgsky Theatre of Opera and Ballet.

Surprisingly she found that Peter had visited Leningrad some years previously and he waxed lyrical about the art in the Russian Museum in the Mikhaylovskiy Palace.

She teased him about being a dark horse and hiding his artistic feelings behind a macho facade.

'We never think of you policemen being art lovers,' she said, 'But I suppose you have the same feelings for fine things as anyone else. I'm seeing you in a different light, Peter. I'm very impressed.'

He smiled sheepishly. 'Just because we have to deal with some of the seedier events in life does not mean that we have to be seedy too, madame.'

She put her hand on his arm and said, 'Oh Peter, I have never thought of you as anything seedy. You have always been a perfect gentleman. Alexei and I have spoken of how helpful you have been to us during this trip to Moscow, and we would be glad to have you looking after us on our next trip.'

'Thank you, madame. I have found this assignment the most pleasant one ever. You and the Professor have been very entertaining for an old peasant like me,' he said with a twinkle in his eye.

'Now you are teasing me,' Katya said. 'Old peasant indeed. I think you are quite a sharp city boy, and I can imagine the girls chasing you when you were a teenager. I'll bet you had to fight them off.'

Peter roared with laughter, 'Not quite true, madame, but there were some good times.'

His face seemed to lose its hardness for a few moments as his mind dwelt in happier days, then he drew himself back to reality as he noticed the driver glancing sidelong at him.

'You didn't forget your ticket, madame? We are nearly at the airport now.'

Katya made a fuss of opening her bag and making a worried search before producing her ticket with a triumphant smile.

Peter helped Katya with her bags. She knew that she would probably have to leave most, or maybe all, of it behind in Leningrad; but she had reasoned that if she was under any surveillance, it would look odd for her to go on a five day trip with anything less than her two bags of luggage.

Once she had checked in, she thanked Peter for his help. Despite her misgivings and her first-hand knowledge of the KGB, she felt that Peter had redeeming qualities and was not all bad. In a more humane society he would probably have been a normal and likeable person. Instead, he was a product of the state, or as some would say the state within the state, since she and Alexei were convinced that Kryuchkov and his KGB were pulling all the strings, including Gorbachev's.

But she had to keep up the front.

'Peter, you won't forget to come and collect me when I get back, will you?' she asked in a slightly appealing way. She didn't want to overact, but she felt she had the measure of charming Peter.

Peter smiled, 'I will be counting the days, madame. You can rely on me. I hope you enjoy your visit to Leningrad.'

She flashed one of her dazzling smiles and left him.

Her flight to Leningrad was scheduled to take an hour and was half the distance which Alexei had travelled that day. The plane was full and she sat beside a grandmother who had been visiting her daughter in Moscow to see her new granddaughter.

For the next hour she was regaled with tales of the baby and its mother, and was shown photographs to which she made the appropriately appreciative sounds. The time passed quickly and they landed at Leningrad without any delay.

A car was waiting for her with Leningrad variants of Peter and his driver, wearing forced smiles. One introduced himself as Vladimir, and was obviously in charge. They whisked her quickly through the city, with Vladimir pointing out landmarks on the way, to the Neva Hotel in Chaykovskovo Street. He was being polite but outwardly helpful.

Katya found the hotel an appealing building, converted from an old mansion. The car crew unloaded her bags and asked if they could assist her further. She played her dizzy blonde role, and said she was looking forward to some tea and an early night.

She booked in and the receptionist confirmed her room as being on the fourth floor, then called a porter to escort her to the room.

Katya followed the porter carrying the bags to her room, and once inside he deposited the bags and asked if she needed any more help. She thanked him and he left.

A few minutes later there was a knock at the door. She opened the door and a maid was there with towels over her arm. She said, 'Excuse me madame, may I check the bathroom, I think you need another towel.'

Katya stepped aside and the girl entered. She closed the door behind her and went into the bathroom. Katya walked to the bathroom door and the girl produced an envelope from amongst the towels.

She handed it to Katya and said, 'This is for you. It is very important that you are there on time. You should visit the

Impressionist exhibition on the third floor of the Winter Palace. Please remember that. I can't say any more.'

She readjusted her bundle of towels and left the room.

Katya opened the envelope and found a ticket for the Hermitage Museum. She saw that it was dated and timed for 11 a.m. next day. There was no accompanying note, and nothing written on the back of the ticket or the envelope.

She sat on the bed, holding the ticket and wondered what was to happen. It couldn't be her escape, since May 8th was still four days away.

If only Alexei was here, she thought, I could talk it over with him. He has promised to telephone tomorrow night, but we can't talk openly on the phone. The 12th Department of the KGB probably eavesdrops on every hotel telephone in Leningrad.

She reasoned that the museum visit would herald some further message or, hopefully, some reassurance that all was well. But she had to remember to keep her guard up; the minders would be shadowing her in the morning.

She had a plain but acceptable dinner in the hotel. Afterwards she chatted to the receptionist about the programmes at the various theatres, and the museums' opening times. She expressed an interest in the Leningrad Philharmonic Orchestra concert at the Mussorgsky Theatre on the 7th, and the receptionist said she would try to arrange a ticket for her. Katya thanked her and went up to her room.

She lay in bed reading for some time, then wondered how Alexei was coping and surprised herself at being so calm, before finally switching off the light and falling asleep.

7

Katya woke early, and had a leisurely bath as she took stock of her activities that morning. The minders and their car would be waiting downstairs - one of the drawbacks of being married to a man so valuable to the system. She would continue her role as the weak female, and utilise their services to transport her around. At the Hermitage, she would just have to play it by ear and hope that the news was good.

Breakfast lasted longer than she would normally take, since she was killing time. She flicked through the newspaper as she savoured the coffee, which was good. She had not seen the chambermaid from the previous evening and thought it prudent not to enquire after her. 'I don't even know her name,' she reminded herself.

She chatted to the waitress, asking her about the sights. The girl told her that the Taurides Palace and Park were at the far end of the street, and the Sheremetyev Palace was only ten minutes' walk along Liteyney Prospekt.

The girl said, 'And, of course, the KGB headquarters are only two hundred metres away, also on Liteyney Prospekt, but not many people choose to visit there.'

'I'll give it a miss, too,' said Katya, and the girl grinned at her.

After she was finished at the breakfast table, she went up to her room and gathered together her map, guide book, and camera; the necessary props to look like the art lover and

52

tourist. When she got to the hotel entrance, Vladimir was waiting for her.

He smiled and said, 'Good morning madame, our car is at your service. I have been told that you might be visiting the sights of Leningrad, and we will be glad to ensure that you get to your destinations safely.'

She switched on the dazzling smile and said, 'Thank you, Vladimir. It's such a long time since I was last here and it seems so much busier now. I'm going to the Hermitage this morning, and I'll probably be there most of the day. I'll bet I couldn't see it all if I spent a week there. It's a wonderful place. Do you go there often?'

He shrugged. 'Not so often, madame. My wife takes the children there sometimes. She likes art, but I like motorcycles.'

Katya smiled as they walked to the car, 'Well, I don't know anything about motorcycles except that they always seem noisy, but I compliment you on choosing a wife who likes art. I hope that rubs off on the children. How many children have you?'

Vladimir was opening the car door, 'Thank you for the compliment madame. We have two daughters, aged seven and nine.'

He closed the door behind her and climbed into the front passenger seat, and muttered 'Hermitage,' to the driver.

As they pulled away, Katya said, 'Is the Hermitage busy at the moment, or is it still early for tourists?'

Vladimir turned in his seat, 'In summer, it's almost impossible to move around the Hermitage. It's not so bad at the moment, but it's one of those places which attracts people all the year round.'

In a few minutes they were crossing Palace Square and

stopped outside the world's largest art collection, housed in the Winter Palace with its associated buildings, the Small Hermitage and Large Hermitage, altogether known as The Hermitage.

Vladimir did not indicate either way whether or not any of his team would be shadowing her. She thought it best to err on the safe side and assume that someone could be watching her.

She told them that she planned to have lunch while she was there, and did not anticipate coming out until around 4 o'clock.

Vladimir nodded and appeared content with that arrangement.

She walked round to the river side of the building where she saw a queue had formed, but she took her timed ticket to the head of the queue and the attendant admitted her immediately. At the information desk she picked up a guide booklet then made her way to the third floor where the famous Impressionist collection was housed. Once there, she duly collected her floor plan and wandered slowly along the galleries stopping frequently to admire the masterpieces of Monet, Van Gogh, Pissaro and others.

She noticed that there appeared to be a lot of foreign visitors, distinguishable by their dress. She found it amusing that nearly all the American ladies dressed in long cream-coloured raincoats and wore trainers. It was undoubtedly a comfortable combination, but she found their uniformity of dress an unusual characteristic of the land of the free. They looked like a uniformed school outing which had disappeared into a time warp and returned, still in uniform, many years later.

She suddenly thought, If all goes well, they could be my

neighbours soon. Perhaps that's how women dress in America now? No, surely that can't be right! It's probably a sensible way of travelling light.

Then she thought, I wonder how light I'll be travelling?

She continued her slow stroll along the gallery, holding her floor guide open.

One of the American women she had been mentally mocking turned to her and said, 'Excuse me honey, do you speak English?'

Katya was taken by surprise. She had been looking for some kind of furtive approach and was taken aback by this openness.

She said, 'Yes, I speak a little, but you must speak to me slowly,' in heavily accented English.

The American woman made no attempt to speak softly. She said, 'My stupid husband has wandered off to the john and I guess he's lost his way back. He has the guide with him. Can I have a look at your guide book?'

Katya had not followed all of the other's speech, but understood the request to see the guide book. She offered it to the woman who looked at it, all the while talking out loud about the pictures she had already seen.

Eventually, the American handed back the guide and said, 'Thanks a lot, honey. I can see where to go next.'

Katya said, 'You are welcome, but I have a question for you. Who is the John your husband is with?'

The American laughed loudly, 'Gee, I'm sorry, honey. I guess that doesn't translate too well. I meant the toilet. We sometimes call the toilet the john.'

Katya said, 'It must be confusing to be named John in America.'

The other woman laughed and said, 'That's a good one. I thought that Russians had no sense of humour. I must write that down and tell my husband.'

She went over to join a group of similarly-clad women and gales of laughter broke out as she related her conversation to them. Two of them detached themselves from the group and came over to Katya.

One said, 'Excuse us, but our friend told us you had a floor guide. May we have a look at it please?'

Katya nodded and the women moved either side of her to look at it with her.

One said, very quietly in Russian, 'Listen carefully. On Wednesday, wear sunglasses because you think you have a migraine coming on, and a headscarf. In the afternoon, go to the Gostiniy Dvor arcade in Nevskiy Prospekt. You will go into the Star Boutique on the first floor at four o'clock. Pick a dress off the rail and ask to try it on. Enter the changing room and do everything you are told. And don't worry, it's going to be okay. Got that?'

Katya kept her composure. She whispered, 'I have a team of minders waiting for me with their car. That could be a problem.' The other replied. 'You're walking everywhere on Wednesday because you need the exercise and it helps your migraine. Insist on it. If they want to follow you in the car that won't matter, but you must insist on walking. It's very important.'

Her companion said, in a normal tone, 'Well thank you very much ma'am for helping us. We appreciate you sharing your guide book.' They walked over to catch up with the other women.

Katya looked at her guide book without seeing it as she went over what she had been told. Her mouth had gone very dry and she would have to find something to drink soon.

Gostiniy Dvor, Star Boutique, first floor, four o'clock. Sunglasses, headscarf, migraine. I must find the coffee shop, she said to herself. She strolled for a few more minutes, to let herself calm down, then asked an attendant for directions to the cafe.

After a cup of coffee, Katya felt more relaxed, and decided she might as well have a light lunch before the restaurant became too busy. The egg salad was fresh and tasty, and she felt much more comfortable when she had finished it.

She sat with another cup of coffee and, in her mind, ran over the instructions she had received. At the same time she was casting a casual glance about the restaurant, which was rapidly filling up. She had her guide book open in front of her and paused to look at it occasionally before looking around again as though to orientate herself.

She saw nothing to concern her. There were no familiar faces, nor any of Vladimir's team around.

That doesn't prove anything, she thought, I haven't met any of the female minders yet. Any of the women in here, including the staff, could be watching me. I'll stick to what I told Vladimir, and have a good look around the place until four o'clock.

The rest of the afternoon passed without incident for her. She enjoyed the parts of the wonderful collection which she was able to visit, knowing that an afternoon was only sufficient time to see a small portion of the enormous display.

When she came out, shortly after four, Vladimir and his

car crew were waiting for her. She smiled and said, 'Well this is a welcome sight. I feel like I have been on my feet for ages.'

Vladimir opened the car door for her and said, 'Where would you like to go now, madame?'

'Oh I'm just looking forward to a cup of tea, then a nice soak in the bath,' she said. 'So it's back to the hotel please, Vladimir.'

Vladimir nodded, then said, 'Would you like to refresh your memory of the sights? We can go back by a round-about route if that would please you?'

'That's a lovely idea,' she beamed at him. 'It's so long since I was last here that I can't remember where everything is situated. I'm in your hands.'

Her smiling response provoked a satisfied smile from Vladimir.

The car moved off and passed in front of the Admiralty with its golden spire, then turned around the square behind it where St Isaac's Cathedral is a beautiful golden confection.

They went as far as the Mariinsky Palace then doubled back and crossed the bigger channel of the Neva via the Leytenanta Shmidta Bridge where they turned right and cruised past the fine buildings of the Academy of Arts, the Menshikov Palace and the Academy of Sciences before crossing the smaller Neva by the Birzhevoi Bridge where the Peter and Paul Fortress came in to view.

It was an impressive sight, symbolising Peter the Great's efforts to modernise the Russia of his day.

Katya was also aware of its history during tsarist times as a notorious prison - perhaps the ancestor of the Lubyanka. However, she made the appropriate and appreciative expressions at every viewpoint.

They circled round by the cruiser Aurora, whose guns signalled the 1917 storming of the Winter Palace, then re-crossed the river by the Troitsky Bridge.

Vladimir gave a brief commentary as they went along. She suddenly heard him say, 'And this is where we join the Nevsky Prospekt. Lots of shops and hotels, the Stroganov Palace, the Mussorgsky Theatre and here,' he pointed, 'the famous Gostiniy Dvor arcade of shops and boutiques.'

Katya's heart missed a beat. Was he dropping a heavy hint? Did they know?

She kept smiling and said, 'Is that where you go shopping, Vladimir? Do you recommend it?'

Vladimir kept a straight face. 'My wife and daughters think it is a wonderful place. They would spend most of their time, and most of my wages, in there, if I let them.'

Katya felt safer. 'That sounds like a recommendation to me. If your wife and girls like it so much, I must try to pay it a visit this week.'

Vladimir opened his hands, palms-upwards, in mock exasperation and said, 'I will never understand the connection between women and shopping.'

Katya laughed and said, 'Don't let it bother you. As long as she lets you play with your motorcycles, why should you complain.'

Vladimir shrugged and smiled.

A few minutes later they stopped outside her hotel. She thanked them for their help and said how much she was looking forward to a cup of tea and a bath. She asked, innocently, if she would see them next day, and Vladimir confirmed that they would be at her service. Later that evening, after dinner in the hotel, she could see Vladimir's car parked opposite the hotel entrance. So, it was the same service as in Moscow.

8

The Coppers for Kids faced a long ride that day - one hundred and fifty miles from St Omer to Charleville. They got on the road early and had a steady ride via Bethune and around Arras, a route they had travelled on a previous trip, before hitting the long straight road to Cambrai. The rolling countryside was good for cycling.

Ron Meadows and Jock Marshall stopped the minibus at the first bakery shop they saw in St Omer to stock up with several sticks of French bread, which, with a huge slab of cheese, would be Ron's basic requirements for their lunch stop. Jock then mounted his bike and joined up with the other riders.

Paddy gave a running commentary on the First World War battles as they passed cemeteries and memorials to that dreadful time of slaughter.

After Cambrai, the landscape changed and some long tiring hills became the norm. They free-wheeled into Charleville at six o' clock and found a friendly welcome at the Relais du Square.

The proprietor's daughter was just about to do the laundry and offered to throw the cyclists gear in the washing machine as well. The chaps accepted her offer gladly and were captivated by her baby son, Kevin.

Pat was intrigued by the child's Irish name and told the little boy that he was his long-lost relative from Dublin.

'I'm your cousin Pat,' he said. 'I'm the black sheep of the family.'

'More like the old goat,' added Tommy.

Of course the little French boy had no idea what was being said.

Dinner was a comfortable affair in a decent restaurant across the square from the hotel, where an English doctor struck up a conversation on seeing Roy and Jock wearing English and Scottish rugby jerseys. When the trip was explained to him, he made a donation to the charity, the Foundation for Conductive Education, which he had some knowledge of and complimented the crew on their efforts. A successful evening and an enjoyable meal put the seal on a hard day's riding.

Alexei took a long time to come to his senses that morning. The previous night's drinking with his friends was taking its toll. A lengthy session under the shower followed by a cup of nasty instant coffee started the stabilising process and he was able to make a reasonably dignified entry to the university restaurant for breakfast.

He spent some time organising his notes for the next day, then was joined by Sasha and Irina who took him to meet a group of their friends for an alfresco lunch. The host was a colleague of Sasha, and his old house had a large garden where a dozen or more were already sampling the beer and wines whilst the hostess was placing trays of food on a couple of tables.

Alexei enjoyed the relaxed atmosphere and the openness and informality with which these Ukrainians conducted their discussions. It appeared that they were already on their way to a more open society, though one would occasionally qualify a statement by adding 'If all goes well, of course', with a smile. There certainly seemed to be an air of optimism about their country's future.

The afternoon flew past and eventually people started to make their goodbyes and leave. Having learned that Alexei was staying in the university halls of residence, the hostess, Magda, insisted on making a hot snack for Alexei before she would allow him to leave.

As they left and went to Sasha's car, he noticed the car and driver from the previous evening parked further along the street, waiting to shadow him.

Keep your wits about you, Alexei, he told himself.

9

Monday morning in Lvov felt like a Monday morning anywhere, thought Alexei.

He had the mediocre fare on offer in the university restaurant for breakfast then collected his paperwork and found his way to the lecturers' rooms where he met up with Sasha. They had a discussion on the mode of introduction for the lecture, and laughingly agreed to disagree when Sasha told of the flowery words he intended using.

Alexei was formally welcomed in the lecture hall by Sasha, who praised his achievements as a microbiologist and pointed out that they had both started out from the same point as the students in the hall. Their determination and ideals had brought them progress and success.

If you only knew, thought Alexei. Determination, yes, but as for ideals; I don't think these kids have any idea of the ideals, or idealism, driving the programmes I supervise.

However, he thanked Sasha for his introduction and made some light-hearted references to the misdeeds of their student days before starting his lecture.

It was a standard lecture, prepared and approved by the Party and *Biopreparat* with little opportunity for any individuality to be displayed. The underlying emphasis was on the superiority of the Soviet system, and the opportunities for medical graduates to show their gratitude by working for the system.

This was threaded through the fabric of Alexei's discourses on medical theories and practices, and despite its sinister intent he found it quite cleverly done. These fresh faces taking in his lecture were also taking in the poisoned seeds created by the spin doctors of Moscow.

The lecture was well received, with an enthusiastic question and answer session following.

Eventually, Sasha rescued him from the earnest students and took him off for lunch.

'Forgive me for saying it, but I got the impression that you were not completely and whole-heartedly in tune with parts of your lecture today,' Sasha said, as they had lunch.

Alexei felt an alarm bell ring in his mind and sought to tread warily.

'After all the wine you gave me last night, I'm not only half-hearted, I think half my brain is still asleep too,' he laughed. 'What did you feel was amiss today?' he asked.

'I thought that when you were referring to working for government departments you did not sound very enthusiastic,' Sasha said.

'No, no, it's just my thirty-nine-years old body rebelling against the travelling and the excess of booze last night. I could do with a holiday,' he smiled. 'Believe me, the department gives me a good living. Katya and I have a comfortable lifestyle. What about you and Irina, you are both state employees. Do you ever feel less than enthusiastic about your work or your bosses?'

Sasha shrugged, 'I will always be enthusiastic about teaching medicine, it is most certainly my vocation in life. My bosses are a different matter. Some of them are career bureaucrats with no feeling for the ethos of medical teaching. It is an uphill battle to keep that teaching focused on purely medical matters. The bureaucrats are always looking for a way to introduce the party line into everything.'

He looked around, but they were out of earshot of the other diners. He leaned forward and lowered his voice, 'Alexei, this is in confidence between you and me, you understand?'

Alexei nodded.

Sasha continued. 'Irina and I are counting the days until Ukraine breaks free. The signs are promising, after the East Germans and the others got out from under the Russian boot. The next two or three years are crucial, but we can see it being possible, and that's without wishful thinking. The problems will arise with choosing the government to follow the Soviets.'

Alexei nodded and said, 'I wish you luck, but do you think you will be given a choice of government when the time comes. As Irina said last night, Ukraine has been linked with Russia so much over the centuries that true and honest separation may be difficult.'

'I agree,' said Sasha, 'But achieving that separation will be the first successful step towards a free and truly democratic Ukraine. We can't expect overnight miracles. I felt from your lecture that you might be thinking along similar lines to me.'

Alexei pondered a moment. He felt almost at one with Sasha, but the path he and Katya were following was more extreme and dangerous by far than trading thoughts and dreams over a lunch table.

He looked at Sasha and said, 'You are my friend and I value your trust in me by revealing your inner thoughts and hopes. I am like many in the Soviet Union today who have seen what has been achieved by our fellow men in the world outside. Those achievements can be realised here, I'm sure, though not under the present system. I hope that a change in the system is on the way and, like you, I can see some vague signs that keep that hope alive. I don't want to say or do anything to support a revolutionary upheaval. I would prefer to see constructive evolution. The 1917 Revolution was a success for human endeavour against oppression, but the driving ideals were quickly taken over by the opportunists and the people found themselves under oppression with another name. So I would suggest evolution not revolution.'

Sasha looked at him with a smile, 'That's a good slogan. 'Evolution not Revolution'. I will use that when the time comes. Yes, I agree with most of your sentiments, though some of us are less patient than you. Like you, I don't think it does any good to advocate bloody revolution. Countries born out of violence seem to develop a violent cycle of life.'

He lifted his coffee cup. 'Here's to evolution.' Alexei lifted his cup and added, 'And friendship.'

Charleville to Metz is a journey of around one hundred miles with the contour lines around Montmedy and Pierrepont giving warning of the climbs to come.

The cycling policemen set off, encountering Sedan in the first ten miles, where Jock's father had been with the 51st Highland Division in 1940, as he told his friends.

They had a good journey that day, despite the anticipated climbs, some of which were hard work. The old fortifications at Montmedy were very impressive and it was worth stopping for a few minutes to enjoy the view.

After Pierrepont, the contours became much more friendly, and they ran down nicely into the northern outskirts of Metz to arrive at the Novotel at Maizieres at three o'clock. The hotel was very helpful in securely storing their bikes.

Their budget would not stretch to a hotel dinner that night, so they had to adjourn to the nearest motorway rest area where they filled up on chips and burgers.

One of their overseas sponsors, Mrs Thelwell from Luxembourg, who had supported them three years earlier on their Great Ormond Street ride, had motored down to meet them and they were very pleased to meet up with her again. Their old friend from the gendarmerie, Bernard Petit, the Adjutant-Chef from Verdun, had left a message of welcome and good wishes for them.

No punctures and no mishaps; another successful day on the road.

10

That afternoon, Alexei spent a couple of hours with Irina in the hospital. She explained her observations on the Chernobyl effects and showed him graphs she had made demonstrating how the patterns of birth defects and childhood leukaemia had altered quite dramatically following the world's worst nuclear accident.

The visible evidence on the wards was both tragic and troubling. The tiny children with grotesque birth deformities were heart-wrenching, and when Irina explained the state's indifference to the plight of those children and their parents, Alexei felt ashamed to have been a cog in that mighty, impersonal juggernaut.

There had been no increase in funds or materials to help cope with the increased problems, and Lvov was by no means in the most seriously affected area. She had anecdotal evidence from colleagues of horrifying effects in other parts of Ukraine, closer to the seat of the accident.

Alexei was full of praise and admiration for Irina and her fellow doctors for their dedication to their patients.

She smiled at him wryly and said, 'Isn't that what the Hippocratic ideal is all about, Alexei. Didn't you make that promise too when you qualified.'

'Of course,' he replied, 'But you have set us all such a splendid example of the Hippocratic oath in action.'

To himself, he was thinking what a fraud he was. His oath to help others was long forgotten. The development of anthrax spores, bubonic plague, ricin and nerve agents were the antithesis of Hippocrates's ideal which he had sworn to adhere to in the heady days of graduation. If the escape to the west succeeded, he hoped he might redeem the Hippocratic oath by nullifying the effects of the horrors he had helped create.

That evening, Sasha and Irina took him for a meal in a traditional Ukrainian restaurant in the Freedom Prospekt. The food was enjoyable and the portions generous. From their table they could see out into the boulevard where small groups of locals were engaged in earnest discussion, games of chess or just strolling in the evening sun. They could also see Alexei's minders hovering.

Sasha explained Alexei's travel arrangements again for him. The journey to Uzhgorod was about two hundred and fifty kilometres, and a car was to take him there next morning.

Alexei asked if it was the same car that had taken him from their home the previous night.

Sasha shrugged, and said, 'It's out of my hands, my friend. It seems that the Party wants to take care of you and they are supplying the car and driver. What should we read into that? Are you a highly respected Party official, are you someone to be protected or is the Party keeping you on a short lead?'

'We had a short conversation over lunch, you recall,' said Alexei, 'I think you can draw your own conclusions. All I will say is that I am not, and never have been, a Party official. The answer lies in the latter part of your question.'

Sasha nodded and said, 'Take care my friend. I feel there is something you are not telling me, and I wish you success.'

Irina said, 'Enough of this mysterious talk. Pay the bill, Sasha, and let's walk along the boulevard like everyone else.'

They strolled along, absorbing the pleasant atmosphere, and stopped for a leisurely drink in Rynok Square, before heading homewards. Alexei was conscious of the time, and that he had promised to telephone Katya that evening. He could sense her waiting patiently for the call.

Katya woke to sunshine that morning. She looked out of her window and thought that the gardens of Leningrad looked attractive with the sun shining on spring flowers. She looked down and saw Vladimir's car, and rapidly came down to earth.

Just two more days. I'm sure I can manage it. I must manage it! After breakfast, she was met at the door by Vladimir.

'Good morning, madame, I believe you are going to the ballet school today,' he said.

'Good morning, Vladimir. Yes, the ballet school, but not any old ballet school; the Vaganova Ballet School where Pavlova and Nijinsky trained. I teach music and dance, and I feel honoured to be allowed to visit Vaganova. I was never a good enough dancer to qualify for such a school, and I am looking forward to seeing their pupils in action.'

Vladimir and his team took only a few minutes to deliver her to Architect Rossi Street where some of the most famous names in ballet had trained. Named after Agrippina Vaganova, the school had been the Petrograd Ballet School until the brilliance of Vaganova and her legacy of balletic training were commemorated by the re-naming of the school. One of her star pupils, Dudinskaya, was still a formidable teacher at the school, and Katya was thrilled to be introduced to her.

She watched a lesson where, despite being nearly eighty-years-old, Natalia Dudinskaya demonstrated the inspired teaching which had produced an endless stream of stars for thirty years.

The following hours were a magical time for Katya. The atmosphere took her back to her days as a young girl full of high ambition to be a prima ballerina. She had been a very capable dancer, but as she matured in her teens, her natural physique had developed and she blossomed into a striking young lady who was slightly too well-built for the corps de ballet. Her teacher was a thoughtful woman who had encountered such a situation many times, and encouraged Katya to keep up her piano playing and to consider teaching that as well as dance. Katya's late parents had seen the sense in the suggestion and had supported that course of action. The initial disappointment was soon dispersed once she reached her qualification as a teacher and started teaching her first pupils. She never lost her love of ballet and the Vaganova was like heaven on earth for her.

The staff members who looked after her were exceedingly friendly and open in talking about teaching methods, and even when she spoke of the school's illustrious pupils, they included Nureyev with pride, not with disdain for his defection. It was apparent that their love of ballet superseded Party diktat.

She had lunch with some of the teachers and pupils and found them all enthusiastic and also interested in the level she was teaching at, and how the next generation of children were disposed towards ballet. She found the atmosphere so refreshing. Nobody talked of politics or the cost of living. They invited her to have lunch with them next day.

She came out in the afternoon feeling quite buoyed up and

enthused by what she had seen and learned. It was unfortunate that she would not be going back to her class near Sverdlovsk. Perhaps, in time, she could continue teaching in America?

The sight of Vladimir waiting for her brought her back to reality. 'I hope you enjoyed your visit to the school, madame,' he said.

'Oh Vladimir, it was wonderful. All those boys and girls are so dedicated and so graceful. It is a truly magical place. Do your girls show any interest in ballet?'

He smiled, 'Yes, they are both attending classes. The eldest one is a natural dancer, I'm told, and the younger one wants to be as good as her sister. I think it is a healthy pursuit for them to follow.'

She clapped her hands, 'Good for you. You must support and encourage the children.'

He smiled again and opened the car door.

She said, 'Is there still time to see the Russian Museum?'

'Certainly,' he said, 'I'm sure it is open until six. It's just the other side of Nevsky Prospekt. It's only five minutes away.'

As they negotiated the streets, they turned by Gostiny Dvor, which Vladimir pointed out. 'My family's shopping paradise,' he said.

Katya said, 'Oh yes, I must try to fit a visit in there. I think Wednesday afternoon would probably be the best time for me.'

She watched for Vladimir's reaction.

He shrugged and smiled. 'I can't think of any time being a best time for visiting a big shopping centre like that.'

She laughed, partly with relief, 'We have been over this before, Vladimir. You poor men don't understand the psychology. Men have always gone out as the hunters while women

73

have been the nest-builders. It's been like that since prehistoric times. You won't change things.'

He put his hands up and said, 'Madame, please, I live in a house with three females, I know when to surrender to female logic. You win.'

'Good,' she smiled, 'I like a man who knows his place.'

He was still smiling when he opened the car door at the Russian Museum in the Square of the Arts.

Katya had a relatively brief visit to this home of purely Russian art. She was captivated by the beauty of the icon collection, and had time for a quick look at some of Kandinsky's works before leaving.

When they got back to the hotel, the receptionist smiled at her and said, 'We are in luck. We got a returned ticket for the Mussorgsky tomorrow night.'

The girl had also got her a copy of the programme.

Katya was delighted. She paid the girl for the ticket and added a generous tip for her, which the receptionist accepted graciously.

Some aspects of this trip were falling into place very well, she thought. As long as everything ran smoothly on Wednesday.

After dinner, she sat in the lounge with a book, waiting for Alexei's call.

Alexei listened to the clicks and squeaks on the telephone line and wondered how much of that was caused by the 12th Department's listening equipment. He was aware of the numbers of personnel employed in that department and reasoned that they must be listening to the majority of telephone traffic throughout the Soviet Union. The bureaucracy required to log that amount of traffic must be staggering.

Suddenly a voice said, 'Hotel Neva. Can I help you?'

He asked for Madame Golovkin, and after a brief pause he heard Katya's voice.

'Alexei? How are you? Are you enjoying Lvov?'

He smiled and ached to hold her. 'Katya, my darling, it's wonderful to hear you. Is your trip going well? Are you managing to visit all the sights? Have you managed the Hermitage yet?'

She replied, 'I'm enjoying myself. I went to the Hermitage yesterday. It's a wonderful place and everything went well. The Impressionist collection was outstanding.'

'So you think it was worth the effort?' he said.

She understood his meaning. 'Definitely worth the effort.' she said, 'I would recommend it. It really felt worthwhile. How about you? Did your lecture go down well? And what about your friend; you haven't told me about him.'

'Hang on,' he said, 'One thing at a time. Yes, Sasha met me at the airport, and he and his wife, Irina, have been excellent hosts. The lecture went well and a car has been laid on for my trip to Uzhgorod tomorrow.'

'Oh yes,' she said, 'I forgot to mention that I have a car at my disposal here too, and I've got a ticket for a concert at the Mussorgsky tomorrow night.'

'Good for you. Are you finding the car useful?' he said.

'Of course,' she replied, 'I could not have found my way around without them. They have even recommended a shopping area on Nevsky Prospekt, but I'll probably leave that until Wednesday afternoon.'

He understood that she was telling him things were in motion.

'Well, enjoy the rest of your visit, my darling, and don't spend too much on your shopping expedition,' he said, 'I'll see you at the weekend. In the meantime I'll try and call you tomorrow night to make sure you are well. I assume they have telephones in darkest Uzhgorod.'

She laughed, 'I'm sure they do, and don't worry about me, I'm just fine. Take care on your journey tomorrow. I love you.'

'I love you too and I'm looking forward to seeing you again.' They hung up.

Alexei felt relieved. He was certain Katya had signalled that she was content with the progress of her stage of the escape, and he assumed that shopping on Nevsky Prospekt was an element in the adventure though he could not imagine how. Tomorrow he hoped he could reassure Katya in similar fashion.

11

Alexei was up, breakfasted and had his bag packed in plenty of time for his nine o'clock start to Uzhgorod. It was a dry, clear morning and he thought, perhaps the scenery might be worthwhile. Sasha said that the second half of the journey had the better scenery.

He went out to the front of the University just before nine and found his car and driver waiting.

He affected pleasant surprise on seeing him, and said, 'Hello again! It's always good to see a familiar face when you are in a strange town. Are you taking me all the way to Uzhgorod?'

The other nodded and said, 'Yes, Professor, and I'll be bringing you back as well.'

Alexei smiled and said, 'Good. I'm glad that's all organised. Will we leave Uzhgorod about this time on Thursday morning, do you think? I'd like to be back in Lvov in the afternoon.'

The driver said, 'That will be no problem. If the road is clear, we can do the journey in about three hours; but tractors seem to live on the road we are using and we have to make allowances for the 'tractor factor'. I would think we can be back here on Thursday afternoon quite easily.'

'Good. Then let's get moving,' said Alexei and moved to take his bag to the boot.

The bag was gently taken from his hand by a bulky man in a dark suit, who appeared at his elbow and smiled saying, 'Allow me, Professor. We are here to take care of you.'

The bag was placed in the boot and the driver held the door open for Alexei.

Once he was in the car, the other two climbed in the front.

Alexei asked a few questions about the quality of the road they would be driving on, and if the weather was likely to change en route. He was assured that the road was of a good standard and that they were fairly sure the weather would stay fine. He also established that the driver was Yuri and his partner was Mikhail.

The first hour of the journey was through farming country and was relatively flat, with a lot of tractors on the road, or crossing it, but beyond the town of Sambir, the road started to rise into progressively higher hills.

Once prompted by Alexei's questions, Mikhail gave a sketchy commentary on the scenery as they moved along. He pointed out that they were climbing over the northern end of the Carpathian range, and would reach over eight hundred metres before they started descending the other side. At one point he told Alexei that the Polish border was less than ten kilometres off to their right, then at a later point, that the Czech border was in their view, also to the right.

The scenery through the mountain section was wild and beautiful. Yuri stopped in the small town of Borynia, at Alexei's request, where they had a cup of coffee and stretched their legs. Mikhail pointed out the reminders of the Polish era in this region, evident in some of the buildings and shop names.

Soon after resuming their journey, they reached the road summit. The views were spectacular, and Alexei teased them about working in such a beautiful region. They agreed that they enjoyed working in Lvov, and looked on their trips out to this region, Zakarpatskaya, as one of the perks of the job.

Their descent gradually levelled out as they approached Uzhgorod. Mikhail gave Alexei some information on the city. It was at the centre of a wine producing region, which was evident as they were passing through numerous vineyards. The River Uzh was navigable and still used for some freight transport. There was a one-thousand-year-old castle on a hill. The city had a theatre of opera and drama, and a concert hall.

Alexei asked about the Cemetery of Heroes, where he believed his uncle was buried. Mikhail said that was also on a hill, the Hill of Glory, and was not far from the centre. Alexei said, 'I am staying at the Verkhovina Hotel, as you probably know. How convenient is that for all these places you mentioned?'

'Very convenient, Professor. That hotel is on the Theatre Square, which also has the Art Gallery. Behind the theatre is the river, and your medical faculty is on the corner of Lenin Quay. There is a Gorky Park here too, like Moscow, with a swimming pool, and a botanical garden nearby.' He laughed, 'You will want for nothing, Professor.'

Alexei said, 'I am overwhelmed. I thought I would be coming to some sleepy little backwater, and you have just described a tourist paradise. I hope the food is good, as well.'

Alexei noticed a number of military vehicles on the road and commented on this. Mikhail told him that Uzhgorod was part of the logistics chain for supplying Soviet garrisons in Czechoslovakia and Hungary.

Alexei looked puzzled. 'Surely that is all finished now since those countries went their own way.'

Mikhail shook his head. 'Not quite finished, Professor. It

has not been possible to withdraw all the troops, because there are not enough barracks in Russia to accommodate them. They are coming out gradually, but there are still a lot of them killing time in Hungary and Czechoslovakia. It seems a silly situation, because they are stationed in those countries but they can't really exercise properly as troops since the regimes changed. The sooner we have them back in Russia, the better. In the meantime, they have to be supplied and Uzhgorod is a major supply point for the eastern part of both those countries.'

They passed through the modern part of the city with the usual concrete and glass monstrosities which passed for Soviet architecture in the fifties and sixties, and came into the older part of the town where the beauty of the Hapsburg era lingered in the pastel colours and pleasing proportions of the older buildings.

About twelve thirty, they arrived at the Verkhovina Hotel, which was also signed as the Intourist hotel. Alexei felt that booking an Intourist hotel was a good move for a servant of the Party.

Yuri and Mikhail said that their needs were already arranged, and they would be at his disposal. He said he was having some lunch, and then he wanted to visit the cemetery that afternoon.

He booked in and was shown to a sparsely-furnished room, with the very bare necessities. It did have a bathroom, but everything had a veneer of grubbiness and decline.

He had a light lunch of a very indifferent standard, and thought he might have to eat out that night.

Cycling through Metz in the early morning was not such a hazard as the bobbies might have imagined. Traffic was free-flowing and they were quickly out of the city into the rolling countryside.

They made good time across the Lorraine countryside, although there were some long climbs. Just as they were starting to tire, and saw the steep hills around Saverne coming closer, their route took them downhill from Phalsbourg to Lutzelbourg and along a level valley bottom, following a canal and avoiding the hills completely.

A relatively short run into the outskirts of Strasbourg found their Police motorcyclists escort who took them through the old city centre and stopped for photographs in front of the cathedral.. Riding over the cobbles by the cathedral was a very rough ride for the cyclists, prompting several uncomplimentary comments about the effect on their anatomy. Ron was having a bouncy time in the minibus, trying to keep pace with them. But they agreed that the cathedral and its surroundings were beautiful and thanked their French police escorts for the diversion. They continued to the European Parliament building where they were officially welcomed and they handed over their letter of greetings from Westminster, signed by the Speaker and Lord Chancellor. Refreshments were laid on for the bobbies and a quick tour of the building, guided by a charming young French lady.

Their motorcycle escorts took them quickly into the city centre again and they settled down at the Novotel that night. A substantial meal and early bed were gratefully welcomed, after a beer or two.

12

Alexei collected a town plan from the hotel receptionist and went out to find his two shadows waiting. He told them his intention of going to the cemetery, and they displayed no emotion; just nodded. Mikhail said he would accompany Alexei while Yuri would meet them at the gate.

They set off towards the Hotel Kiev, Alexei buying a bunch of flowers along the way, then up Tykha Street towards the Hill of Glory. They passed under a memorial arch and into the Cemetery of Heroes which seemed to be fairly modern. With Mikhail's help, a clerk was found in an office, and he was able to show them the burial plans and lists of the dead. In response to Alexei's query, he pointed out that the cemetery had been modernised in the 1950s and was constantly maintained in honour of the heroes buried there.

'What is the name of the person you are looking for?' he asked.

'I have his name, Alexei Golovkin. He was my father's eldest brother, and I was named in memory of him.'

The clerk was able to trace the name and the plot number, and directed Alexei to the row where his uncle lay. It took him several minutes to find the correct row and then a slow stroll to identify the headstone.

Alexei found it very moving as he stood in front of a grave-stone with his own name on it. This was the grave of a man he had never met, who had died nearly ten years before he had been born, but Alexei's father had spoken often of his elder brother. It had been obvious that the two of them had been very close before the war had separated them.

There was a feeling of some permanence about that plain headstone. Both Alexei's parents had been cremated, at their own request, and their ashes scattered in a forest they both loved, near Moscow. Alexei sometimes felt that he had nothing tangible to focus on when reminiscing about his parents. But his uncle Alexei was here for eternity, for anyone to visit.

Mikhail had withdrawn some distance, leaving Alexei some privacy. He squatted down to place the flowers on the grave. He thought of his father who had hoped to visit this spot himself, but had been stopped from even reaching retirement by a sudden stroke. He could feel a lump in his throat, thinking how his father had plodded along through life, uncomplaining, facing the many obstacles and setbacks life threw at him and doggedly clawing his way through them. He had always talked about 'the good time coming' and of all the things he and Alexei's mother would do when he retired. Sadly, the good time never came for him, and Alexei's mother did not long survive her husband when cancer took her.

He muttered softly to the headstone, 'Uncle Alexei, you and my parents had your chance of good times snatched away from you. I respect your sacrifice in the war. In that situation I would have responded like you. My parents too had little opportunity to make their lives different, but they left me their dreams. They could never realise those dreams, but Katya and I have the chance of that other life where some of the dreams come true.'

'We love Russia, but not the Soviet nightmare that Russia has become. We will never give up the hope that Russia can change into a society where people matter more than the Party and its political dogma. But we can't wait forever. The years go by and I cannot see a distinct light at the end of the tunnel, only the faint glimmer of hope. I don't want us to follow my parents' route, forever dreaming of times which never come. As long as I am part of the *Biopreparat* programme, I can see that those good times are jeopardised by the nightmares I am helping create. I cannot neutralise that danger from within the Soviet Union, therefore I must try to take my knowledge where it can be used to cancel out the wrongs I have helped create.'

'It would have been good to discuss this with you and my father; I feel you would both have understood and supported me. But that is just another good time which did not happen, so I must take my own road to clear my conscience. Goodbye, old soldier. Sleep in peace.'

He stood up and looked around the cemetery with its never-ending rows of headstones and thought of the dreadful waste of lives. Mikhail strolled up to join him.

Alexei turned towards him.

'What do you think of all this, Mikhail? The world must have gone mad, I think.'

'It was those Nazis who were mad, Professor, following the insane ideas of Hitler and thinking they could rule the world. The heroes of the Soviet Union took everything that was thrown at them and turned the savages back in the Great Patriotic War. It was a glorious success for our people.' Mikhail looked like a man inspired.

Alexei thought he had best bite his tongue.

'Yes, Mikhail, we are all thankful for that successful defence, but we should also be a bit sad at the loss of friends and family, don't you think?'

Mikhail pursed his lips, 'I suppose we should not forget them, but we should build on the success and go forward to a glorious future.'

Alexei thought, the bloody war has been over for forty-six years and where is the glorious future that these poor bastards died for? What is there to show for our advancement? The Chernobyl disaster and an arsenal of biochemical poisons.

He turned towards the gate and Mikhail fell in beside him.

'Thanks for your help, Mikhail. My father always hoped to make this journey, but he did not live long enough, so I feel that I have done it for him as well as myself.'

Mikhail said nothing.

They walked for a few minutes, then Alexei said, 'Is the Castle worth seeing, and have we time to visit it?'

'If you like history, then it is worth a visit. I would suggest we use the car to save a half hour walk,' Mikhail replied.

Alexei smiled, 'I prefer to walk, but since it's now mid-afternoon I suppose it makes sense to use the car.'

Yuri was waiting at the entrance, with the car, and soon whisked them all up to the castle founded by Prince Laborets in the ninth century. Alexei enjoyed the museum of local history within the castle walls, which helped explain the presence of the statue of the mythical Turul bird, the messenger from the gods of the Magyars and their predecessors. He had not known that Uzghorod was a Hungarian city for centuries before becoming Ukrainian and that the Turul was a creature of Hungarian mythology.

They made their way back to the hotel where the receptionist handed him an envelope with his room key. Alexei looked at her quizzically.

She said, 'It was delivered from the Philharmonia Concert Hall. I assume you ordered a ticket.'

'Of course,' Alexei bluffed, 'It had slipped my mind. Thank you.'

He asked her about the dinner menu, and her unenthusiastic response prompted him to ask about other restaurants in the vicinity. She quietly suggested a restaurant on the other side of the square which was popular with local people.

He went up to his room, opened the envelope and took out the ticket which was for eight o'clock. No other communication was in the envelope. He looked at the ticket and ran over the possibilities. Was it a gift from the medical faculty or from Sasha and Irina? A treat arranged by Yuri and Mikhail? Both options were possible, he thought, but unlikely.

Was it the next piece in the jigsaw, the part he was waiting for? He hoped that tonight would reveal the final stage of the journey.

13

It was a grey morning in Leningrad, with the threat of imminent rain. Katya felt pleased that she had planned her itinerary with indoor visits for that day. She was not planning an early start. She had decided that her best policy was to keep busy, in an effort to stop worrying too much, but she reasoned that she had to keep herself focused and that keeping busy did not mean rushing headlong at things. That way could lead to errors, fatal errors. So, she had chosen her visits to places where she felt that the sights and their contents would be sufficiently interesting to keep her mind occupied.

When she eventually breezed out of the hotel after ten o'clock, Vladimir was waiting patiently. They greeted each other with smiles as he held the car door for her.

She told him that she wanted to go first to the Smolny Cathedral and that she had been invited for lunch by the teachers she had befriended the previous day at the Vaganova Ballet School.

Vladimir nodded and asked, 'Are you planning anything for this afternoon?'

She told him, 'Your little tour past the Peter and Paul fortress on Sunday has given me the idea to visit there this afternoon. Is that a good idea?'

Vladimir nodded approvingly, saying that it was one of the sights which local people were proud of.

She would have liked to visit Peter the Great's Grand Palace out at Petrodvorets, west of the city, but her guide book indicated it was closed that day.

The Smolny Cathedral was an impressive building. As they drew near, its pale blue and white decor made it look like a mirage floating on the Neva. The building was currently used mainly for concerts and exhibitions, but the original mixture of baroque architecture and Orthodox decor made it a work of art.

She asked Vladimir to show her the Smolny Institute next door, which had started life as a school for daughters of the aristocracy and had won another kind of fame when Lenin and Trotsky established the Bolshevik Central Committee there in 1917. It was now the municipal offices of the city, but Vladimir was able to show her some of the building and relate some anecdotal history of various parts.

Lunch with the friendly teachers and pupils at the Vaganova was a pleasure. Katya felt at home with these kindred spirits who shared her love of dance and music. Thinking of Vladimir's daughters, she asked if there were any souvenirs she could buy for them. Two illustrated books of ballet, suitable for children, were found and she was also given a book for herself as a personal gift. She was very touched by their kindness and expressed her thanks with sincerity. She was given an open invitation to call at the school on her next visit to Leningrad.

She replied, honestly, that she had no idea when she would next manage a visit.

If they only knew what that means, in my case, she thought.

Vladimir was waiting for her and she was taken smoothly to her next choice of landmark.

The Peter and Paul Fortress was a vast sprawling place

overlooking the river. Much of the fortress, especially the Trubetskoi Bastion, had been the prison of the tsars and there were plaques alongside many of the old cells denoting famous occupants, such as Gorky and Dostoyevsky.

The Peter and Paul Cathedral with its soaring golden spire was the undoubted showpiece within the fortress. The interior was as magnificent as the exterior, with the white marble tombs of the Romanovs standing out against the walls of pink and blue marble, and an ornate gilded ceiling giving a rich glow to everything. Katya found it all beautiful, and said so.

Vladimir said, 'How many peasants wasted their lives building this ornament?'

Katya rounded on him, 'Vladimir! How can you be so cynical? We cannot change history, so we should appreciate what history has bequeathed us. Your daughters would probably think this is a beautiful building. They would not be looking for anything sinister in it. Try seeing it through their eyes.'

Vladimir looked uncomfortable. 'I apologise, madame. I did not mean to offend you.'

Katya waved her hand at him. 'Don't be silly,' she said, 'I don't offend easily. The point is not that I take any offence, but that you are less cynical and more catholic, with a small 'c', in how you view the relics of pre-revolution times.'

Vladimir gave a wry smile. 'I shall try madame,' he said.

'Just listen to your children,' she said. 'We can learn so much from them, and as your two daughters grow older they will almost certainly try to re-educate you, I feel sure.'

'They have started already,' said Vladimir, pulling a face. 'They say I'm old-fashioned and don't understand anything. I certainly don't understand girls.'

She patted his shoulder. 'Just roll with the punches, old chap, and you'll survive.'

They dropped her at the hotel in late afternoon, giving her plenty of time for an early dinner before her concert.

Alexei had a shower and got himself tidied up for the concert. Before leaving the hotel, he put through a call to Leningrad and was connected to Katya quite quickly.

'Katya? Are you still enjoying yourself? What have you been up to today?'

She related her outings that day, then asked, 'How about you; was your journey all right? How are things in darkest Uzhgorod?'

'The journey was fine. We crossed the Carpathians, and some of the views were terrific. The co-driver gave an excellent commentary. And Uzhgorod is a very pleasant place. With a bit of help I found Uncle Alexei's grave, and put some flowers on it.'

'Well done', she said, 'That was a nice touch. Your father would have liked that. How did you feel when you were there, at the grave?'

'It is difficult to describe. I felt a bit emotional, probably because it made me think of my father and how he would have liked to be there too. I felt I had settled something within myself; some kind of debt of honour I suppose.'

'I can imagine it would be touching, but then I cry easily,' she said. 'What are you up to tonight?'

'I'm going to a concert, too. It's the Uzhgorod orchestra playing several operatic pieces, with some choral sections being sung by a local choir. I don't know how good they will be, but

I'm looking forward to going there.'

He stressed the last sentence.

Katya understood. She knew Alexei's tastes in music, and that he would not normally be looking forward with great enthusiasm to operatic selections sung by a small-town choir. He usually referred to such performances as pop-opera. He felt that such extracts, in isolation, failed to portray the mood or continuity of the story line in the opera. So, he was going there for another reason. Everything was coming together.

'I hope you enjoy the performance, and don't forget to tell me all about it tomorrow. I'm listening to the Leningrad Philharmonic tonight, and I know the performance will be first class.'

'Well, I'm sure we will both enjoy our separate performances. I don't know what I will be doing tomorrow night. The university may have something arranged. I'll find out tomorrow. Don't be surprised if I don't ring, I may be out late.' he said.

'As long as you are not chasing Ukrainian girls,' she laughed.

'I'm looking forward to chasing you, and catching you,' he growled.

'You big bad wolf!' she said, 'Behave yourself. We might be on a crossed line and you don't know who might be listening. Enjoy yourself tomorrow, and take care of yourself.'

'You too, my darling. I'll see you soon.'

He hung up. He felt that events were propelling them with increasing momentum, but he knew this was of their own choosing. He just wished it was over.

14

Vladimir was surprised by Katya's gifts for his daughters when he picked her up at the hotel.

'I got them at the Vaganova today, but I had to wrap them before I gave them to you,' she said. 'Children enjoy unwrapping presents, as I'm sure you know.'

'Madame, this is very kind of you,' said Vladimir. 'I was not expecting anything like this.'

'The children enjoy ballet, you said. I love ballet and I hope that your girls will continue to enjoy it.'

She smiled. 'If these books give them some encouragement, then I'm happy.' Vladimir seemed to be knocked off-balance and could only smile and say,

'Thank you.'

Katya enjoyed her evening with the Leningrad Philharmonic Orchestra in the Square of the Arts. The programme was one of their best. They opened with Roslavets's 'Hours of the New Moon', and the second half of the evening was Shostakovich's Symphony No.7, 'Leningrad', which provoked prolonged applause from a predominantly local audience.

Katya felt tears in her eyes as she clapped her hands. A mixture of pride and sorrow, she reasoned. The beauty of the music and the skilled presentation by the orchestra cheered her Russian heart, and she felt a slightly breathtaking sorrow at leaving her homeland.

Then she thought of the KGB minders waiting outside for her, and regained her resolve. She and Alexei were not quitting some Utopian wonderland.

She flashed her smile at Vladimir when she came out, and he held the car door for her. 'I can see that you enjoyed the performance, madame.' he said.

'Vladimir,' she said, 'That is an understatement. It was a magnificent performance. You are fortunate in Leningrad to have such an orchestra. Have your girls dragged you here to listen?' she teased.

'When we were newly-married, my wife and I came here several times, but since the children arrived, we don't seem to have much free time. Everything revolves around the children.'

She laughed at his down-trodden expression.

'I think you are a fibber, Vladimir,' she said, 'You pretend that having the children is a big drag, but you take them to ballet lessons and, I'm sure, to other events. You are just a proud dad who does not want to admit it. You men like to put on a macho front and pretend that you don't care about the beautiful things in life. I'll bet you enjoy a hug from your kids as much as your wife does.'

He had a big smile on his face. 'Nonsense. Those girls will make me a pauper before they are very much older.'

'You're a fraud,' she laughed.

They were still laughing when they arrived at her hotel.

She told Vladimir she wanted to visit the Dostoyevsky Museum next morning.

He told her that it did not open until eleven, and she replied that she would get some letters written in the morning before going out.

Alexei crossed the square to the restaurant indicated by the hotel receptionist. He found the place filling up and a waiter seated him at a small table facing across the room towards the window. He could see Mikhail and Yuri in their car about a hundred metres across the square.

The menu was mainly Ukrainian dishes with a few Hungarian additions. Alexei settled on a creamy fish soup, allegedly made from local carp. He enjoyed it and went on to the main course, a Budapest steak. This was a grilled steak covered in a rich sauce of paprika, mushrooms and chicken liver, which he found delicious.

He relaxed with a coffee and observed people around him. Judging by their complexions and the men's coarse hands, they were mostly outdoor workers, probably engaged in farming. He imagined that the extensive vineyards he had seen on the journey into Uzhgorod needed a fairly large workforce. They all seemed cheerful and looked well fed.

He remembered Katya's warning about his worried face betraying him, and tried to appear more relaxed.

After paying his bill, he made his way across the square to the Philharmonia Concert Hall. He was directed to his seat and found that the hall was nearly full.

He sat down and noticed that the seats on each side of him were vacant.

A short time later, he saw two young women, in their twenties, coming along the row towards him.

As they drew level with him the first smiled and said, 'There you are. We thought you had run off and deserted us. We should have known better.'

She squeezed past him and sat down.

The other woman sat down and said, 'We were waiting in the foyer for you. We thought that's where you said you would be. One of us must have got it wrong,' and both women laughed.

Alexei had a bemused smile on his face. He felt like that time in a school play when he forgot his lines and was too shy to ad lib.

He finally said, 'Well we are all here now, so no harm has been done. I'm sorry if I kept you waiting.'

The girl on his right patted his arm and said, 'Don't worry, Alexei, Tina and I are getting used to you.'

Tina said, 'Jana and I thought you might have forgotten the time. That was silly of us, wasn't it?'

Alexei thought, 'Good. They have introduced themselves; Tina and Jana. What next, I wonder?'

The two young women chattered about the musical programme, then Tina said,

'Have you heard this orchestra before, Alexei?'

He shook his head and smiled, unsure how the plot would unfold.

Jana leaned towards him, holding a copy of the programme at waist level. She said, 'I think you will like the first choral piece.'

He looked down at the open programme and saw a small square of paper in the fold.

Jana said, 'Here you are, hold the programme yourself; you can read it better that way.'

She leaned across to speak to Tina, who also leaned forward, effectively screening him from view at each side as they chattered.

He quickly opened the folded piece of paper and read the

brief instructions. 'Art Gallery. Theatre Square. Enter 4.10pm. At 4.15 go to toilet. Emergency exit next to toilet. Go out. Motorcycle waiting. Climb on.'

He quietly folded the paper again and Tina gently retrieved it with minimum of movement.

Jana said, 'What do you think of the selection then?' pointing to the programme.

He nodded and said, 'It seems quite varied, with some pieces I don't know. I'm sure I will follow them once the performance gets under way.' Jana smiled and nodded approvingly.

The orchestral pieces were good and the choral performances were full of enthusiasm. Alexei was quite charmed by the choir.

The refreshment facilities at the interval were functional but limited. Alexei secured soft drinks for the three of them and found the girls in a quiet corner of the bar, with nobody in earshot of them. They all smiled and toasted each other, Tina covertly scanning their surroundings as they did so.

She said softly, 'Have you got the details in your mind?'

'Yes', he said, 'But it doesn't tell me much.'

'Don't worry,' said Jana. 'You know all you need to know for the moment. Just make sure the minders don't come in with you. Tell them you will be inside for about an hour.'

'Won't they see me on this motor cycle?' he asked.

She shook he head. 'The emergency exit is at the back, in a lane. They will have the car out front and stay with it. KGB minders don't like exerting themselves by walking around.' said Jana.

Tina added 'Your route away from there will not enter the square and you will be wearing a crash helmet. Smile, it's all going well. Are you enjoying the concert?'

'Yes, of course,' he said, looking slowly around and noticing that other concert-goers were getting closer as the bar area filled up. 'I'm pleasantly surprised at the choir's performance.'

The girls laughed, and Jana said, 'Enthusiasm covers up a lot of mediocrity.'

'Don't be unkind,' Alexei laughed, 'The end result is quite pleasant.'

The girls grudgingly agreed with that opinion.

They talked about the university and Alexei's visit next day, which was public knowledge and therefore a safe subject to discuss. Both of them were training as teachers, having already graduated in languages, and were able to describe the university to Alexei.

Alexei asked where they hoped to teach, having language degrees. 'Would you like to travel abroad, perhaps?' he asked.

Tina said, 'That is a possibility, in the longer term. Nobody knows what the future may bring in the way of opportunities.'

She looked him straight in the eye as she spoke.

He guessed he should change the subject and asked about the sights of Uzhgorod.

In a normal tone, Jana said, 'Have you visited our art gallery yet?'

He shook his head, and she continued in a voice loud enough for public consumption, 'It is surprisingly good. There is a mixture of old and modern, with some excellent eighteenth and nineteenth century pieces from the Hapsburg era. There are some very striking local rustic, or primitive, works which you should see and tell your friends about. It's a place everyone should see when they visit Uzhgorod.'

'I'll try and see it tomorrow afternoon,' he said, playing along with her charade, 'I'm not going back to Lvov until Thursday morning. It sounds very interesting.'

The bell sounded to call them back to the hall. As they returned to their seats, he asked the girls about the hall and the tale he had heard about it formerly being a synagogue.

'Oh yes,' said Tina, 'That is true. After the war, there were no Jews left. The Nazis had liquidated all of them around here, so the building was converted and has been the Philharmonia Concert Hall ever since then.'

The second part of the concert followed the format of the first, with some light-hearted moments during the choral renditions where some soloists found their shortcomings exposed when the collective voices of the choir were not hiding them.

At the end, when they stood up to leave, Jana said quietly, 'We are going to collect our coats. To avoid any questions or suspicions from your minders, you should leave alone. We may see you tomorrow at the university, but if you don't see us, don't ask after us. Understand?'

'Perfectly,' said Alexei.

Mikhail and Yuri were waiting, as usual, outside the concert hall. He greeted them, and chattered enthusiastically about the performance as they walked to the hotel. Both minders looked less than interested in his praise for the city's musical accomplishments.

He told them his timetable for the university next day before going into the hotel. The bar was open and he got himself a beer. He sat and ran over his instructions in his mind. It was frustrating to him that he did not know the full game-plan. He liked to feel in charge of his life, and he was being spoon-fed the plan in tiny portions. He had to trust that they knew what they were doing.

It was probably too dangerous to reveal the whole plan, he reasoned to himself, as it could be betrayed and all its players with it. He had to agree it was probably safer for each person to know only the segment affecting them.

'This time tomorrow', he thought, 'everything should be over and we'll be safe.'

He finished his beer and went up to bed.

Lights burned late that night in the third floor rooms of the Regional Security Office in Grosvenor Square, London. Jack Bergen was detailing the current situation to his colleagues, who all enjoyed a variety of euphemistic titles concealing their secretive roles.

'You already heard that all the pieces are in place in Leningrad. The lady seems to be a really cool cookie; she's not showing any nerves. Our team are as happy with the situation as they can be. It looks like a reasonably smooth ride there, tomorrow.'

He paused and looked around the table, but no questions were raised.

'Now for the main man,' he continued. 'The word just came in that he has been briefed for tomorrow. I have to say that the people down there have pulled all the stops out to make the game plan work. They feel that it should go like clockwork.'

Harvey Fletcher, Jack's deputy and friend, asked, 'How confident are you, Jack?'

'You know me, Harvey. As my old European grandma used to say, 'don't put all your faith in a recipe, you have to taste the finished dish'. To be fair, we have used this route before, mainly for moving our own people back and forth, and it's always worked well. No problems, so far.'

He looked over his glasses at Harvey who nodded and repeated 'So far.'

David Sanchez frowned as he said, 'Is there something you guys aren't telling us here? We are not putting this guy out on a limb, I hope.'

He looked towards Jack and Harvey.

Jack shrugged and looked at David. 'Come on buddy, you know that there are never any guarantees in this business. We have covered all the angles as far as we can. We are using a tried and tested system which has always delivered. In theory, it should be a piece of cake. It's just me; I never count my chickens.'

Harvey interjected, 'Don't worry too much, David, he's always like this in the last stages of an operation. I blame it on that European grandma!'

The others laughed.

Harvey asked, 'The reception's all fixed, I hope?'

Jack turned over a sheet of paper and said, 'A good team of Czechs; they are in position with two of our people. They will helicopter him up to the German border, near Passau. Our friends in the Federal Border Guard, the Bundesgrenzschutz, will help us there, and we'll fly him straight into our facility at Frankfurt. As soon as he is aboard that first helicopter, we will get the message.' He looked around.

The Senior Regional Director, Cliff Holmes, had been quietly turning his pen over in his hand as he listened to the unfolding story. He looked towards Jack.

'This is your baby, Jack. Are you comfortable with things as they stand?'

Jack leaned back from the table. 'The straight answer? Yes, but with reservations. As I've already said, we've used this method before and it's always been a success. This guy is a high profile prize, we are told.'

He looked questioningly at Cliff Holmes who nodded in reply.

Jack continued, 'That being the case, I'm too long in the tooth to be complacent and I figure that if ever there is a chance for things to foul up, it will happen when we least need it. But that's just my personal pessimism talking. We have gone over this thing time after time. The people we are using have never let us down. On the face of it, we should not worry.'

Cliff nodded and said, 'What time can we expect that phone call tomorrow?'

'Around nineteen hundred hours, London time.' replied Jack.

'Okay,' Cliff concluded, 'I think we have all the bases covered. Pray for success gentlemen.'

15

The eighth of May dawned bright and cool in Leningrad. Katya had lain awake for some time, her mind troubled by the situation she found herself in.

She and Alexei had led a relatively comfortable and protected life as a result of his status, and now they were about to leap into the unknown.

Would it all be as wonderful as they hoped? Could they be absorbed, anonymously, into another society? Would Alexei's knowledge be useful in making life safer for everyone?

Yes, she thought. If the Western powers are serious about peace and stability, Alexei and I know that his knowledge can help neutralise any threat from the Soviet biological and chemical weapons. So, on that count alone, our escape is worthwhile. We can only hope that the quality of our lives will also be worth the danger and effort.

Well, she concluded, whatever happens, the decision to go ahead was ours. The signs, so far, are all positive so I must be positive too.

After a late breakfast, she ran over the things she wanted to take with her. She realised that, of necessity, she must travel very light. Vadimir and his cohorts would be sure to suspect her motives if she suddenly went out with a bulky bag. The weather forecast was that the afternoon would cloud over and remain cool. That meant she could quite reasonably wear her padded coat, and if she zipped out the inner lining she would be able to conceal some of her sentimental treasures quite easily. She continuously wondered how she was to be spirited out without the minders missing her, and was unable to imagine a plausible scenario.

She wrote some postcards, as she had told Vladimir she would, and asked the receptionist to post them, then she set out to brave the morning.

The car trip to the Dostoyevsky Museum in Kuznechny Lane was again quite short. She was intrigued to hear that in this unremarkable, middle-class house Feodor Dostoyevsky had written Crime and Punishment and The Brothers Karamazov which she remembered from her college days. The curator was happy to discuss with her at length the writer's realistic style and his grasp of the psychological forces driving some of his characters, and to show her the exhibits with pride. He also brought Crime and Punishment to life for her by pointing out locations from the book which were real and nearby. Sennaya Square and Sadovaya Street were part of the run-down area in the book, and were still a bit run-down and disreputable, lying to the south of Nevsky Prospekt.

The curator's infectious enthusiasm prompted her to ask Vladimir to go via Sennaya Square, en route to the Maryinsky Theatre where she would see some of the Kirov company's collection of ballet history.

The square was in a dilapidated area, and she could picture Dostoyevsky's Raskolnikov in this place. She felt more comfortable when they moved on.

The Maryinsky Theatre, home of the Kirov Ballet, was another pilgrimage point for lovers of Russian ballet. It was part of the history of dance, and had staged some of the first ballets. Nijinsky and Pavlova had made their debuts there.

Katya was grateful to her new friends at the Vaganova for setting up this visit. She was able to watch some of the dancers practising. The theatre supported three companies who tended to rotate their performances. The first company, formed from the cream of the dancers, was frequently touring the world.

Katya felt at home amongst these dedicated artistes and could have spent all day watching their constant progress towards perfection.

The history collection was interesting through its connections with the many and varied personalities who had performed at the Kirov. To her it was a delight to see shoes which had been used by the magical Nijinsky or by Kschessinska.

She was invited to have lunch with some of the staff, and enjoyed talking 'shop' with them. Like the staff at the Vaganova they were full of encouragement for teachers such as herself to act as the nursery for the future stars of companies like theirs.

Mindful of her timetable, she eventually thanked them for their hospitality and encouragement and left.

She told Vladimir that before starting her shopping trip to Nevsky Prospekt, she needed to change her shoes at the hotel, and take some headache pills as she felt that a migraine was coming on, probably caused by the bright lights in the theatre. Vladimir showed some sympathy for her and she was whisked back to the hotel.

The temperature was significantly milder in Uzhgorod. Spring showed itself in every garden and window-box.

Alexei was not feeling the joys of spring that morning. He

was consciously forcing himself to act normally despite the breathless excitement - or was it fear? - that he felt.

There was no backing out now, he told himself. Katya was already committed to the plan, and for either of them to renege on their agreed course would expose the other to fatal dangers. She had not contacted him to say she had any doubts; he was unlikely to get hold of her, and even if he could speak to her, what would he say on the telephone?

No, he thought, we must press on and succeed. As Irina quoted from the Ukraine anthem *'we are not dead yet'*.

He had breakfast, then collected his briefcase with his lecture notes and went out to meet Mikhail and Yuri. He greeted them, as normal, and they nodded in return.

'Well gentlemen, now I have to sing for my supper, or in this case, my lunch. I have no idea what time I'll be finished. It all depends on how long the chatting goes on after lunch. Sometimes it can drag on.'

Mikhail smiled, 'It's not a problem, Professor. We are at your disposal.'

'Good,' said Alexei. 'I think we should go now.'

Yuri drove along the riverfront pointing out the colourful old houses overlooking the River Uzh, and Alexei enjoyed the sight of them.

They crossed the river into Lenin Square with its enormous City Hall and the Trade Unions House, then round to the Medical Faculty on the corner of Lenin Quay.

As Mikhail opened the car door, Alexei was met by a small delegation of lecturers and administrators from the university.

The principal lecturer was rather effusive in his welcome, and would have rambled on if Alexei had not tactfully interrupted him by expressing his grateful thanks for the warmth of the welcome and then starting to introduce himself to the others in the party.

The principal, Professor Tereskov, was unabashed by Alexei's diplomatic interruption and took over the introductions.

They all went inside and Alexei had the obligatory short tour of the faculty, before he joined the others for coffee in a committee room, where Professor Tereskov launched into the remainder of his interrupted speech of welcome, and thankfully finished quickly.

Alexei gave a short address of thanks, and explained, as usual, the thinking behind his lectures.

Firstly, the lecture was meant to encourage students to apply themselves to their studies and secondly, it was a veiled recruitment plug for government departments.

He asked them not to be judgmental on the cynicism behind that train of thought, but to listen to his lecture and have an open discussion with him over lunch.

This seemed to take the wind out of a few sails, since he had noted some individuals with notes in front of them and expected them to have a go at him.

He made complimentary remarks about the city in general, and about the setting of the medical faculty with its river views in particular. He told them that he envied their pleasant environment and hoped he might include Uzhgorod in future lecture tours.

This went down well with the majority, and the meeting quickly gravitated into small groups talking amongst themselves with Alexei being the centre of a polite circle discussing medical and social trends.

At eleven o'clock, Professor Tereskov led Alexei into the lecture hall and, with his uncontrolled effusiveness, introduced him to the students. Alexei thanked the Professor and repeated some of his earlier compliments about Uzhgorod.

His lecture was identical to that he gave in Lvov, and followed the Party diktat. He rarely deviated from the script except when answering questions, which allowed him to introduce a modicum of individuality. He was always aware that amongst the administrators attending these lectures were Party apparatchiks who would report on any signs of veering off the approved path.

However, he was an expert in the field of virology and displayed this in the comprehensive way he covered so many aspects of the subject. The students attending the lecture, who were all in their final year, were well able to follow his theories and explanations. He did not see Jana or Tina in the hall.

The question and answer session which followed was lively and in some cases, almost adversarial, where some students thought they could beat Alexei with questions on obscure aspects of virology. Alexei treated all the questions with the same good humour. He thanked each questioner for the quality of their question, then proceeded to answer it to such a depth that made them realise their own limits of knowledge.

He closed by pointing out that he, and many like him, had started from the same point as the students. He encouraged them to keep learning, since they would find that all sciences, including medicine, were pushing their frontiers further back continuously and perhaps their generation would eventually find that there were no limits to what could be achieved.

He had not finished a lecture quite so enthusiastically before, and was surprised at the warmth of the applause he received.

He did not milk the situation, but quietly walked off. Professor Tereskov appeared to be ready for curtain calls, but Alexei would not return to the lectern. 'I would like the students to appreciate the importance of their studies,' he said. 'That is more important to them than any speaker. I'm sure you agree, Professor Tereskov, that medicine will outlive us.'

The Professor nodded vigorously. 'That is so true, so true,' he replied. 'It's a message I am always trying to get across to them.'

Alexei could not imagine this pompous little man ever agreeing that he was any less important than the content of his lectures.

Lunch was quite a splendid affair, with a variety of Ukrainian and Russian dishes, and plentiful supplies of local wine. Several of the lecturers were authoritative on the varieties of wine.

Alexei resolved to keep his wine consumption to a minimum. He wanted a clear head for the afternoon. Nevertheless, he was amused to see how the opinions of the 'wine experts' became more divergent as their consumption increased. He managed to survive with a glass of fruit juice in his hand, refusing any topping up from the wine bottles.

From his talks with many of the lecturers there, he gathered that the medical faculty was of a high standard and well regarded in the Ukrainian medical circles. He had to use his glib tongue to slip past the uncomfortable questions about his current work, describing his work as 'humanitarian research for the common good'.

He never failed to surprise himself at how easily the lies slipped out of his mouth.

From tomorrow, he thought, I should not have to lie any

more. My life will be clean and, hopefully, I will cleanse my conscience too.

The time was coming up to three o'clock, and he felt he should make a move. He thanked Professor Tereskov for his hospitality, especially the outstanding lunch. The Professor was equally grateful for Alexei's lecture and urged him to return to Uzhgorod as soon as possible. Alexei said he would try to arrange that.

He collected his briefcase and said a few goodbyes as he left. The wine experts were too far gone to notice his departure.

Yuri and Mikhail were waiting at the entrance for him and set off for the hotel.

Mikhail asked if the lecture had gone well, and Alexei told him that it had, then went into some detail about the lunch he had received. He hoped they had had some lunch, and Mikhail assured him that they were fine.

'I have a few notes to write up,' Alexei lied, 'Then I'm going to have look at the art gallery. Several of the lecturers were telling me about it and insisting that I must see it before leaving. Have you chaps been there?'

Mikhail and Yuri looked at each other. Mikhail said, 'We are not great art lovers, Professor. We enjoy sport more than anything.'

'That's fine,' said Alexei. 'Each to his own interests. It would be a funny world if we all liked exactly the same things.'

The others nodded.

'When I have finished my notes, I'll stroll over and see what they've got,' said Alexei.

At the hotel, he went up to his room and sat down to let his mind clear. There were several pages of notes which were essential to him and must be taken on his trip. They detailed several processes and test results which would help him in the new life he hoped to make, counteracting his efforts for *Biopreparat*.

He had some dollar bills he had been acquiring in very small amounts over the last two months. He didn't know what use he would need to make of them, but felt reassured by having them.

He folded the papers and inserted them into several plastic bags which he sealed to make small flat packages. He put them into various pockets of his jacket and trousers and, after examining his appearance in the wardrobe mirror, was satisfied that his clothing showed no lumps or bumps and looked normal.

After an early breakfast in the Novotel, the Coppers for Kids cycled out of Strasbourg at eight o' clock towards the Pont de l'Europe and into Germany. The route alongside the Rhine was straight and level and they set a good pace in the sunshine.

Somehow, let's blame human error, they took the wrong fork in Rastatt and it suddenly dawned on them that they were approaching Karlsruhe from the southwest instead of bypassing it to the south.

They stopped for a snack and looked for a way back on course. A laboured conversation with a German shopkeeper put them in the right direction very quickly.

They were just congratulating each other on getting things right, when they found themselves running down a ramp and joining a road with very fast traffic. Some of the passing cars were sounding their horns as they passed. Roy looked over his shoulder at the others and shouted, 'I think we're on a bloody motorway.'

Jock rode alongside him and said, 'I hope you're wrong. It's probably a bypass, but we'll err on the safe side and get off it as quick as we can. Stay on the hard shoulder and we'll set a stiff pace.'

So, it was heads down and tails up again for a couple of miles until the next junction when they turned off and found themselves on their original planned route, heading in the right direction on highway 10. A long stiff climb followed, from Durlach up to Pforzheim, which strung the team out a bit.

As they approached the outskirts of Pforzheim, Jock and Paddy were trailing the others and caught up with the group where the minibus had stopped and a Police motorcyclist was chatting with Ron.

Ron called out, 'Jock, you could be in trouble. The Police are looking for some cyclists who were seen on the autobahn near Karlsruhe.'

Jock and Paddy drew alongside the others and stopped. Jock said, 'I see no cyclists.'

'What's an autobahn?' said Paddy. The German officer was grinning, and Ron burst out laughing. 'I think you were half believing me,' he said.

Paddy said, 'After climbing that long drag from Durlach, a night in the cells would give me a decent rest.'

They were escorted into Pforzheim to a splendid reception by the local Police. Lots to eat and drink; lots of exchanging of pennants and cap badges and other souvenirs.

They got back on the road at last, for the hilly final run into Stuttgart, where they found their hotel, the Novotel, on the outskirts of the city, but got a shock when the receptionist said there was no booking for them.

A long discussion took place, with Jock asking the manager to contact the London office of Novotel. Finally the hotel manager went back through his paperwork and found the fax from London relating to the cyclists' visit.

They booked in with great relief and were given a free drink as a gesture of apology.

At that stage all they wanted was a bath and a rest, but the rest was not to be. Local members of the International Police Association arrived to welcome them to Stuttgart, and one of the German officers, who spoke English with a wonderful New York accent, took them off for a tour of the city by night and an excellent pub meal. One of the local highlights was a night view from a high tower overlooking the city.

16

Katya unzipped the lining from her padded coat and hung it in the wardrobe. She put on a cardigan with large pockets and used this for some of the lighter things she wanted to carry, such as photographs of her and Alexei's parents, and birth and marriage certificates. She had stitched temporary pockets into the inside of her coat, and used these for her few pieces of jewellery, and those her mother had left to her.

She put on the coat, tied a headscarf over her hair and carried her sunglasses as she went downstairs. At the door, she donned the sunglasses and went out with a glum expression.

Vladimir stood by the car and she walked over to him.

'Vladimir, this migraine is not very good.' She said. 'I'm feeling queasy, and the light is straining my eyes, but I must get some shopping done. I don't fancy riding in the car while I feel like this. I'm sure I'll throw up. So, I'm going to walk to Nevsky Prospekt. It's only about ten minutes away, isn't it?'

'Yes madame,' said Vladimir. 'I'm sorry to hear you feel unwell. What can we do to help you?'

'Vladimir,' she said, a little sternly, 'I'm not dying. I've got a damned migraine, which I've had before and lived through, so please don't fuss. It will get better on its own. Walking in the fresh air will probably help.'

With that, she stalked off along Liteyniy Prospekt. Vladimir hurriedly spoke to his car crew then walked quickly after Katya.

When he drew level with her, she said, 'I'm sorry, Vladimir, but I don't feel like talking to anyone at the moment. While I have this migraine you will just have to put up with me.'

'No problem, madame,' said Vladimir.

They turned into Nevsky Prospekt and she stopped outside Yeliseev's, and admired the huge windows with the Modern Art surrounds. It is a food store, but unlike any food store she had ever seen. Inside, she admired the marble counters, the stained-glass windows and crystal chandeliers, and the sculptures and bronzes which decorated the fascinating interior. It was like a shopping centre in a museum of modern art, and she didn't know how she had missed it on previous visits to the city.

She looked around a few more stores on the north side of the street, then crossed over towards Gostiniy Dvor with its yellow stone arches and porticos. Inside, it formed a huge quadrangle of stall and boutiques.

'So this is where your family spend your money, Vladimir.'

'Yes indeed, madame,' he replied, 'I think I own half of it by now.'

She wandered around and bought one or two cheap items; tee shirts for her and Alexei, some sports socks, things she guessed she would be leaving behind. All the while, she studiously ignored Vladimir. She had already noticed where the Star boutique was, and as the time approached four, she drifted in that direction.

She turned to Vladimir, who was following behind, and said, 'Look here, Vladimir. I am sure that your wife does not enjoy having you trail along with her when she is shopping, and I certainly am not enjoying it today. I am going up to look at some of the clothes in the boutiques on the first floor and I don't want you coming around with me looking like an undertaker. If you won't clear off, at least get out from under my feet. Is that understood?' she snapped.

Vladimir looked like she had slapped him. 'Yes madame,' he spluttered, and hung back as she went up to the first floor.

She looked in several shops as the clock swung towards four. Behind her sunglasses she saw that Vladimir was still hovering on the ground floor keeping an eye on her.

At four o'clock, she entered the Star boutique.

It was not large inside, and there were two women serving some customers who all appeared to be dressed like the American women she had met in the Hermitage. Several racks of clothing were lined across the shop. Katya looked along a rail, found a black dress in her size and asked one of the assistants if she could try it on.

The woman directed her towards a curtained-off area at the back of the shop.

When Katya went around the curtain, she saw that there were three women already in the changing area. All turned towards her and she suddenly recognised one of them as the chambermaid from the Neva Hotel who had passed her the Hermitage ticket.

The women waved her forwards and the chambermaid said, 'Don't worry, just do as we tell you. It's all going to work perfectly. I am Teresa.'

The other two women were dressed in the light raincoats and trainers she associated with Americans, and they took up a position blocking anyone else from entering.

'Quickly,' said Teresa, 'We must change your clothes. Take off your outer clothes and give them to me. You will put on these ones here,' and she indicated a bag.

Katya quickly divested herself of her clothes, putting on the trousers, jumper and trainers from the bag.

Teresa, meanwhile had donned Katya's clothes, removing the personal belongings and handing them to Katya. On Katya's instructions, they removed the contents of the temporary pockets from the inside of the coat, then Teresa put on a blonde wig, the headscarf and sunglasses, and Katya felt that she was looking at herself in a mirror. The effect was startling.

'Tell me what you have been saying and doing with that minder on your way here.' asked Teresa.

Katya related her migraine charade and grumpy behaviour towards Vladimir.

Teresa nodded and said, 'Well done. You have made my job easier.'

Katya was concerned. 'What are you going to do? Won't we be discovered?'

Teresa said, 'We haven't much time. This is what will happen. You will put on this dark wig and the glasses and go with these women. I will play your role and walk grumpily back to the hotel. I will go to your room without speaking to anyone and telephone the reception to say I don't want to be disturbed and that I'm going to bed early. Then I'll change into my chambermaid outfit and slip out of your room and out of the hotel, and disappear.'

She picked up the bags Katya had been carrying, then strolled out of the changing area and back into the sea of shoppers.

One of the American women helped Katya into a curly brunette wig, then put on a pair of tinted glasses with a winged frame which altered the shape of her face quite considerably.

116

The ubiquitous light-coloured raincoat followed.

'Okay honey,' she said, 'You'll do. From now on you are Connie Newhart. Can you say that?'

Katya said, 'I am Connie Newhart.'

The other woman smiled, 'That will do. I'm Jean and this is Freda. Put all your bits and pieces in this shoulder bag. You will find your American passport in there. We are going to catch the coach now, so let's go.'

Jean linked arms with Katya, and Freda followed in their wake.

Katya saw Vladimir on the ground floor, but he was looking away from them towards the staircase. She saw Teresa descending the stairs and walking off towards Nevsky Prospekt. Vladimir followed her.

The three women came out of Gostiniy Dvor into Nevsky Prospekt and met up with a group of men and women who were obviously tourists. Jean and Freda took Katya aside and explained the next stage.

'We are going on a coach, which should arrive any second now,' said Jean. 'We must have our passports ready when we go on the coach, and the Intourist guide ticks us off as we go aboard. Don't worry, your name is on the list, Connie Newhart.'

Katya had started opening the shoulder bag and found the passport. She was amazed to find her photograph, with dark curly hair, inside.

'Never mind that for the moment,' said Jean. 'When we board the coach, just follow Freda to the back, where you can sit between us and you'll be hidden from the street.'

'But where are we going?' asked Katya.

'I'm getting to that. Once we have all been checked into the coach, it remains closed until we reach the port. That's about three miles from here. It's a secure area, apparently, which is why we have to be checked in and out. The coach will take us directly to the cruise ship, and we'll all go aboard together. Tomorrow evening we will be in Stockholm. Now hold your handkerchief up to your mouth. You are feeling sick.'

Katya did as she was told.

The coach drew into the kerb, and Freda stomped forcefully through the others to the door, closely followed by Jean, arm-in-arm with Katya.

Jean was saying, 'Don't worry Connie, we'll soon have you safely in your bed. I told you not to eat that pancake thing. Keep taking deep breaths.'

She turned to some of the people near the coach door and said, 'This is just in time. She ate one of those *blini* things from a stall. I told her it was a mistake, and now she is feeling bilious. We'll get her sorted out aboard ship.'

The people she spoke to expressed concern and ushered them towards the coach. The Intourist representative was at the door with his check list.

Freda produced her passport then turned to face Jean and Katya saying, 'Our friend's not feeling well. She ate one of those pancake things. Get her passport out, Jean.'

Jean produced her passport with the fake one for Katya, and the guide waved them aboard without comment. They went to the rear of the coach where Katya sat with Jean and Freda forming a shield on either side of her.

'Keep the handkerchief up, and don't speak to anyone,' muttered Jean.

Katya thought: This has been an afternoon of play-acting, but I have not been able to enjoy it so far.

She sat back with her handkerchief to her mouth and after a few minutes, the last of the party came aboard and the coach moved off. Katya resisted the urge to look out of the windows and see if Vladimir or any of his team had spotted her.

One or two of her fellow passengers turned and expressed their sympathy for her. To each of them she just waved her hand slightly, and kept the handkerchief in place.

Within ten minutes, the coach pulled up at the port entrance where the Intourist guide produced his list for the uniformed guards, and they carried on into the port.

They stopped at the foot of the gangway of a Swedish liner. Again the Intourist guide produced another copy of his list to more uniformed guards who counted the passengers as they came off the coach, then allowed them to walk aboard ship.

Jean and Freda guided Katya up several flights of stairs to a passageway where they walked to a cabin door, produced the key and ushered her inside.

'This is it, honey. Your home until tomorrow night. Welcome to freedom.' said Jean.

Katya looked around her. The cabin had four berths and an open door led to a bathroom. She could see the roofs of Leningrad through a window.

Freda opened one of the small wardrobes and said, 'We have done our best with clothes sizes. These are for you. Underwear and toiletries are in the bag, there.' She pointed into the wardrobe where several items of clothing were on hangers and a holdall was on the floor.

Katya sat down and looked at the other two.

'Am I safe yet? The ship is not leaving. When will it go?' she asked.

'You are safe, Katya. Believe me,' said Jean. 'The ship is due to sail in twenty minutes. Once we have moved out into the sea, we can take a walk around the deck, then we'll have our dinner served here in the cabin.'

'There are four beds.' said Katya. 'Who else is using this cabin?'

'Just us. Things have been planned this way.' replied Jean. 'As soon as we sail, Freda will go up and send a telegram to her sister, asking her to buy some flowers for their mother's birthday. That is the message confirming your safe departure. Now how about a cup of coffee, or would you like something stronger?'

Katya smiled, 'Coffee is fine. Do you know when I will hear that Alexei is safe?'

'We'll have to wait until we get to Stockholm, tomorrow night.' said Freda, following her instructions. She knew that if Alexei's move went to plan, a message would be sent to them; but if it came unstuck they would get no details until their arrival in Stockholm. So, no point in having Katya waiting and worrying in expectation of a message. Hopefully, everything would turn out fine.

'Let's get some coffee brought down, and then you can relax,' smiled Freda.

17

Alexei walked casually out of the hotel into the square. He smiled to Mikhail and Yuri and said, 'I might as well see as much as possible whilst I'm here, and several of the university staff suggested visiting their art gallery. I'm told it also has a gift shop, so I should be able to find something for my wife there.'

The others smiled, and Mikhail said, 'And it is only a hundred metres away, Professor, so you don't have to hurry.'

'Indeed not, Mikhail. The pace of life in places like this has a lot to recommend it after the hurly-burly of some of the places I have to work in.'

Mikhail agreed, 'It certainly has a peaceful feel to it.'

Alexei had noted the time on the clock tower and knew he must move. His stomach was turning somersaults, but he would have to keep up the front.

'The medical professors reckon that a satisfactory visit to the art gallery takes about an hour.' he said. 'So, we'll see if they are right. I'll see you soon.'

He walked across the square towards the gallery, his ears pricked to hear if the minders were following him. He heard nothing, and as he came to the front of the gallery he was able to see a reflection in the front window of Mikhail and Yuri still lolling on the car.

He entered the gallery, and from the shaded interior ventured a quick look back. They were still by the car, deep in conversation and not looking his way. He collected a guide book and looked through it at length until the clock came round to four fifteen, then he followed the sign towards the toilet, walked past the toilet door and found an emergency exit.

A young man was standing by the exit, and Alexei hesitated. Should he go back, pretending he had missed the toilet door?

The young man waved him forward and hissed, 'Quickly, Professor.'

Alexei walked towards him and the young man swung the door open, pushed him gently through and closed the door behind him.

Outside the door a motorcycle was ticking over. The rider handed Alexei a crash helmet and an old army smock to wear.

He quickly pulled them on and climbed on the pillion seat. Not a word had been spoken. The bike pulled away steadily, without excessive revving, and headed from the rear of the art gallery towards the north of the town. Alexei could not resist looking behind them, frequently, but saw no sign of pursuit.

After five minutes, the bike pulled up in a lay-by on the outskirts of Uzhgorod. The rider switched off the engine and opened his visor.

'Okay, Professor, give me the helmet,' he said.

As Alexei pulled off the helmet, the rider handed him an army forage cap.

'Keep the jacket on, and the cap.' he said. 'Everything is going fine. In a few minutes, an army truck will pull into this lay-by and the driver will wave you aboard. He is carrying supplies to an army camp over the Czech border. It's a regular trip, with nobody scrutinising passports. The driver has his official paperwork which will get the truck over. You will be dropped off soon after you cross over and collected there. I wish you safe journey.'

With that, he started the motorcycle and rode off, leaving Alexei feeling exposed and slightly ridiculous in the army smock and cap. He sat on the kerb in the lay-by, reducing his profile, and within a few minutes, an army truck came growling into the lay-by. The driver waved to him and he got up and climbed into the cab.

The truck moved off immediately, and Alexei sat, looking ahead with his mind whirling. The driver was a man in his late twenties.

He glanced at Alexei and said, 'Worried?'

Alexei nodded and said, 'You bet I'm worried. Aren't you?'

The soldier just grinned, 'What is there to worry about? I've done this trip several times and it's always worked. The military police don't bother much anymore since we started pulling out of these countries like Czechoslovakia. I don't know how long the situation will last, but I'm making my money while I can.'

He had a streetwise, opportunist air about him and was obviously one of life's survivors.

They had only gone a couple of kilometres when the driver suddenly looked in his mirror, then looked again and said, 'Shit! I don't believe it.'

Alexei was alarmed. 'What's happening?

'There's a military police jeep coming up behind me fast. If he signals me to stop, you duck down on the floor and I'll try to bluff my way through.' he looked grim.

The jeep came alongside and Alexei leaned down to keep out of view. The driver swore again and started to slow down. Alexei dropped to the cab floor, his heart in his mouth.

He heard the footsteps approaching and the driver leaned out of his window and called, 'What's up? Have I forgotten something?'

Alexei could hear the military policeman say, 'It's a good job we don't have a war on. These stupid bloody conscripts would lose it for us before we start. You have the wrong load. The thick bastards have given you the Hungarian delivery, so we are redirecting you.'

The driver said, 'Shit. Do you want me to take this truck back and get reloaded?'

'No,' said the policeman. 'We have the necessary paperwork here to get you through the Hungarian border. So, you can take your load down to the Kisvarda camp. You have done that run before, the transport officer told us, so you can cope. Follow us, we will explain it all to the guards at the border.'

'Are you escorting me all the way to the Kisvarda camp?' asked the truck driver.

'Yes. We were due to go there anyway, but this cock-up has brought it forward by a few hours. We have all had our day mucked up so don't bloody grumble at us. Just follow us.'

Alexei listened in disbelief. The months of indecision before grasping the nettle, and the weeks of worry leading up to this day had all been turned into a crock of shit by some dozy conscripts who had loaded the wrong lorry. How was it possible? What should he do now?

The driver started the truck and pulled out onto the road again. He looked down at Alexei sitting on the truck floor and said, 'Well it could have been worse. You were not spotted, so the game goes on.'

Alexei spluttered, 'But Hungary. Will there be a contact

124

point for me there? Are you going to drop me off at a pre-arranged point? I think not.'

'Look,' said the soldier, 'There is no going back for you, if I am guessing right. You are almost certainly in a situation where you have to keep going forward or you will probably be locked up, or worse.'

Alexei was still shaking his head in disbelief.

The soldier continued, 'You wanted to get to the West. The routes to get there go through Czechoslovakia, Germany, Poland and Hungary. So, you are now going via Hungary, instead of with the Czechs. I'll drop you off as soon as I can, once we cross the border. It should be getting into dusk by then and that will make it easier. I'll let my contact know what's happened as soon as I can, but that will probably be quite a bit later tonight. I don't think I'll be doing a return trip tonight, and the telephone link isn't always reliable. I promise I will do my best.'

'How am I likely to fare in Hungary? Does everyone speak Russian, because I sure as hell don't understand Hungarian?' Alexei looked miserable.

'My friend, don't blame me for this cock-up. We are in the Soviet Union. It's a disorganised shit-hole of a country, which is possibly one of your reasons for leaving. The bottom line is that you are leaving, though not necessarily in the ideal manner. Just lighten up, man. You are not dead yet.'

The driver was defending himself, and Alexei was fair-minded enough to grant that what he said was right. He had expected a smooth well-oiled operation, but as with many other things, it was human frailty which had let things down; the single unpredictable element which can lighten, or blight, our existence. But, as the soldier had said, and as Irina had said in Lvov - he wasn't dead yet.

The driver asked, 'Have you any money; dollars or deutschmarks?'

Alexei replied, 'I have some dollars, but not a lot,' he said guardedly.

'That's good,' said the soldier. 'Dollars will open all sorts of doors for you, so you should survive okay. Once we clear the border, it's about a half hour run to the camp outside Kisvarda. That gives us plenty of opportunity to drop you off. Look on the bright side, you'll still be out of the Soviet Union.'

Alexei was finding it extremely difficult to raise any enthusiasm for his present situation. What had happened to the slick operation he had imagined the Americans would engineer? How would he fare on the Hungarian side? How would his Russian language fare? Who could he approach? He turned to the driver.

'What do you suggest as a good course of action after you drop me off? Should I find the nearest police station and ask their help?' he asked.

'No, no,' said the driver. 'That's not a good idea. Just think of it. They have been a Soviet satellite state for over forty years until their recent separation. The KGB had the police and secret police under their control. Since then, they may have changed their cap-badges, but not all of them will have forgotten old allegiances, and you can be sure that some of them are still on the KGB payroll. There is no way of knowing who the good guys are, especially at this end of the country where the Russian Army still occupies a few bases. You will have to play it by ear and use your wits. Don't take any stupid risks now.'

126

His advice did not help Alexei's state of mind a great deal. It had only served to show him how naive he was about surviving by his wits. He realised how his sheltered existence under the KGB had ill-prepared him for this adventure he had embarked on, but he thought of Katya, who might be in equally dire straits, and forced himself to believe that he could win through.

The truck bypassed the town of Chop, which the driver told him was also an army town, and they approached the Hungarian border. A line of trucks was waiting to cross, but the military police jeep drove past them and up to the control point. Alexei's driver chugged along behind them.

They passed through the Soviet side of the border without a hitch and rolled across the River Tisza bridge to the Hungarian border. The military policemen went into the office of the border guards, and in the fading light, Alexei raised his head from under the dashboard to see a heated discussion taking place in the lighted office. Eventually the Hungarian officer appeared to grudgingly acquiesce with the dogmatic Russians, and he stamped the papers they were holding. They came out of the office, and as they approached their jeep they waved to Alexei's driver to follow. He was in Hungary.

The Russian soldier, who had still not volunteered his name nor asked Alexei's, turned to him with a grin and said, 'We got away with that, my friend. It's all looking good for you.'

'I hope you are right,' replied Alexei, 'But what are we going to do about dropping me off with that military police jeep in front of us?'

'Should not be a problem. You look reasonably fit.'

Alexei's eyes widened. 'Reasonably fit! Just what are you

planning to do with me?'

'Stop worrying,' the driver chuckled. 'I'm not going to throw you out on the motorway, or do anything really dangerous, but you will have to look lively when the opportunity arrives.'

'What opportunity are you talking about, and when is it likely to arrive?' Alexei's worries were resurfacing.

'Look,' the driver pointed to a signpost. 'We'll soon be passing Zahony, and I remember the road has a few bends in it. After those bends, the road is almost dead straight to Kisvarda, so there won't be much of chance then. I'll be able to let the jeep pull ahead a bit before a right-hand bend, then slow down enough to let you jump out. Simple!' he grinned.

'Simple? I think you can appreciate that I don't share your optimistic assessment of the situation I am in.'

Alexei's expression portrayed a seriously worried man.

'I can only hope that I survive a leap in the dark from a moving truck; I'll be landing in a country whose language I cannot hope to understand, and whose geography I have no knowledge of; and, you think the local police might still be sympathetic to the KGB, who are probably starting to look for me now. It does not sound simple to me!'

'Make the best of it,' the soldier retorted. 'I am just a little cog in a big machine. I have done my best, and I have got you out of the Soviet Union. So, the plan went a bit shitty. Nothing's perfect. If you wanted someone to take your hand, blow your nose and wipe your arse, you've got the wrong man. My best advice to you is, that when you jump from this truck hit the ground running and you will be all right.'

'But where the hell are we?' pleaded Alexei.

'We are in the north-east corner of Hungary, and you must

128

head roughly south-west to reach Budapest. If you can get yourself into Kisvarda, you can catch a train all the way. Once you are there, it should be easy to establish contact with your friends.'

'Budapest,' repeated Alexei, 'And how far away is that?'

The driver pursed his lips for a moment, then said, 'About three hundred or three fifty kilometres. Something like that.'

Alexei groaned. 'This is the icing on the cake.'

Before he could bemoan his lot any further, the driver patted his shoulder with his right hand then pointed ahead.

'Look! Just up there, a right hander with a wood on our side. Your jumping off point, I think.' The driver grinned at Alexei who was removing the army cap and smock.

He peered ahead through the half-light and saw the road disappearing to the right behind a fairly large wood. The driver had eased off the accelerator and the military police jeep was pulling away from them. As they drew nearer the wood, Alexei felt that the truck was still travelling a bit too fast for him to try jumping out.

The jeep was suddenly lost to view behind the trees, and the driver braked a little more and called, 'Go on, it's now or never,' giving him a forceful push towards the door.

Alexei opened the truck door to see a grass verge rushing by. It crossed his mind that even if he fell, the grass would cushion his fall.

The driver was shouting at him, by now.

'Jump, you fool. There won't be another chance.'

Alexei pushed the door against the force of the slipstream and leapt out. He heard the door bang shut as the truck accelerated away. His feet touched the ground and he tried to make his legs keep up with his speed. He careered along briefly until his shins cracked against fallen timber and he shot headlong through a jumble of broken branches into a ditch. There was a sensation of searing pain and he blacked out.

18

The mood in Grosvenor Square was distinctly funereal. Jack Bergen was talking quietly into a telephone, whilst Cliff Holmes and the others stood in front of a map of Eastern Europe and tried to make optimistic hypotheses of escape routes, but without much conviction.

Jack put down the phone and rubbed his brow. The others turned towards him. 'Anything?' asked Cliff.

Jack shook his head. 'Frankfurt office has been chasing all the contacts we have, but there is not a trace.' His shoulders sagged.

'Okay,' said Cliff, 'Let's all just sit down and evaluate what we have.'

The others sat around the desk with Jack who straightened up and rearranged the sheets of paper in front of him.

'Let's have the positives first, Jack,' asked Cliff.

'The Leningrad operation went like clockwork,' began Jack. 'The wife played her part perfectly and is on her way to Stockholm. Our girl who doubled for her drew the minders back to the hotel, then got herself out safely. She'll be in Berlin by morning.'

Cliff smiled across the table, 'I think we all agree that you deserve praise for the planning and execution of the Leningrad job. That was exactly what we would expect of you Jack. Well done.'

Harvey Fletcher and David Sanchez said, 'Hear, hear.'

'Thanks, gents,' replied Jack, 'I appreciate your kindness, but hold off the praise.'

He grimaced as he turned over the next paper and looked at the faces round the table.

'Now we come to the main course, which could be called Operation Foul-up. The positives, if we can call them that, are that our man appears to have followed all the instructions given him. He was safely delivered to the point where the transport was picking him up, and was seen boarding the truck.

On the negative side; the truck has not been seen crossing the Czech border, and our reception team haven't seen nor heard anything.

However, what is a glimmer of hope is the news from Uzhgorod. We have been told that the KGB minders have been tearing around looking for our man, which would tend to suggest that he is not being held by them. There hasn't been anything back from the truck driver yet, so we should not write things off completely, just yet.'

David Sanchez showed some enthusiasm. 'Hey, it sounds like there could be a silver lining just waiting round the corner. Maybe the truck just broke down, and everything will get back on track any time now.'

Cliff Holmes looked at the clock. 'We are four hours behind your anticipated time check. That's not completely disastrous when we consider that, for the present, we have no direct evidence to suggest that our man has been put in a dangerous position. Until our sources give us the details, we should at least keep an open mind on the outcome.'

'I hear all you say, and I can't logically argue against you,' Jack replied. 'If we can only get some information soon, we might be able to take some positive action and reach the conclusion we want. Our communications in that area are not ideal because of the safeguards which have to be exercised to avoid the phone-tapping and to protect our people. Everything takes a bit longer to come through.'

'That reinforces Cliff's line of thought,' said Harvey.

'We can't do any more at present,' concluded Cliff. 'As and when we get the information, we'll decide the next steps. Jack, you'll be organising a listening watch in this office and liaising with Frankfurt. Have we enough personnel for a relieving roster?'

'I'm staying here tonight,' said Jack, 'And one of my team is coming in at midnight to give me a break. I'll have a snooze on the fold-up bed in the other office.'

'Make sure you get some rest; I want you clear-headed when we get any news, and let me know what's developing as soon as you hear,' said Cliff.

'Understood,' replied Jack.

They all stood up and started heading towards the door when the telephone rang on Jack's desk. Everyone turned and looked at it, until Jack scooped it up in his left hand and grabbed a pen with his right as he sat down, all in one fluid motion.

He spoke quietly, a by-product of his many years as an agent in the field, scribbling on a fresh sheet of paper in front of him. He quietly asked a few questions then put the phone down.

The other three had drifted back to the table and were standing around it as he looked up.

'Well, there's bad news and there's not so bad news,' he said, looking bemused.

'Come on, Jack, spell it out,' said Cliff.

'Our man got the transport as arranged- not bad. The transport got re-routed - bad. It was re-routed into Hungary - bad but not too bad. He is somewhere in Hungary and we've no idea where he is - bloody bad!' Jack was still looking at the notes he had made in disbelief.

Cliff sat down. 'Next move?' he asked.

'I'm calling Frankfurt to co-ordinate things directly for us. They will alert our people in Budapest and may stand down the guys in Czechoslovakia. It will be like the proverbial needle in the haystack until or unless he gets in touch with us.' Jack said.

David Sanchez said, 'What about the other side, Jack? How soon will we know what they are doing?'

'I think we can safely assume that they will be working out the possibilities as we speak. They know he can go via Czechoslovakia or Hungary, from that location. A message has probably gone via Moscow to check up on his wife. They have probably found her hotel room empty in Leningrad and the hunt will be on. They still have personnel in army bases in Hungary and Czechoslovakia, and they have rights of access for all their personnel. You can be sure that a lot of KGB will be crossing those borders in the guise of Russian troops. The race is on.'

19

Alexei opened his eyes and felt pain stabbing him all over. All around him was darkness, with stars overhead. He could hear the occasional sound of traffic passing quite close. He could recall jumping from the truck and feeling elated, then nothing.

Have I broken anything? he wondered, and consciously started to try moving parts of his body.

His toes and feet reacted, so his back was in one piece. Both shins felt like they had been whacked with a club. His left shoulder was extremely painful and he was unable to move his left arm.

His right arm seemed fit and he gently felt around his left shoulder joint. The left arm was dislocated. He was lying in a ditch, with fetid water partly covering his legs, and he felt cold. He realised he was lucky to have landed with his face out of the water or he might have drowned when he passed out.

Alexei struggled into a more upright position. After buttoning his jacket, he gently placed his left forearm inside the front of the jacket to act as an improvised sling. He was going to need help to sort out that shoulder.

He raised his head above the ditch, and by the lights of a passing truck, took stock of his whereabouts.

The road was about five metres away, and a tangle of branches and roughly cut timber lay between him and the road. This must have been the obstacle he blindly blundered into and caused his present condition.

Using his good right arm, he hauled himself backwards out of the ditch and sat against a tree trunk. He felt that he was in no condition to undertake any adventurous travel; his body seemed to hurt everywhere. He wiped his brow and felt crusted blood on his face. The occasional traffic was a tempting option, but with the luck he was having he was likely to flag down a KGB car.

The River Tisza was about a kilometre away from the road, he remembered, and the countryside was flat. If he could get himself moving, that might be a promising option. He had seen boats on it as they crossed the bridge at the border.

The KGB would not be patrolling the river, he thought.

He struggled to his feet and turned away from the road, heading through the trees. He was soon into fields, negotiating gates and fences with difficulty. He could not see any lights indicating farms or houses, but it was a clear night and he was unable to cover the ground quickly, so he did not rush into any more obstacles. He came to a minor road running across his path, and stopped to listen before crossing. There was no traffic passing, and he painfully shuffled across and over another gate.

He could see the sheen of open water ahead and after fifteen minutes came to the bank of the river. He sat down to rest, feeling dreadful.

Here I am at the river. What am I going to do now? I must have scrambled my brains when I fell. What irrational impulse made me think the river would be my salvation?

The river traffic had stopped, it appeared. He got himself up again, wincing at the pain this induced, and started off along the river bank, heading downstream.

After shuffling along for more than half an hour, he smelt cigarette smoke in the air. He stopped and peered ahead. A cigarette glowed suddenly on the river bank and he heard distant voices. He veered away from the river in an arc past the cigarette smokers. As he passed some distance behind them, he was able to see two figures with fishing rods on the bank. He kept going and hoped he had not been noticed.

He was having to stop frequently to rest. The pain in his shoulder was severe, and his shins were badly bruised, making walking a laborious business.

After another half hour, he could see lights in the distance on the far bank, which must indicate a town or village ahead. Indecision hit him. Should he try to make some contact or was it too early, and still too near the Soviet influence to trust anyone?

He felt a complete idiot. He knew next to nothing about Hungary or its geography. He might as well have been walking on the moon, he told himself.

Walking along the bank, still trying to reach a decision, he found himself at a tiny landing stage. He stopped to sit on a bollard, and saw that an old boat was tied alongside. He looked into it and saw that there was a pair of oars, and it was obviously reasonably sound as it rocked with the current. Not really knowing what he planned to do, Alexei lowered himself gently down into the boat. There was some water sloshing in the bottom, but not enough to worry him. He looked around but could not see a farm house or any other building in view. There were some clumps of trees, so perhaps there were houses hidden from view.

With his good arm he untied the painter and pushed himself away from the stage. He put an oar over the stern, thinking it might act like a rudder, and drifted into the current. Alexei sat in the stern and watched the dark shapes on the bank drift by. He saw the town lights off to his right grow nearer, then recede. There were several ferry stations along the river, but they seemed to be closed for the night.

The river current was steady and gentle and the lapping sound of the water on the boat was quite soporific. Alexei was feeling quite bad. The pains had not receded, and he felt feverish. He wondered if the foul trench water had infected any of the cuts he had received. Propped against the stern, he eventually fell asleep.

20

The brisk Baltic breezes brought a flush of colour to Katya's cheeks as she walked around the deck with Jean and Freda. In her new, and strange, environment she had not slept well; partly caused by the motion of the ship but mostly because of her worry for Alexei. A substantial breakfast had helped restore her equilibrium, and the stroll in the sun and breeze bucked up her spirits.

The American women had advised her to wear the wig and glasses when she came out of their cabin, to maintain her image and avert awkward questions. She felt some surprise and relief that nobody appeared to notice anything special about her. She seemed to blend into the background.

As they leaned on the rail and watched the seagulls wheeling around them, Katya asked the others, 'How soon after we get to Stockholm do you think Alexei will join me?'

'You won't be staying in Stockholm, honey,' Jean said. 'It's a great place, believe me, and the food is terrific, but we have to move on. We are due in around ten tonight. We'll be picked up at the dock and taken to the airport, then fly by Lear jet to Frankfurt where the debriefing will take place. If all has gone to plan, you will meet your husband there.'

'What will the debriefing be about? Is it a form of interrogation?' Katya looked concerned.

Jean put her arm around Katya's shoulders. 'Stop worrying,

honey. You are out of the KGB's shadow now. The debriefing will mainly centre on your husband and his knowledge of the circles he moves in, but you'll probably be asked similar questions about the current policies in your education department or anything else that helps build up-to-date pictures of what's going on. I promise you, there will be no pressure on you, it will be like a chat among friends. Consider yourself among friends.' And she gave her a friendly hug.

Katya shook her head slowly. 'For ages, this venture has been a dream for us, and now that it's happening it still feels like a dream. I can hardly believe we have done it.'

'It's real,' said Freda, 'And so is the chill in that wind. Let's get inside and have some coffee and a slice of gateau. I've got an appetite.'

Jack Bergen looked at the scribbled notes and fax messages spread across his desk, the product of a busy night for him and his staff. They had not found any trace of Alexei yet and their agents on the ground had told them of a surge in KGB activity in the area. It looked like they still had everything to play for.

He and Harvey Fletcher were looking at a large-scale map of Hungary when they were joined by Cliff Holmes.

'What's the latest?' he asked, joining Jack and Harvey to peruse the map.

Jack told him how Alexei seemed to have vanished and that local intelligence was reporting a lot of Russian activity.

Cliff nodded. 'That would tie in with what I've just been told. I spoke to our liaison contact in British intelligence, Joan Jenkinson, and it seems that their listening station at Cheltenham is reporting a big surge in radio and telephone traffic in that corner of the Soviet Union bordering on Hungary and Czechoslovakia. There hasn't been anything in the information to narrow the search and it looks like the Russians are searching in both countries. So, we have a slight advantage in knowing that the man is in Hungary. All we have to do is find him.' He smiled ruefully.

Harvey opened the folder he was holding and said, 'I have some signals here from Frankfurt. They have been pumping all the German sources, and their friends at the *Bundeskriminalamt* at Wiesbaden have come up with some interesting material coming out of Moscow. Kryuchkov, the KGB chairman, has gone ballistic. He is kicking ass all over the place. His deputy, Grushko, and Shebarshin from Foreign Intelligence are leading the hunt.' He continued, 'The Germans are getting snippets from all over the place. Yegorov from Counter-Intelligence has allegedly been seen in Prague, and that young guy, Putin, has left Dresden - presumably to join the hunt. This is a high priority operation by the Soviets.'

Jack added, 'In anticipation of something like this, I got word to our reception team in Czechoslovakia to act a little more obvious. They might act as a diversion and keep the Russians chasing them, giving us a chance to find the man in Hungary. The network in Hungary is starting to feel around and we could be lucky.'

'How do you feel about flying out there and taking control on the ground?' asked Cliff Holmes.

Jack grimaced. 'It may have to come to that, eventually. For the moment, I don't want any new people charging into Hungary. There is no doubt that the Russians would spot new arrivals, add it all up, and they'd concentrate their efforts in

Hungary. We have some good people out there and I think we should give them a free hand, initially. If there is no progress, we might have to send in some more specialists. Has any contact been made at official level?'

'The State Department are marking time on this,' said Cliff. 'It's always a time for delicate diplomacy when these operations go wrong. The Hungarians are doing well since they broke free from Russia, and the United States has been very supportive. We know that, unofficially, the Hungarian Government will give every assistance if and when we ask them. They are still treading a fine diplomatic line with the Russians, and they know that there is probably a deep-cover fifth column within the layers of their society. We don't want to push them into a position of support where Kryuchkov and his xenophobic theories of Western plots could force Gorbachev to engineer a confrontation. The crap is on our own doorstep, and we have to clear it up.'

He looked at Jack's tired face and turned to Harvey Fletcher. 'Harvey, why don't you take this weary old soldier for a coffee and a doughnut, or whatever he wants. Take him out of the office, I'll mind the shop,' said Cliff, removing his jacket and starting to fill his pipe.

Jack looked grateful and walked with Harvey to the elevator.

The cafeteria in the basement was always fairly lively and today was no exception.

As they walked towards a vacant table, a voice called, 'Hey Jack! We haven't seen you in here since last Thursday. Are you confining yourself to weekly visits?'

Jack shook his head wearily and smiled towards his questioner, Marine Sergeant Paul Rook. 'You're right, Paul. It's a week since I was last down here. Pressure of work; you know how it is.'

Paul smiled sympathetically in return, then added, 'We've been charting the progress of those crazy bobbies on bikes. You remember, you gave some sponsorship to Jock Marshall last week. If they are still on schedule, they will be making the trip from Stuttgart to Munich today. It looks a helluva long bike ride on the map.'

'It sure sounds like it,' replied Jack, his interest kindled, as he and Harvey joined Paul and a couple of his Marine colleagues at their table.

Paul had the bobbies' itinerary in front of him. 'We've been getting daily updates from our contact at Saville Row, David Fitzpatrick, and these guys are still bang on schedule. We looked at a relief map yesterday and agreed that none of us fancied the climb they were making from Karlsruhe up to Pforzheim. They've been getting great receptions along the way, and seem to be a big hit.'

Jack smiled and said, 'Yeah, everybody loves the bobbies. You say they are going to be in Munich tonight. That's certainly some achievement. That guy, Jock, gave me a copy of their itinerary. I must have another look at it.'

Harvey looked at Jack thoughtfully, then turned Paul's copy of the route towards him and read it slowly. They sat and drank their coffee and ate their doughnuts, enjoying the conversation of the Marines who soon rose as one and excused themselves, since their break was over.

Harvey looked at Jack. 'You have a copy of that itinerary. Have you looked at it in any detail?'

'I'm with you, Harvey. Maybe even one step ahead.' said

Jack. 'You heard what Paul said about them getting a great reception. As far as I can gather, these guys are going way beyond anything normally associated with cycle trips. The further they go, the better the receptions will get, and...'

'Their potential for creating a diversion, or a cover, will increase greatly, always provided it coincides with any of our events.' concluded Harvey.

'Two minds with one thought,' grinned Jack. 'Let's get back up to the office and find that itinerary, then we can dream up some possible scenarios.'

At eight o'clock that morning, blissfully ignorant of any nefarious plans for their future, the London bobbies followed two of their German colleagues in a Stuttgart Police patrol car through the centre of the city and out onto the road towards Esslingen. The Germans wished them luck when they parted company.

First stop was at the first baker's shop they spotted in Esslingen to stock up on fresh bread for the day. Then they settled into a steady pace, passing through Eislingen and Geislingen before turning off across country on a minor road.

The scenery was pleasant rolling farmland, the sun was shining and traffic was light. They had their first snack when they stopped at Langenau and chatted with some local people who spoke English. The locals advised them on the route ahead to Gunzburg, advice which they found helpful since the quiet country route they were using was very short of direction signs. They had already experienced navigational problems with their route map getting through Weidenstetten.

After Gunzburg, they joined a major road where they bunched together with Ron driving the minibus close behind as protection. They hit their rendezvous outside Augsburg fifteen minutes early.

Their German motorcycle colleagues were extremely welcoming, and amazed that they had reached that point after only five days. Paddy regaled them with his tall tales of the journey so far, but some of his tales were lost in the translation, which was maybe for the best.

Their passage through the city centre of Augsburg was swift and efficient, though they did admire the fine buildings as they passed, then they dug in for the final fifty mile leg to Munich.

A lot of water and Lucozade was drunk that afternoon as the weather stayed warm, and they were relieved at last to see their motorcycle escorts waiting at Germering on the outskirts of Munich. The thought of navigating a city of that size was very daunting.

Following their German escorts, they skirted the south side of the city, adding about fifteen miles to their projected total, to be welcomed at Perlach by Herr Jens and other officers of the Munich Police, and also by the Lady Mayoress of Munich.

An excellent buffet meal had been laid out for them in the Novotel and copious amounts of Bavarian beer. It was their best reception to date.

The German Police officers were very interested in talking 'shop' with their London colleagues, and the Lady Mayoress, after making a very warm welcoming speech, accepted a formal gift of a police shield from the bobbies and a London Policewoman's hat which she wore with a smile during the reception.

The hospitality was enjoyed by all, and the lady mayoress spoke to each officer, enquiring about the contacts they were keeping with their families whilst travelling and complimenting them on their levels of fitness. All the time she was also enjoying the Bavarian beer and was very jolly when she left.

The Munich police officers were fascinated by an operations map of the Metropolitan Police District which Dave explained to them. Friendships were made.

21

The River Tisza meanders back and forth as it crosses the north east plain of Hungary, so it was hardly surprising that the small boat containing the unconscious Alexei finally grounded itself amongst some willows on the left bank of one of the lazy loops of the river. He was unaware that he had travelled more than forty miles on the gentle current, and still lay slumped in the stern with his good arm draped over the shaft of the oar.

Daylight was breaking by now with the promise of early sunshine, and had he been able to raise his head and look around he would have seen only low farmland with some vine-yards, and clumps of willows flanking the river. No buildings were visible, and his boat was barely visible to river traffic when that started running again.

As the morning brightened, a dog came trotting along the river bank, stopping to nose thickets on its way. A hundred metres behind, a young woman was walking in the sunshine with the coiled-up dog lead in her hand. Every so often the dog, a Hungarian Viszla, stopped and looked back at the girl. Once reassured that she was following, it trotted on, sniffing the scents of nature as it was bred to do.

When the dog came under the willows partially concealing the rowing boat, it stopped and sniffed the air before moving towards the boat. The dog backed away, then advanced again as its curiosity won over. It moved from under the trees until it could see the young woman and gave a short bark.

The girl did not appear unduly concerned and called out to the dog, 'What have you found, Pasha? Is it a duck's nest again?'

The dog showed some agitation, ducking into the trees and reappearing to look towards the girl. She quickened her pace slightly until she came up to the dog which looked at her expectantly and ducked into the trees. She forced her way through the drooping withies of willow and saw the boat. She was trying to avoid the twigs scratching her face and watching where she was putting her feet and did not at first notice the boat's contents.

She talked as she negotiated her way through. 'Good boy, Pasha, you found a boat. Someone up the river will be looking for it. Let's see if there is a name on it.'

The sight of Alexei stopped her short and she called the dog to her. At first glance, with his face encrusted with dried blood, his ghastly pallor and the dishevelled state of his clothing, he looked dead. She waded into the shallows and pulled the stern nearer to the bank, then had a closer look at its occupant. There was a visible rise and fall to his chest. She noticed the left arm inside the jacket and checked his pulse on his right arm. It was strong but a bit fast, she thought. Up close, she could see that the facial injuries were fairly superficial and merely scratches.

She tried to rouse him, but he only moaned in return. When she put her hand on his neck she noticed the high temperature. He was going to need help, and she was unable to lift him from the boat.

She grabbed the painter and tied it to a substantial willow branch, then turned to the dog and said, 'Come on Pasha, we

148

will have to get father to help us.'

The girl and the dog emerged from the clump of trees and both ran off across the fields.

Twenty minutes later a tractor with a flat trailer came to a halt alongside the willow clump. The girl jumped down from the cab, followed by the driver, a middle-aged man with the broad shoulders and thick forearms of one who worked the land.

The farmer was surprisingly gentle in his handling of Alexei. With his strength he was able to rock the boat close against the bank, then he stepped in and started to lift him. As the farmer straightened up, Alexei's left arm flopped out from the restraint of his jacket and his face creased with pain. The girl quickly supported the arm and placed it across Alexei's chest, and between them they carried him to the flat trailer. The girl climbed up beside Alexei while her father started up the tractor and they moved off.

The girl kept speaking to Alexei in attempts to wake him. At one point he seemed to be trying to speak and she leaned close to him. She heard what sounded like Russian, and she thought he was saying, 'No police.' He said nothing more, and they arrived at a single storey farmhouse.

With the father doing a major part of the lifting and carry-ing, and the girl supporting the left arm and shoulder, they got him into the house and on to a bed. They had been joined by the girl's mother who had been busy in her kitchen and was now wiping her hands on a towel.

The father turned to the girl and asked, 'What do you think?'

'He is quite sick,' she said. 'His left arm is dislocated, I'm sure, and he seems to have a fever which could be an infection or any one of several reasons. I can't put his shoulder back on my own, and I don't have the necessary antibiotics to do anything about the fever. We will have to get Doctor Hasz to come along.'

Her mother said, 'Where could he have come from? I don't recognise him.'

The girl said, 'When we were coming back on the tractor, he was muttering something in Russian which sounded like he did not want the police and he wanted to stay secret. That's what it sounded like to me.'

Her mother looked unsympathetic. 'Bloody Russians! I thought we were finally getting rid of them. Why doesn't he want the police? He must be a criminal, and we should hand him over right away.'

The man smiled gently, 'We are not going to rush into anything. The man is sick, and Josefina here says he has a dislocated shoulder and a fever. He might be on the run, as you say, but a lot of good people are on the run from the Russians. I will go over to my brother's place and telephone Doctor Hasz. I won't tell him too much; I'll say that one of our visitors has had a fall and I want him to take a look.'

He looked at his daughter, Josefina, and she replied, 'I think that is the safest course to take until we know more. We must tend to the poor man's injuries, and then we can decide what else to do. Go on then father, mum and I will clean him up a bit and see if he is going to talk to us.'

The farmer went off and the two women set about tidying up Alexei. Despite her apparent reservations about Russians, Josefina's mother was an able assistant to her daughter. They gently removed his outer clothes; the jacket being a particular problem, as his face showed great pain when his left arm was moved. The trousers, smelling of rank ditch water were dumped outside the back door, to be dealt with later. Josefina cleaned the dried blood from his face with a disinfectant solution and shook her head when she saw the black and yellow bruising and abrasions on his shins.

'I don't think there are any breaks there, but we'll leave that to Doctor Hasz. My expertise is growing, but there are some things I'm not yet confident of,' she said.

Alexei moaned and opened his eyes. He looked up at the two women, then cast his gaze about the room.

Josefina, speaking in basic Russian, said, 'You are safe. A doctor will be here soon.'

'Where am I?' asked Alexei, trying to gather his jumbled thoughts together.

'You are at my parents' farm near Tiszavany. We found you in an old boat on the river. What has happened?' asked Josefina.

Alexei looked around. 'My jacket! Where is my jacket?'

'Your jacket is here. Did you think we would rob you? We have not had time to look in your pockets, so whatever you had will still be there.' Josefina looked offended.

Alexei was too distraught to think of the feelings of others. He tried to reach out his arm but slumped back against the pillow.

The girl held out the jacket and said, 'Shall I help you? Where would you like me to look?'

Waves seemed to be rolling over Alexei's consciousness and he felt his concentration ebb and flow.

'The papers,' he said.

Josefina emptied out all the pockets. His eyes lit up when

he saw the flat plastic parcels he had made up in Uzhgorod.

'What are they?,' asked the girl. 'You are not carrying drugs in these are you?' She looked at him sternly.

He closed his eyes and tried to moisten his mouth.

The girl's mother suggested that he looked like he needed something to drink, and went to the kitchen, returning with a cup of hot coffee. They helped Alexei to sip from the cup which seemed to revive him a little.

He looked at the girl. 'Who are you?'

She sat on the edge of the bed and began, 'I am Josefina Huba and this is my mother, Margit. My father, Zoltan, helped me bring you up to the house from that old boat we found you in. My parents are farmers here. I am a student at the Semmelweiss University of Medicine in Budapest, but I am home for a week. You appear to have dislocated your left shoulder, your shins are severely bruised and you have superficial scratches to your face. I think you also have an infection, since you feel feverish. My father has gone to call Doctor Hasz, who is an old family friend.'

Alexei closed his eyes again and nodded. 'Your diagnosis is good, young lady, how far are you into your course?'

'I am in my third year.' she replied. 'Why do you ask?'

'I trained in medicine too, and I know how much hard work you must be doing.'

'Are you still in medicine?'

'That's why I'm in this situation,' he said. 'You could say that medicine has brought me to the position I am in today.'

He looked directly at her. 'You realise I am Russian?'

She laughed. 'Isn't that stating the obvious? You may think of us as peasant farmers, but we are not simpletons. We have

152

lived with Russians in our country for more than forty years, so you are not exactly a novelty. Are you an army deserter?'

He shook his head slowly. 'No, it is more complicated than that. I need to know if I can trust you to keep my identity hidden until I can move on. The KGB will be looking for me by now.'

Josefina snorted, 'The KGB? You don't have to worry about them in Hungary any more. They have all gone now.' She waved her hand dismissively.

Alexei reached his good arm towards her in exasperation. 'You must listen and realise the danger I have put you in. The KGB will be looking for me. They will have guessed I am either in Hungary or Czechoslovakia and they will move heaven and earth to find me.'

Josefina looked questioningly towards the plastic packages of papers. He nodded and continued.

'The contents of those papers can go a long way to protecting life on earth and ensuring a future for your generation. The KGB will do anything it takes to find me or stop me. If they find me, they will destroy all evidence of me and that would include witnesses. So, just in case you were thinking that there might be a reward for handing me over, I would suggest you think carefully what that reward could be! You and your parents would disappear.'

Josefina hugged her arms across her chest. 'What the hell have you got in those papers?'

'You realise that once you have completed your degree in general medicine, you may show an aptitude for specialisation in one aspect of medical practice?' he asked.

'Yes, of course.'

'That is what I did.' He sighed. 'I showed an aptitude and understanding of microbiology and virology, and was invited to join a department specialising in those subjects.' He looked at her. 'As the years have gone by, that specialisation has not been directed at the welfare of my fellow man. The department I worked in was the antithesis of the Hippocratic ideal. Do you understand me?'

'I understand enough Russian to realise what you are telling me, but why are you on the run? Where are you taking this information?'

'I have little option but to trust you, since you now know that we could share the same fate if I am caught.' He paused and asked for another sip of coffee.

'I want to cancel out the effects of the work I have been doing, by giving the information to the Americans who have the resources to do that job. They arranged my unofficial exit from Russia last night, but at the last minute things went wrong and I ended up jumping from a moving truck. I landed in a ditch and lay there unconscious for some time. I managed to walk in the dark and found an old boat by the river. You seem to have found me and I'm in your hands. I need to get to Budapest or to let the Americans know where I am.'

Josefina said, 'That should be no problem. I can telephone the American Embassy and tell them you are here, and they can collect you.'

'No, no.' moaned Alexei, still in great discomfort from his injuries. 'The KGB will have reactivated agents and subversive police contacts. They will be keeping a listening watch on the telephone system as they did when they controlled your country. They will be listening to your call and be round here before the Americans get out of Budapest. I know I am a burden, but if you could keep me safe until I am fit to move, perhaps later today, I will get out of your lives and keep you out of danger.'

The girl considered what he had told her, and gave her mother a watered down version of his account in Hungarian. Margit's hand flew to her mouth in shock. She spoke hurriedly to Josefina and, whilst Alexei could not understand what she said, he heard 'Doctor Hasz' and 'Zoltan' from amongst the incomprehensible words.

Josefina turned to him. 'I've explained the situation to my mother, as best I can without panicking her. We will speak to father when he returns, and he will probably be here before the doctor. Mother agrees with me that we have no option but to help you. We need a story to explain your presence here. I'll think about it; we don't have a lot of time.'

She left the room with her mother, and Alexei could hear their voices arguing back and forth in the other room. Then he heard the tractor stopping outside and the father, Zoltan's, voice joining the discussion.

They all came back into the room, Margit looking pale and worried and Zoltan with his perpetually calm look. He looked at Alexei's injuries and carried on a brief conversation with Josefina who appeared to agree with him.

She sat on the edge of the bed again. 'This is what we have decided. I hope you can agree with us. You are an exchange lecturer at Semmelweis University in Budapest, and I have been in several of your classes. During this weeks' holiday, several of us have invited you to visit us to learn something of Hungarian life. You arrived with us yesterday and decided to try some dawn fishing in the river this morning. You had a fall

155

down a steep piece of bank and we found you. Your Hungarian is not very good, but all your students speak some Russian. How's that?'

'You should take up story-writing in your spare time, if medical students get any spare time these days,' Alexei replied.

'Never mind the compliments,' she said. 'Even as a visiting Russian lecturer you should know some Hungarian, but it might be best if you act dozy and concussed.'

He agreed and suggested she tell the doctor he had concussion, since he found Hungarian too difficult to pronounce. They settled on a new identity for him of Sasha Petrov, and put his plastic-wrapped papers and belongings out of sight.

They were all on tenterhooks as Doctor Hasz arrived. A tall slim man of about sixty, the doctor spoke to Alexei, but his Hungarian was too much for the patient. Speaking slowly in Russian, Alexei detailed his pains and symptoms. The doctor listened to Josefina's version of events then looked Alexei over. The shoulder was obviously the major problem.

'This should really be replaced in hospital,' he said, 'although it looks fairly uncomplicated.'

'I've seen it done on my attachments to the Casualty Department,' said Josefina, brightly. 'And it doesn't look all that difficult. I was tempted to try it earlier, but I'm not sure I have the physical strength. I'll be glad to assist you if you think we can manage it.' She added eagerly.

The doctor pursed his lips then looked at Josefina's pretty face. He had a soft spot for this eager youngster who had sought his advice before embarking on her course at university.

'Very well, young lady. We'll do it the old way, like my father and his colleagues used to do, when a journey to hospital took all day and the country doctor performed all sorts of services. First we will have look at the other damage.'

He examined Alexei's face and then the bruises and abrasions on his legs. He prodded about and was satisfied there were no breaks. He agreed that the feverish symptoms were from some infection, and suggested that he might have swallowed ditch water. He would leave a course of suitable antibiotics for the patient.

In stilted Russian he explained to Alexei that he proposed to relocate the shoulder joint. Alexei knew what that would entail and the likely pain he would suffer. However the doctor produced a syringe and injected Alexei in the arm. He felt himself losing consciousness and all went black.

Doctor Hasz turned to Josefina, 'Quickly, that won't keep him under for long.'

He called Zoltan over to help lift Alexei onto the floor, then with Josefina and her father keeping Alexei's head and shoulders in the correct position, he sat on the floor, took hold of Alexei's left arm and placed his own left foot in Alexei's armpit. Leaning back, he steadily pulled on the arm while telling Josefina how to guide the ball-joint back into its socket. He released the pressure and checked the shoulder, gently manipulating the arm.

'That's perfect,' he announced. 'That's something you won't see demonstrated in such a manner at university,' and smiled to the girl.

They lifted Alexei back into bed and made him comfortable, with the arm in a proper sling.

Doctor Hasz delved into his bag and produced a bottle of capsules, the antibiotics, giving instructions to Josefina and Margit on their dosage. He suggested the country remedy of chicken soup; Jewish penicillin he called it, and plenty of liquids would be the best course of action to help the patient. He dressed the abrasions on the shins with antiseptic cream and bandages, and guessed that it might be two or three days before their guest would be up and about.

Alexei was starting to come round from the anaesthetic drug, and the doctor checked his pulse. He appeared content with Alexei's condition.

'Will you let the University know about the accident, or would you like me to telephone them for you?' he asked Josefina.

She smiled, 'No, mother and I are going shopping at the market tomorrow, and I'll phone then. I have to phone one of my friends to let him know that Dr Petrov is unable to visit him next. He doesn't like fuss and is embarrassed by this accident. You would be doing him a favour if you kept quiet about it. We aren't due back to classes until Wednesday, so he hopes he will be able to get back to Budapest without anyone knowing of his accident. And I would be glad if you didn't tell any of the neighbours.' She added. 'He is only a tutor, nothing more, and as I said he is visiting a number of us at our invitation to find out about country life. You know what the gossips round here are like. They will make too much of it and ruin my reputation. I have a boyfriend at university, and he knows all about our visitor.'

'My lips are sealed,' said the doctor. 'I know exactly what you mean.' He turned towards Alexei who was staring sleepily around. 'Good luck, Doctor Petrov. Come back and see us again.'

Josefina accompanied Doctor Hasz to the door.

'Thank you for your help. Will you need to see him again?' She asked innocently.

'Unless the fever develops into a chest infection, I don't think I'll be needed. He is a fit man and should recover well. If you are worried, then call me.' He smiled at Josefina and said, 'No charge for the special lesson on dealing with dislocations.'

She laughed in return and said, 'I wonder if anyone will believe me when I tell this story at classes.'

When she returned to her parents, Zoltan, with his perennial genial expression, was talking soothingly to his wife. Margit was obviously worried by the situation which had engulfed them. Josefina joined Zoltan in the effort to reassure Margit and, whilst not completely won over, their reasoned arguments eventually mollified her to a great extent. She busied herself warming up soup for Alexei.

Zoltan and his daughter talked over their possible course of action, with the girl asking Alexei for clarification as they went along. At last she was able to present a scenario for Alexei to consider.

'Tomorrow we are going to the market in Nyiregyhaza. That's more than thirty kilometres from here. It's a big town and is the centre for people of this area, the Nyirseg, to go to market. The town will be busy tomorrow, and we could telephone from there without anyone tracing us. Who is it you want to get a message to?'

Alexei looked at their honest faces. 'I don't want to place you all in any more danger than I have already brought on you.' He paused, 'Where would you telephone from in this town you are going to?'

'There is a line of public telephones at the market,' said the girl. 'I could make a short call and hang up before anyone might come looking for me. Who do you want to call?'

'I think the military attaché at the American Embassy would be the best person to contact,' he replied. 'But we have to think what you should say. Do you speak any English?'

'A little,' she replied. 'It's something the young people do in Budapest. We watch television and films and try to pick up the language. I have managed to hold little conversations with tourists in the cafes. As long as it's nothing complicated, or technical, I think I could pass on a message.'

'All right. If you think you can do it, but we will keep it very short. Let me think about it,' he mused. 'As I said, I cannot put you in any more danger, so you must not say anything to identify yourself or where I am staying. I have to know if my wife is safe; she was coming over by a different route. If you were to let them know that I am safe but delayed, and ask if my wife is safe, that would be enough. Whenever I am well enough, I will be on my way and leave you good people in peace. I am really sorry that my problems have endangered you.'

She translated this for Zoltan, who smiled and spoke to Josefina.

'My father says that it's the country way to help a person in difficulty and share their troubles. He asks if you are a believer.'

'A believer? Believer in what?' replied Alexei.

'In God. A Christian.' explained the girl.

'I was raised in the Soviet Union and I am a product of that godless society. I sometimes felt that there was more to our existence than the Party, but I never had the opportunity to do anything more. Once I joined the department, my life and work were dictated by the needs of that department. So, I can't

160

claim to be a believer.'

She listened to Zoltan then added, 'My father says it's not necessary to be a believer to be a good person. He says that he feels you are finding your own form of faith and it looks like you are suffering for it, just like the early martyrs.' She giggled as she concluded. 'Forgive me, I just found that thought funny. What do you think I should say on the telephone?'

'Something like, 'Alexei is safe. He will move when he is ready. Is his wife okay?' Do you think you could manage that?'

She ran through it several times and Alexei was satisfied that she had grasped it.

'You will have to find the telephone number for the American Embassy,' he said. 'How are you going to do that without attracting attention?'

She shrugged, 'I have my guide book to Budapest, which I bought when I first went to university. It has all the embassies listed. I told you already, we are not country bumpkins. We can read.'

'Of course you can. I apologise. But, one more thing,' he said. 'Don't let anyone delay you on the phone. Good or bad, they could be trying to trace you. Just tell them there is no time and you have to go. Understand?'

In a comic American accent she replied, 'Sure thing, man!'

Alexei slumped back, closed his eyes and smiled at her irrepressible spirit. He guessed she had inherited her father's optimism. The shoulder still ached, although he now had some slight movement in his left arm.

Margit came into the room and gently fed him from the bowl of soup, then he slipped back to sleep.

22

It was mid-afternoon when Alexei opened his eyes. The re-located shoulder felt quite fragile and it hurt to move his left arm, but he felt reassured that it could move a little. His mouth felt parched, his legs ached and the glands in his neck felt uncomfortable. He could guess that the time he spent in that stinking ditch had started the infection which was now coursing through him. Provided there had been nothing too outlandish in that foul water then he reckoned that the antibiotics should kick in and control things in the next couple of days. He would have to resign himself to a spell of feeling pretty rough.

Margit appeared in the doorway. She came over and tidied the bedclothes then said, *'Kavet?'* miming a drinking motion as she did so.

He nodded and she came back with a cup of coffee which she helped him to sip. He lay back and said thanks in Russian, German and English before shaking his head and saying, *'Kein Ungarn*. No Hungarian.'

She understood him and entered into the game. *'Koszonom - spasebo. Spasebo - koszonom.'* She said.

Alexei then thanked her in her own language, *'Koszonom,'* which brought a bright smile to her face.

She then made a supping motion and asked, *'Tyukhusleves?'* He guessed she might be talking about soup, and nodded.

'*Koszonom,*' he responded, and she clapped her hands and bustled off to the kitchen.

He did not feel particularly hungry but knew that he had to keep up his fluid intake and that the chicken soup was as good as anything in giving him suitable sustenance for his body to fight the infection.

Margit spoon-fed him the soup, then she was joined by Zoltan and Josefina. The girl enquired as to how he was feeling. He detailed his symptoms and weakly suggested that she make a diagnosis.

She pouted and said, 'It would not take a doctor to tell that you have a bug in your system and that it is working its way through you. It also doesn't take a doctor to tell you that your body needs rest and that you should get off to sleep soon. You can take another antibiotic capsule and we will leave you in peace. There will be a glass of water by your bed. We will see you in the morning.'

Alexei thanked them in Hungarian, much to their amusement and they left him to sleep. He drifted off quite quickly.

'This does not look too promising,' said Cliff Holmes. 'I thought we might have got something, anything, by now.'

He was sitting on the edge of the desk, looking at a map of north-east Hungary for the umpteenth time, as though something inspirational was hidden in the unpronounceable names.

'The old clichés are the best in this situation, Cliff,' said Jack Bergen from his chair behind the desk. 'How about 'no news is good news'?'

Harvey Fletcher called across the room, 'Don't count your chickens until they're hatched.'

David Sanchez chipped in with, 'Every cloud has a silver lining.'

Cliff Holmes shook his head and laughed. 'You guys are all nuts.'

Jack responded with, 'Working for this salary, you have to be nuts!'

They all laughed, and Cliff put his hands up in mock surrender, 'Enough, enough,' he cried. 'But seriously,' he continued, 'the wife will be arriving in Stockholm tonight. The team accompanying her will stall her questions, I'm sure. What are the guys and gals in Frankfurt going to tell her when she lands there?'

'We'll delay the flight from Stockholm as long as possible,' explained Jack. 'If the situation still has not improved, we can arrange for the flight crew to give her a special cup of coffee before she lands. She'll be sound asleep by the time she reaches Frankfurt and the girls can make her comfortable in her room. That could buy us time until tomorrow morning. Beyond that, when she wakes up, is just another part of the problem, which is not my main worry. I want to find this poor bastard and get him out of trouble.'

There was silence in the room for half a minute, broken by one of the signal girls knocking at the door and entering.

'The latest from Frankfurt,' she said, placing a handful of papers on the desk. The men all gathered around the table, as Jack scanned them quickly.

'Same position,' he said. 'The Russians are still scurrying around in Czechoslovakia as well as Hungary, which should mean that they are in the dark. So that's hopeful. Our guys in Czechoslovakia are doing their Inspector Clouseau act and

164

are being shadowed by the Russians, but you can only keep a deception going for so long and the Russians could see through it soon. The news out of Moscow is much the same; the KGB leadership sounding off in general terms about conspiracies by the West. Gorbachev hasn't joined in yet, but he'll do as he is told when they need him to make a noise.'

Harvey asked, 'How much do we know about our man's ability to survive in the field? I mean, is he an ex-serviceman or does he have any kind of training that would help him?'

'The guy's a trained doctor. He is thirty-nine years old and in good health, so he should be able to stand up to a bit of hiking if that's necessary,' replied Jack. 'On the other hand, he has been working in an elite and protected government department for a number of years, so you can interpret that any way you want. By all accounts his wife is good looking and they are nuts about each other, so I would guess he will be trying to survive and meet up with her again. He is a bright boy; he is going to work things out. Unless he's fallen down a mineshaft, my money's on him making it.'

'Okay,' sighed Cliff, 'We'll just have to go into a holding pattern until the guys in the field come up with the goods. Christ, Jack, this can put years on you.'

Jack grinned, 'Come on, Cliff, we can do it.'

He looked at the telephone and said, 'Please ring. Just give us one little glimmer of hope, just enough to give us something to home in on.'

'So say all of us!' enthused Cliff. 'I'll see you in the morning unless you wake me with good news in the night, Jack. And don't be shy about ringing if word comes through.'

'You got it,' said Jack.

23

I t was approaching eleven o'clock that night as the cruise ship
tied up in Stockholm. Katya had been ready to disembark
since the ship had first started negotiating the islands on the
winding inlet leading to the city. In her wig and tinted glasses
as Connie Newhart, she was eager to get on with the business
and meet up with her Alexei.

At last an announcement over the public-address system
brought her waiting to an end and she followed Jean and Freda
through the passageways to the exit. At the dockside a car was
waiting for them and they were whisked through the city to a
hotel near the city centre.

Katya was confused by this development and turned to Jean
and Freda. 'What is happening? Why are we not going to the
airport?'

The driver explained that their plane was delayed as a technical fault was being rectified at the airport and could take an
hour. The embassy thought that it would be more comfortable
to wait at the hotel than at the airport.

Jean and Freda affected a pleased and nonchalant air.

'There you go, honey,' said Freda. 'It's just one of those
things. We can have a nice rest here, it's better than a draughty
old airport terminal.' She rubbed her hands, 'And everything's
on Uncle Sam, so let's enjoy ourselves.'

A suite at the hotel was at their disposal, and staff brought in food and drinks for them. The driver was joined by several other alert young men who had been following the women's car from the docks. They positioned themselves to secure the suite.

Katya was unable to relax. Jean and Freda seemed at ease with the delay, but she knew they were professionals and would say anything they were told to say. She questioned the driver and the embassy staff there, but none of them could help her. They told her they had received no messages from Frankfurt, but also told her that was not unusual in these special circumstances. They were all trying to cheer her up and act as though everything was fine, which would not work in her case without some positive news of Alexei.

It was gone midnight before they climbed back into the car and headed out to Arlanda airport, north of the city. The car drove onto the runway and stopped by a Lear jet where another alert young man stood at the foot of the boarding steps. Jean and Freda accompanied Katya aboard and they were welcomed by a man who introduced himself as Fred Delaney. He explained to Katya that he represented the State Department and went on to praise her and her husband for the brave actions they had taken.

'My husband?' said Katya. 'What news have you of Alexei? Is he safe?'

'I can't help you there, ma'am.' said Delaney. 'That's all being handled by the Frankfurt office, and for security reasons we are keeping all radio and telephone traffic silent about your escape. I'm sure you know how efficient the KGB are at listening in to telephone and radio messages.'

She nodded without enthusiasm. This was not what she wanted to hear.

'You must have a coded system of messages,' she insisted. 'There must be a way of communicating. You are hiding something from me. What has gone wrong?'

Delaney spread his hands wide and smiled, 'What's gone wrong? You are here, safe and sound, as arranged. These things take a lot of planning and are designed to work. You saw that for yourself, I'm sure, when the team brought you smoothly out of Leningrad. We'll get all the news when we get to Frankfurt, and I'm sure your mind will be put at ease there.'

A steward appeared and told them to put on their seat belts as the engines began to whine. A few minutes later they were aloft, and the same steward reappeared with a tray of coffees and pastries for them.

Jean and Freda kept the conversation lively on the flight, distracting Katya from her worries about Alexei. They went through some American magazines with her, showing her some of the sights of their country and commenting on places to visit.

As they came towards the end of their two hour flight, Delaney went forward to the cockpit. On his way back, he spoke briefly to the steward in passing, then sat with the others. The steward came into the main cabin and announced that they would land in about twenty minutes. He suggested a cup of coffee to keep them all awake until their business for that night was finished.

'Good idea,' said Jean. 'I'm starting to get a bit tired. A cup of coffee should perk me up.' She looked at Katya and added, 'You want to stay awake, don't you?'

Katya nodded and said, 'Yes, I want wrap my arms around Alexei when we land.'

'We'll all have coffee, please.' Jean said to the steward.

The coffees were handed to each of them individually. Delaney picked his up and said, 'I'm going to enjoy this.'

Katya picked up hers and started sipping, whilst the conversation with Jean and Freda ebbed and flowed.

After a few minutes, the steward returned and said, 'Can I ask you folks to drink up and we'll get everything stowed away before landing.'

Jean and Freda reached for their cups and said, 'Bottoms up,' to Katya, who drained her cup. She sat back in her seat and suddenly felt very drowsy. She struggled to bring herself back from the brink, but slipped away into a deep sleep.

Freda patted Katya's hand and said, 'Just you have a snooze, honey.

Everything might look brighter in the morning.'

'We can only hope you're right,' responded Fred Delaney gloomily.

24

The bedroom door opened, creating enough sound to wake Alexei who peered over the bedclothes to see Josefina approaching him with a mug of milky coffee and a slice of thick bread spread with honey.

She smiled brightly and said, 'Good morning, Doctor Petrov, how are you feeling?'

Alexei smiled at the use of the fake name. 'Despite your smile brightening the room, I still feel terrible.'

'Aha; a flatterer I fear,' she countered. 'That probably indicates that you are recovering. Well, you will just have to be a patient patient,' she punned. 'You heard Doctor Hasz say that it could be a few days before the antibiotics make a difference. Mother and I are off to the market in Nyiregyhaza. I have the telephone number, and I remember what I should say. Father will be going out to the fields soon, but he will help you to the toilet before he goes. We will be back this afternoon and tell you how everything went. Keep taking your medicine and drinking water. Now eat your breakfast, such as it is. Goodbye.'

She breezed out of the room, singing as she went.

Alexei slowly forced the bread and honey past his lips, and washed it down with the coffee. He had no appetite, but knew he had to keep his body ticking over until the effects of the infection started to wane. He had just swallowed his capsule when Zoltan came in with his calm smile and indicated that he was ready to help Alexei out of bed.

He felt as weak as water, but Zoltan's brawny arm held him up and guided him through the house until he was seated on the toilet. Zoltan left him to it.

Alexei managed to reach over to the wash basin and turn on a tap, then gripping the edge of the wash basin he pulled himself up in front of it. He felt very unsteady, and got a shock when he saw his reflection in the mirror. His face was very pale, that paleness accentuated by the dark stubble, and the scratch marks running down his face from his hairline to his chin. He splashed his face with water and dried it on a towel. This movement made him wobble and he grabbed the basin again to steady himself, then turned to open the door and call weakly to Zoltan.

The farmer got his arm around Alexei and slowly helped him back to bed. After smoothing the covers over Alexei, Zoltan spread his hands in a calming motion and indicated that the patient should sleep. An exhausted Alexei needed no persuading.

Margit and Josefina caught the early bus - the market bus - and found themselves as usual amongst a crowd of local people, most of whom they knew well. There was a barrage of questions for Josefina; about university, Budapest night life and boyfriends. She had grown up in this environment and coped with the friendly curiosity without embarrassment. In such an atmosphere, the half-hour bus trip passed quickly.

It was not yet nine o'clock when they arrived in town, the largest in that region, and everyone headed for the market. Margit was looking for bargains on the meat and produce stalls, and Josefina kept sliding off to look at the modern clothes and music stalls.

As nine struck on the clock tower, Josefina told Margit she was going to the telephone booths on one side of the market. They agreed a meeting point and the girl headed off with her mother's whispered advice to be careful. Looking at the telephones from a distance as she walked through the various stalls, she saw no sign of anyone hanging around.

She went into the first booth and closed the door behind her, then opened her purse to get some forint coins out and to read the telephone number on a small piece of paper in the front of the purse.

After inserting the coins and dialling the number, she heard the ringing tone and a woman's voice answered in accented English, 'United States Embassy; can I help you?'

'Military Attaché, please.' Josefina said.

She heard a few clicks then a man's voice came on. 'Military Attaché's office; what can I do for you?'

She realised her hand was clenched around her purse, and tried to relax before speaking. 'Are you military attaché?' she asked.

'Yes ma'am. David Samek at your service,' was the reply.

'Listen please,' she began slowly. 'Alexei is safe. He will contact you when he is ready to move. He wants to know that his wife is safe.'

'Who is this, please?' She could hear a sound like someone rapping a pen on a desk.

She could not see the frantic activity at the other end of the line as David Samek waved a colleague to an adjacent phone.

'Could you repeat that message please, ma'am, and tell us where we can get back to you?'

Josefina took a deep breath.

'No time. Is dangerous. Is his wife safe? I must go.'

'Wait, please. Yes, his wife is safe, but we need to talk to him. Please hang on and I'll take some details.'

'He will contact when he is ready. Is dangerous.'

She hung up and turned and left the booth. She wondered if her face was as flushed as she imagined, and quickly blended herself into the crowds. The excitement and sense of danger were very real and she stopped at a stall to look at records and tapes, and try to calm herself. She glanced about her casually, but nobody was paying her any attention. It was just like any market day in Nyiregyhaza. She found a music tape she liked and haggled with the stall holder before agreeing a price, then set off to find Margit.

Her mother had several bags of groceries when Josefina found her. To her questioning look, she muttered that everything was fine, then she took some of Margit's bags and the pair of them went into a bustling cafe for a drink before the journey home.

The phone rang on Jack Bergen's desk just as he sat down with a bundle of fax messages. He laid down the messages and picked up the receiver.

'Jack Bergen here.'

'Hi Jack, it's David Samek in Budapest, how are you?'

'I'm okay, David. How's Helen enjoying Budapest?'

'She's happy spending money, even if it's foreign money. Listen Jack, can we go on the scrambler?'

'Sure, David. Line three.' He pressed a button on the telephone console. 'Shoot, David. What have you got for me?'

'I just got a call from a woman, sounded like a young woman.

I'll play the tape to you.'

Jack listened carefully, then said, 'That sounds promising. Not as comprehensive as I would have liked, but it sounds like our man is holed up somewhere. Did you trace the call?'

'Not completely,' came the reply. 'We know it's from the north-east area, which fits in with the little we know.'

'How secure is this information?' asked Jack.

'It isn't. It came on a public telephone through our switchboard which is manned with a mixture of American and some local personnel. We've vetted them as far as we can, but with a language like Hungarian, we don't have enough fluent speakers and have to employ some locals. It's a calculated risk.'

'We have to accept that perfection is a long way off in this business.' said Jack. 'I think we should assume that the news might leak, and watch for the signs. In the meantime, get some of our people up into that area and start fishing. Keep me informed.'

He called Cliff Holmes and the others on his ad hoc group and fifteen minutes later they were sitting down in his office. He replayed a tape of the conversation he had had with David Samek. They all listened intently, then he gave them transcripts of the conversation.

He opened the discussion. 'What do you think?'

Cliff Holmes was first to respond. 'It's not much, is it? On the other hand, it's short and to the point and on that score it could be genuine.'

Harvey Fletcher observed, 'She asked twice if his wife was safe. You told us, Jack, that they're nuts about each other. I think it could be the real thing.'

Jack turned towards David Sanchez, who was drawing

interconnected diagrams on a pad. 'I hear all you say, and it does sound genuine.' said David. 'Why isn't he ready to move? Does he think he's under surveillance, or is he holed up waiting for some kind of specialised transport? I just don't know.'

Jack pointed his finger at David. 'Transport, you said. That could be it. The last we heard of him, he had jumped from a truck and nothing's been seen of him since. Now jumping from a truck is not quite an Olympic sport, and this guy is an academic. He could have taken a fall when he jumped and he may have broken something or just be badly shook-up. Maybe that's what she meant by 'he will contact you when he is ready to move'. Could be that he has to patch himself up before he can move.'

Harvey added, 'If he has to get himself fit, how long might that be? A few days, a week, a month?' He laughed. 'Jack, maybe you'll need those cycling bobbies after all.'

Cliff and David looked puzzled until Jack explained the previous week's encounter in the basement restaurant at the embassy.

David raised his eyebrows. 'Well that would certainly be a diversionary tactic to dine out on for years. A bunch of London bobbies on bikes. Who would ever believe you?'

'Precisely,' said Jack. 'Just think it through. I'm a cyclist, and I'm fairly certain that this ride - London to Budapest - hasn't been done before. So that will attract positive publicity to these guys. When was the last time a bunch of bobbies were able to go that far into Eastern Europe, and to set up some kind of cycling record at the same time?'

He looked at the others. 'They're going to be heroes, of a sort; five minute wonders. But they'll be above any suspicion and almost untouchable. They are qualities I like to have up my sleeve. If they fit into the timescale, I'll try to use them.'

'Always provided they are willing to play along with us,' David added. 'What about the wife; have we told her what's going on?' asked Cliff.

'That's in hand,' replied Jack. 'I spoke with Frankfurt as soon as I got the message and Fred Delaney will do his best to put her at ease.'

Cliff Holmes had a grim smile on his face. 'Jack, I can see you heading east before the week's out to back up David Samek. If, as you suspect, the information leaks then we'll need to face up to the opposition on the ground. The State Department have an open budget for guys of this calibre. They really want him.'

'I thought you might say that. Mind you,' he smiled, 'it's years since I was last in Budapest and it was a depressing place then, under the Communists. As we said, every cloud has a silver lining.'

The Coppers For Kids faced a ride of 145 miles from Munich to Linz, so another early start was in order and they took to the road at eight o'clock. Their motorcycling friends from the Bavarian Police guided them through the suburbs of Munich and led them across country to get them safely on to Route 12. The small towns and villages they passed through were decorated in the Bavarian blue and white with large decorated maypoles in most village centres. They crossed the border into Austria near Braunau and encountered some long climbs.

At Grieskirchen, the taxi drivers' association from Linz met them and treated them to coffee and cake with schnapps whilst the local television station filmed a few shots for their news summary. Of course, they wanted someone in a bobby's uniform, so Ron the driver was pressed into action since all the cyclists were grubby and sweaty by this stage of the day's journey. Ron rode back and forth for the cameras while the cyclists drank his glass of schnapps.

'Sure now you can't drink and drive,' admonished Paddy.

'No bloody chance of that with you gannets about.' moaned Ron.

Another thirty miles took them safely into Linz, escorted by several taxis from the local drivers' association, to the Novotel in *Wankmuellerhofstrasse*.

An old friend was waiting for them. Len Coles, who had served as a bobby for many years at Westminster had retired to Austria with his wife, who was a local girl, and he had motored up from Steyer to greet them. The national directors of the Austrian Taxi Federation had also motored over from Vienna to have dinner with the bobbies. The director of the association, Ernst Schlecht and his co-director, Christine Trs, were excellent hosts and, despite some slight language difficulties, they enjoyed the evening. A joke about garters taught the bobbies the German name, *strumpfbande*, and Christine was nick-named *Fraulein Strumpfbande*. She enjoyed the joke. The further east the bobbies travelled, the welcomes got warmer.

25

Katya felt like she had a bad hangover. She peered grog-gily around this strange room, trying to recollect how she could have arrived here. The digital clock on the bedside cabinet told her it was nine-thirty, and since there was daylight filtering through the curtains she guessed it must be morning.

She swung her legs out of bed and sat up. Her head seemed to spin and she sat still for a while until the room stopped rocking. Then she ran through her memories of the previous day. She remembered everything until the flight was nearly over and she had a cup of coffee with the others on the plane. There, her memory switched off.

Could there have been something in the coffee? Surely not, she told herself. After all, she was among friends now; friends who were going to look after her and Alexei.

Alexei! Why wasn't he with her? They were supposed to be meeting in Frankfurt after the flight from Stockholm. Was this Frankfurt?

She stood up, went to the window and opened the curtains a little. The view was of two and three storey residential blocks, with neatly mown lawns between. There were some men and women in blue American uniforms passing by.

There was a knock at the door, and Jean put her head around and called, 'Anyone awake in here?'

'Where am I? How did I get here? Did someone drug me?'

Katya demanded.

Jean thought: This one is no dumb blonde. She looks like she could fight her corner.

To Katya she said, 'Honey, I have to apologise. We got the feeling that you were getting a bit anxious about what you might find in Frankfurt, and thought that a mild sedative in your coffee would just calm you down a little and stop you worrying so much. The steward misheard the instruction and gave you a knock-out drink. We are so sorry; this is not the kind of welcome you should have received. We'll try to make it up to you. If you have your shower and get dressed, I'll take you down for some breakfast and some real unadulterated coffee.' She smiled sheepishly.

Katya was not to be diverted. 'What about Alexei? Where is he? Can I see him?'

'He isn't here, but there is news of him.' She waved away the flurry of questions she anticipated from Katya and added, 'Fred Delaney will give you all the details at breakfast. Let's get moving.'

This was not how Katya had imagined her arrival in the promised land of the West, but she decided to go along with things, for the present. She showered and felt much livelier after it. The wardrobe had a small selection of clothes in her size. She selected a shirt and trousers, which fitted comfortably, then after brushing her hair she and Jean went downstairs and across to an adjacent building where there was a dining hall.

Jean tried to help her choose food from a wide selection on display. She did not feel very hungry and settled for yoghurt and fruit. They both went into a smaller dining room where they found Fred Delaney and another man seated at a table

180

drinking coffee. Both men rose as she entered.

'Good morning, Katya,' said Delaney. 'And welcome to the United States air base in Frankfurt, Germany. I hope Jean has explained our little error of last night. We thought that we were acting in your best interests and someone put the wrong thing in your coffee.' He tried to look contrite, knowing that he was lying outrageously.

Katya sat down, unconvinced, and looked Delaney in the eye.

'Where is Alexei? I want to see him and I don't want to hear explanations about little errors,' she said pointedly.

Delaney appeared unruffled. He indicated the man sitting with him and said, 'Let me introduce Jim Bakker. Jim is one of our top men in the intelligence field and he will update you on your husband.'

Bakker was a fair-haired, fresh complexioned man of around thirty-five. He had a pleasant smile as he shook Katya's hand.

'May I add my apologies ma'am for the hiccup in your welcome. We truly want you to know that we are really glad to see you and will do everything we can to make up for this bad start to things.' He oozed charm.

Katya's uncompromising demeanour had not altered. 'Where is Alexei? All I hear is apologies and promises.' She spoke slowly and deliberately, 'Where is my husband?'

'Yes ma'am,' said Bakker. 'In your husband's case, everything went according to plan until the last minute. He is out of Russia, but a confusing set of circumstances developed which was beyond our control, and he went seriously off course. This threw our reception arrangements out of sync, and we had to rush to alternative methods to attempt to stabilise the situation.'

'My English is not very good, and I think you are trying to confuse me.' She was now looking at Bakker with cold anger. 'We believed the promises of safety and care that you people made. What do we have? I have been drugged and you are refusing to tell me what has happened to my husband. These are the tactics of the KGB. You are no better than the KGB.'

Her face had gone very pale, and the barely controlled anger was obviously rising to the surface.

Delaney stepped in to try to calm the imminent storm.

'Come on, Jim. Tell the lady the good news,' he said with a forced smile. Bakker repositioned his slipping smile, and resumed his narrative.

'Ma'am, the good news is that we have heard this morning that your husband is safe. We are not yet in a position to get him here. As I said, the position is complicated, and it may be a few days before we can complete the operation. We expect to update you as soon as we hear.'

'You don't know where he is,' Katya confronted them. 'That's the truth, isn't it? You lost my husband.'

Delaney adopted a confidential manner. 'That's not how we see it Katya. As Jim explained, and as you have to understand, operations like these are made up of many, many different parts and it just takes one of those parts to slip slightly out of place and the whole chain of events can take a different direction. This is what happened in your husband's case. We received information this morning indicating that he is in a safe place but cannot be moved at the moment. I can't go into any more detail for you. As soon as the conditions are right, we'll move him and complete the operation.'

'When will this be? Are you sure that I am going to see him? Tell me everything!' she cried.

'I assure you ma'am,' said Bakker. 'We have told you as much as we can at the moment. I can't stop you worrying but I promise you that everything is being done to bring this to a happy ending for you both.'

'I want to believe you, but I feel you are hiding something from me,' Katya accused them. 'Where is Alexei if he can't be moved safely yet? He must still be in Russia, and there the KGB will find him. That will be the end.' Tears welled in her eyes.

Delaney spoke earnestly, 'I swear to you, Katya, your husband is out of Russia. The problem is that he's in one of the former Russian satellites and we are forced to tread very carefully. We are confident of succeeding in this.'

Katya let the tears fall. 'My poor Alexei. He trusted you, but only after I persuaded him that the Americans would not let us down. I should have kept my mouth shut. You are like all the government departments, everywhere, you deal in politics and do not consider peoples' lives of any value. We are only commodities to be traded for whatever advantage you think you can make.'

'We have to go now, Katya,' said Delaney. 'But Jean and Freda will show you round the base and you can use all the facilities here. Please be realistic. We are confident that your husband will be joining you soon. We are working flat out to achieve that result. Whether you have faith in us or not, will not stop us from working to save your husband.'

The two men left and Jean did her best to console Katya, but quickly realised that the lady was not for consoling, just yet.

Josefina and her mother, Margit, were glad to drop their shopping bags and sit down when they arrived home that afternoon. Perched up on his tractor, Zoltan had seen their arrival and made his way to the farmhouse.

By the time he arrived, Margit had started to empty the bags and stack her purchases on the kitchen table. In his easy-going fashion he asked them how their trip had gone.

Margit pointed out some of the bargains she had purchased, and told him of how busy it had been in the market that day.

He patiently listened to his wife, with a contented expression on his face, then looked at Josefina. She sensed the unspoken question and told him of her brief telephone conversation, stressing how she had taken care before making the call, she had not identified herself and she had got off the line quickly.

'How is our patient?' she asked her father.

'He was just the same when I came in for some lunch. He managed to swallow some soup and some apple juice. I looked in before I went back to the fields and he was asleep. He is a sick man.'

'I'll peep round the door and see how he is,' she said, walking quietly towards Alexei's room. She opened the door slowly and peered round. Alexei looked flushed and had thrown the covers off his chest. Josefina went to the bed and gently replaced the covers and tucked them in. Alexei stirred and partly opened his eyes. Her image took a moment to register in his sleepy brain, then he opened his eyes fully and said,

'You're back. Did you make the call?'

She smiled and nodded to him, 'Yes I made the call.'

'Did you take care, and not put yourself at any risk?' he asked.

She sat on the edge of the bed. 'I did it just as you told me, and hung up when they started asking questions. There was nobody hanging around the telephone booths, so I think it went fine.' She smiled at him.

His eyes were pleading. 'And did you ask about my wife?'

'Of course I did. They did not answer me the first time, so I said I would hang up. They wanted to keep me on the line, and said your wife is safe. I hung up then.'

His haggard face softened. 'Thank you. This means everything to me. Now I can relax.'

'That's it,' she said. 'Relax and get better, then we'll see if we can get you on your way to join your wife.'

Alexei's pains and discomfort seemed to recede as he relished the relief of knowing that his Katya was safe. If only he could speak to her and reassure her.

He drifted off to sleep again and Josefina slipped out of the room.

The family sat around the table while Josefina related to them the details of her conversations with the Americans and how Alexei had reacted.

'He has told us the truth, I am sure,' said Josefina. 'The Americans seemed to know who I was talking about immediately, and told me that his wife was safe.'

'I'm sure they do know him, and I agree with you that he is telling us the truth. I'm not so sure that the Americans were being honest when they said his wife was safe. They would say that anyway, just to keep you on the phone, so we can't be certain that the news is genuine,' said Zoltan.

'For his sake, I hope it's true,' added Margit.

'When I told him the news, he looked like he had won a

million dollars,' said Josefina, 'so I think we had best keep our opinions to ourselves. He still doesn't look too good, but perhaps we should wait and see if he makes any progress over the weekend.'

Margit rose from the table. 'He needs time to recover. Don't be too impatient. I'll be making up a fresh pot of soup this evening, and that will help his pills to work on him. Take my word on it. You can't beat home-made soup.'

'And nobody can make soup like you, my love,' added Zoltan, as he rose and gave her a hug.

'I know you,' she teased. 'You only married me for my cooking.'

'That's true,' he said, 'but what a pleasant surprise I got.'

He winked at her, forcing a sheepish smile to her face. She waved her hands at him. 'Get back to the fields, you dirty old man.'

He went out the door singing an old folk song about girls and May flowers.

26

Morning brought another bright start along the banks of the River Tisza, with the faint morning mists disappearing quickly in the growing warmth of the sun.

Alexei felt slightly better than the previous day, though his body was lethargic and his appetite poor. However, he benefited from the ministrations of Margit and Josefina when they came into the room and propped him up in the bed for few minutes while they sponged his face and upper body. Their actions did little to improve his physical strength, but his spirits were lifted by their kindness and, in conversation with Josefina, he found his mind and attention much sharper.

Josefina told him that her mother suggested he have a bath that day, if he felt well enough. He answered that he thought it was a good idea, well enough or not!

After a breakfast, where he forced down some more bread and honey with his milky coffee, Josefina sat down with him.

'Do you feel any improvement this morning?' she asked him.

'My body feels much the same, pretty useless. My mind feels much more active this morning and I'm noticing things.' He pointed, 'I've only just seen that fine icon on that wall. Was it there yesterday?'

'It has been there for years,' she answered. 'It was my grandfather's, and he spent his last few years with us here. He was a fine old man, and very proud of his family. You would have liked him. Perhaps he has been looking kindly on you,' she smiled.

'I think he has every reason to be proud of his family. You are all very good people. With my background, I don't really deserve to be in the same room as any of you. I have a lot of guilty secrets to make amends for.'

Alexei felt slightly foolish starting to confess his guilt to this young woman, but as he went on to tell her just a little of what he had been involved in, and of how he earnestly hoped to put his wrongs right, he felt the load on his conscience lightening.

Josefina was enthralled to hear of their guest's murky past in the biochemical nightmare that was part of the Soviet war machine. Her youthful tolerance and optimism coloured her reaction to Alexei's soul-searching admission.

'It all sounds like a horror story, or a bad dream,' she said. 'It's difficult to believe that such things happen. Thank goodness you had the sense to see that what you were doing was not a good idea, and you want to put things right. You should be telling the world what is going on, so that everyone can understand.'

'I don't want to be centre-stage. My work has been secretive and I would prefer to remain in the background. I will do everything possible to neutralise the effect of the work I have been involved with, but I won't be thumping any drums or appearing on television. My wife and I just want to have a quiet, normal life, and hopefully to have children and bring them up in a peaceful environment. It's not a lot to ask.'

As he mentioned his wife, a more gentle expression came over his face.

Josefina saw the softness appear in his face and smiled at him. 'I think you are very fond of your wife, and as soon as you are fit enough we had better try to get the pair of you together. You are the qualified doctor,' she teased gently, 'What is your prognosis for your rate of improvement?'

His laughter was somewhat laboured and ended in a bout of coughing.

'This is what I am concerned about,' he eventually said when he recovered his breath. 'The effects of the infection coupled with my lack of activity lying in bed, could settle the infection on my chest and seriously delay recovery. I must spend some time sitting up, and even trying to walk a little. If I can keep away from chest infections, then I will probably be mobile very quickly.'

'That's good. My father is very philosophical about everything, and does not worry at all, but my mother is very protective of us and is worried by your presence here.' She went on, 'Mother will do all she can to help you, and would never try to throw you out, but we must think about helping you on your way as soon as is reasonable.'

'My apologies to your mother, and please tell her as strongly as you can that I am very grateful to her, and indeed to you all, for the kindness and help you have given me. I am very eager to move on and complete my journey, but I realise that my physical condition isn't up to that effort just yet. As soon as I am well enough, I will be on my way.'

'We will help you get to Budapest, where your friends can look after you safely.' She smiled at him and added, 'Then you can live happily ever after.'

'I'll believe that when I'm holding my wife again.' He looked wistful.

In the office overlooking Grosvenor Square, a mood of frustration had permeated all conversation. Jack and Cliff had put into place everyone and everything they felt could possibly contribute to the successful conclusion of the operation. On paper, their efforts were a copybook for success, but everything was held in suspended animation whilst the vital element, the location of Alexei, remained unknown.

They ran over the information that was coming in, much of it repetitive. Their team in Czechoslovakia was still operating as a successful diversion and drawing Soviet resources to keep an eye on them. Unfortunately, the Soviets were also making covert moves in the sensitive area of north-east Hungary.

'Do we know to what extent they are active in that part of Hungary?' asked Cliff.

Jack was upbeat. 'It's all pretty low-key and general at the moment, and mostly concentrated within an hour's drive of their camps, which covers a fair bit of the border area. Our people in Budapest have seen an increase in activity there, and there is more surveillance on our embassy and personnel. The same thing's going on in Prague. So it looks like the Soviets are still trying to find him and have nothing positive to go on.'

'A bit like us, I suppose.' Cliff looked gloomy. 'Sure, we know he went into Hungary, and we think that anonymous phone call is genuine, and that he is alive and well, but we are still in the dark. If only the phone would ring again.'

'We are here for the long haul on this one, I feel,' said Jack. 'The more I think of it, the more I suspect that our man was injured jumping from that truck. He must have had some good sense and got himself into a safe situation; how safe we don't know. It's now a matter of how badly injured he is, and how good this girl is who phoned the embassy. We don't have control of events, at the moment. As soon as we hear something, we have teams poised to go into action and bring him out.'

'That's always provided the Soviets don't get in the way,' added Cliff. Then he smiled and said, 'Of course you might always use your cycling bobbies to save the day. They could bring him out on a crossbar, I suppose.'

Jack laughed with him, and said, 'Come on, don't laugh. Nobody knows how things might turn out. We have them up our sleeve along with a lot of other tricks.'

Alexei lay in the hot bath, enjoying the water's soothing effect on his weakened body. Zoltan sat in the corner of the room, smiling and making signs that Alexei should wash himself. The left arm was painful to use and he could not raise it to his head, so he slowly soaped his body with his right hand, then sponged himself. He felt exhausted after this slight effort, and Zoltan came over to the bath. He took the sponge and wiped over Alexei's shoulders and back, then squeezed out the sponge several times over Alexei's head before soaping his hair then rinsing it in similar fashion.

Zoltan helped Alexei out of the bath and wrapped a towel around him before helping him back to the bedroom. Margit had laid out a nightshirt on the bed and Zoltan slipped it over Alexei's head, then helped him back into the bed.

The effort had refreshed Alexei and exhausted him at the same time. He looked up at the smiling Zoltan and said, '*Koszonom*. Thankyou.'

The farmer smiled in acknowledgement and called to Josefina

who came in with a bowl of soup and a piece of bread.

'I hope you are feeling better after your bath,' she smiled brightly.

'I certainly smell better,' said Alexei. 'Please thank your father for his help. He has made me feel much more human again.'

She passed on the message to Zoltan whose brief reply she translated to Alexei.

'My father says he was glad to help you, but don't get used to it. He prefers washing a lady's back.' She laughed.

Alexei laughed, 'I am in total agreement with that.'

Zoltan went out, singing gently.

Josefina said, 'Take your soup. It must be getting a bit boring by now, but you are looking brighter, so it must be working. We will see how you are tomorrow, and perhaps you will get something more substantial to eat.'

Alexei smiled, 'Something to look forward to - solid food. Now I know how babies must feel.'

The girl giggled, 'Just eat it up and take your medicine; then get some rest.'

Jack Bergen decided to call it a night after a short conversation with David Samek at the Budapest embassy.

David had no news of any consequence. The field workers were out posing as birdwatchers, anglers and tourists in north-east Hungary, but without any success.

There was an increase in personnel at the Soviet embassy and their radio traffic had increased.

Jack told him that the UK listening centre at Cheltenham had already confirmed the rise in radio messages, although the interpreters had also found nothing of any great importance in them. Both the Americans and the Russians were like a crowd of competing hunters waiting for the game to break cover.

Jack and his team had theorised over possible routes that Alexei might have taken, but the field workers in Hungary had not yet found anything to support their hypotheses.

He picked up his coffee cup and realised it only held cold dregs. Time I went to bed, he told himself.

27

In a modern flat in Frankfurt, Katya lay in bed, unable to sleep, and trying to pray for Alexei's safety. She realised how ironic her efforts would appear to her old friends in Russia where religion was only slowly surfacing after more than seventy years of repression.

She didn't care what anyone else might think of her. Alexei was all she wanted, and she could not imagine life without him. Their hopes and dreams of the preceding months had formed a vision in her mind of how their life together might be. She was not prepared to surrender that vision by giving up hope for Alexei, but they needed help, and prayer was all she could think of.

I don't know who I'm supposed to pray to, she said to herself, but one of those nice ladies on the icons, or the angels in the cathedrals might help. If any of you are listening, save my Alexei, please.

She felt a bit foolish, but decided that next day, Sunday, she would visit one of the churches and see how it felt. Maybe she could light a candle for Alexei; it would do no harm, and might do a lot of good, for all she knew.

Eight o'clock in the morning, and the rain fell steadily on Linz as the Coppers for Kids followed their motorcycle colleagues of the Austrian Police across the Danube bridge to follow the left bank on their one hundred and forty miles to Vienna.

The rain continued until lunchtime, but they kept to their schedule and made good time. The scenery along the left bank of the Danube was quite sensational in places.

The only problem they encountered was when a very officious police officer stopped them and ordered them to use the cycle paths which meandered up and down the hillside. The bobbies explained what they were doing and that they had a deadline to get to the Parliament building in Vienna, but the pompous officer was adamant that they would not be permitted on the main road, which seemed like a country road.

They could not persuade him to turn a blind eye to fellow police officers and so they went on the cycle path for a few miles until they reckoned that the pompous one was well behind them then got back on the main road to make up lost time.

A change into dry clothes before Klosterneuberg helped refresh their spirits for the fast run into Vienna, where they were expected at the Parliament at four o'clock.

As promised, a party of Viennese taxi-drivers, who were also supporting the charity ride, met the team on the road out of Klosterneuburg and formed an escort with Police outriders up to the Parliament.

After a very hearty and sociable welcome from the Speaker of the Parliament, with copious draughts of Austrian beer, and a brief tour of the main sights of the building, the motorcycles and taxis escorted the cyclists to their hotel at Vosendorf.

The local International Police Association from Modling laid on an early evening reception at the hotel where gifts were exchanged, toasts were made, and a considerable amount of beer was consumed. A party from the British Embassy had also come along and enjoyed the evening immensely. The Modling police officers then ushered everyone out to the car park to be taken to a wine cellar in one of the nearby villages.

Jock Marshall had to clear up an administration problem with the hotel staff, and to thank them for their involvement in the reception. When he came out, everyone had gone except the organisers of the taxi escort, Ernst and Christine, who offered to try to find where the others had gone. A fruitless search of several villages meant that Jock returned to the hotel where he had dinner with Ernst and Christine.

A telephone call was put through to the restaurant, and Jock found himself receiving a good-luck message from the House of Lords. The Earl of Winchilsea and Nottingham, who shared an interest in several charitable ventures with the police officers, wanted to know how their trip was progressing. He finished by telling Jock to pass on his best wishes to the team, and that some associates at the United States Embassy were following the trip with interest. Jock felt flattered at their interest and asked Chris Winchilsea to pass on his thanks.

He had an early night, disturbed only by his team-mates rolling in about two-thirty, having attempted to empty the Austrian wine lake.

28

The sound of distant church bells drew Alexei from his slumbers. Gritting his teeth, he sat himself up then slowly got his legs over the side of the bed. He paused to get his breath back and stop his head spinning, then very gingerly stood up while holding on to the bed. He felt less wobbly, and was pleased with the small progress he was making. He reached for the window ledge to steady him and stepped over to look out.

The landscape undulated slightly, and he saw the rows of vines on the south-facing fields. The church bells continued to ring faintly but he could not see any sign of a church, it must have been beyond the slightly-rising fields. Zoltan walked across the farmyard with the dog, Pasha, trotting along at his heels. He appeared to be heading out into his fields.

Josefina was in the chicken enclosure, with a bowl of stale bread and other scraps which she scattered for the scampering hens to fight over. She turned and saw Alexei at the window. Surprise showed on her face, then she gave a big smile and waved to him. He automatically tried to wave back by raising his left hand, but found that his balance became slightly uneven and the left arm was still very painful and difficult to move. That shoulder was still mending. He slowly turned round and headed for the door with his right arm out to steady himself against the wall. He managed to reach the bathroom where the long mirror reflected his unflattering appearance in the long nightshirt.

I don't care, he said to the scarecrow in the mirror. I am getting better, and I'll be looking like Alexei Golovkin again soon.

After washing his face, he retraced his slow route back to the bedroom and had only got himself back into bed when Josefina came into the room.

'It looks like the church bells have brought Lazarus back from the dead,' she said. 'I was really surprised to see you at the window. Do you feel that much better?'

He shook his head. 'Not really, I forced myself to get to the bathroom under my own power, and now I feel completely exhausted. I have to move on, and I'll keep trying my strength until I'm able to go. Perhaps I can try to get up again later.'

'You should not need me to tell you that over-exerting yourself, in your condition, can be a bad move,' she reproved him.

'I know, I know,' he answered, 'but desperation, and perhaps optimism, can make a fellow take risks, and now I'm paying for it. I apologise to my lovely nurse.'

'Flattery again!' she said. 'Just concentrate on getting well, and leave the flattery until then. I'm not complaining,' she added, 'but you had better hope I don't meet your wife or I'll tell her all about you.' she teased.

He smiled wearily, 'In this condition, I'm all talk and no action, sad to say.'

'Just as well,' she said. 'My mother and I think you are a handsome man. It would be interesting to see you when you are fit.' She rolled her eyes at him in an exaggerated fashion.

He tried to enter the spirit of her teasing. 'Help. I'm being kept as a sex slave. Go and find someone your own age, young lady,' he pulled the bedcovers up to his chin in mock horror.

She laughed and left the room calling, 'Don't worry. We'll be gentle with you.'

He turned to the breakfast she had left for him, his spirits lifted by the banter.

The church on the American air base in Frankfurt was a plain, modern building with very little decoration. Katya saw the large cross on the wall, above the plain wooden pulpit where the Presbyterian padre in his black surplice spoke to the large congregation, but she saw none of the icons and traditional symbols she had seen in the old Russian churches.

She was able to follow some of the preacher's sermon, but felt nothing inspirational in the words. Jean was singing the hymns along with the others, and pointing out the words to Katya as she sang. The devotion and sense of dedication was apparent in many of the faces, but Katya felt she was in an alien environment. She felt that prayers for Alexei would not be right in this strange setting.

As they strolled away from the church after the service, she asked Jean, 'Does everyone in America go to a church and look so enthusiastic about it?'

'Hell no, honey,' Jean laughed. 'This is a military base, and it's part of military life to attend church. Most of those guys in there know that when promotion time comes round, attending church adds some extra brownie points to their chances. It's just a cynical game, following the accepted line; it's probably something like the party politics in your country.'

'I thought that religion was some deeply-held conviction, that some people were prepared to die for. That's what the history books suggest.' Katya said.

'Don't get me wrong; a lot of people are sincere in their beliefs,' Jean replied. 'But you will find that a lot of the people who turn up at church in their best clothes on a Sunday, don't show much love or compassion for their fellow men during the rest of the week. They seem to think that going to church for an hour cancels out all their shitty behaviour. Don't be misled by people pushing themselves forward as pillars of religion, they are usually propping up their own ego and ambitions.'

'Why did you go to church if you feel it's a false atmosphere?' asked Katya.

'I'm just playing the system like the rest of them,' said Jean, 'And it won't have done me any harm to escort you there today.'

'Do I qualify as a brownie point for you?' asked Katya.

'It's quite likely,' nodded Jean.

'It all seems more like politics than religion,' declared Katya.

'You are a lot nearer the truth than you can possibly imagine,' Jean smiled.

That afternoon, Alexei woke feeling considerably more human. He sat up without too much trouble, though his shoulder was still sore. He got out of bed slowly and stood still for a moment or two, still feeling somewhat wobbly, but without the light-headedness which had worried him. He walked the few steps to the window without mishap and looked out. The view was pleasant and peaceful with sunshine across the fields, and he could see Josefina in the distance walking towards the house with her dog.

He looked around the room slowly and found his trousers which Margit had cleaned for him. With slow deliberate movements, he sat on the edge of the bed and gradually got the trousers over his legs then stood up and pulled them up. His muddy shoes had been cleaned and were beside the door. He slid his feet into them, but couldn't be bothered to bend over and tie them. Feeling nearly presentable, he walked slowly out of the room and into the yard, leaning on the wall as he went.

Outside the door was an old wooden bench which he flopped down on, feeling like he had performed an arduous task. The sunshine was a wonderful fillip and made him feel that his recovery was under way.

Josefina came bounding into the yard, teasing the dog which was leaping to catch the lead she was holding. The dog stopped abruptly and looked at Alexei. Josefina looked too, then clapped her hands.

'Bravo,' she said, 'The hero is ready to continue the battle.'

Alexei smiled. 'There is not much about this battered wreck that is heroic. The good doctor's treatment seems to be winning against the infection, with the help of your mother's magic soup, of course,' and he smiled towards Margit who had appeared in the yard when she heard the voices.

The sound of a car approaching spoiled the relaxed atmosphere. Margit looked troubled. Josefina jumped up on the log-pile and looked along the lane leading to their farm.

'It's all right,' she called, 'It's Doctor Hasz, and he seems to be alone.'

Alexei relaxed; he could not have seen himself running into the house in his present condition.

A few moments later, Doctor Hasz walked into the yard,

greeting Margit and Josefina before looking at Alexei.

'Well Doctor Petrov, you look a great deal better than when I last saw you. How is the shoulder?' he asked in fractured Russian.

Alexei kept his response minimal. He rubbed the shoulder with his good hand and nodded, 'Better.'

Doctor Hasz felt Alexei's pulse and felt his brow and seemed content. He turned and spoke to Josefina and Margit, but Alexei could not follow the conversation. Both women looked concerned.

Josefina turned to Alexei. 'Doctor Hasz says that the Russian garrison near Kisvarda has alerted the police that a dangerous prisoner has escaped. They say he is a soldier who has gone mad and is very dangerous. He escaped before he could be returned to Russia, and he is likely to claim he is a doctor. The local police are working joint searches and roadblocks with the Russian military police.'

Alexei looked at her, and spoke quietly, 'It looks like they have worked out my escape route. You know the truth, the Americans are expecting me. Does your doctor suspect me, do you think?'

Josefina shook her head. 'He is a good friend and he trusts us. I think he just wants to make sure we are safe. We must hope that you recover soon, for your own safety.'

Doctor Hasz strolled over to them. 'Doctor Petrov, I was talking to a colleague at the Semmelweiss University and he could not recall meeting you. Are you a recent member of staff?'

Alexei understood his broken Russian sufficiently to realise what was being suggested.

Before he could formulate an answer, Josefina broke in; 'Doctor Hasz, you have been our doctor and friend for all my

202

lifetime. We have always trusted you as I hope you have trusted us. The story I told you was to cover up why my friend was here. You know what people are like around here. Doctor Petrov is a very good friend, and that is the sum total of our relationship. This does not cause a problem in a city like Budapest, but the old-fashioned people around here might not approve, and would have made more of it than there is. We did not think it fair to involve you in a personal matter so we stretched the truth a little. That is why I made up the story.'

She shrugged her shoulders. 'I hope you don't think badly of me, but perhaps it would make sense to take him back to Budapest as soon as possible.'

The doctor smiled at the girl and shook his head. 'I don't know what the truth is, and I don't want to know. My judgement is that you might benefit from my help. Your friend here could well be fit enough to travel by tomorrow, by the look of him, although he will still not be back to normal.'

He looked at the girl whose sad eyes silently confessed her guilt at lying to this man she respected.

'I will be here at seven-thirty tomorrow morning and we will see if we can get to Budapest. We will need a rug to cover your friend whilst he lies on the back seat, don't you think?'

Josefina threw her arms around the doctor and hugged him. 'Forgive me,' she whispered to him.

He kissed her cheek and said, 'Don't worry, us old-timers were able to survive the Red terror for forty years. I'll take care of it. It is important for us that your generation learn to survive and keep Hungary free.'

He turned and shook Alexei's hand and smiled at him. 'Until tomorrow, my friend,' he said in Russian.

Jack Bergen looked down on the green oasis of Grosvenor Square, illuminated by the early morning sunshine, then turned towards Cliff Holmes. 'Cliff, this thing has got to start moving pretty damned quick, or I can see us losing out.'

'I respect your experience in these situations, Jack, but don't you think you could be a bit pessimistic this time?' replied Cliff.

'On the contrary, Cliff, I'm still optimistic that we can get a good result, but,' he grimaced, 'the longer we are stumbling around in the dark, the better the odds get for the other side to strike lucky. We need a call from this mystery girl, or better still, we need contact with the man himself.'

Cliff shrugged his shoulders. 'Jack, you are starting to state the obvious. We aren't achieving anything here. Don't you think you could be of more use on the ground? I think that's where we could get the best out of you. Let's face it, it would not be the first time your hands-on treatment has turned a situation to our advantage.'

Jack smiled thinly and wandered over to the window again where he stood with shoulders hunched, his hands in his pockets. Suddenly he looked at his watch, then turned to Cliff.

'OK. Let's get things moving. You and Harvey can manage things this end.'

He picked up the phone and pressed a button on the console. 'Can you get me on this morning's flight to Vienna - use the name Jack Spalding. Ring me back.'

Cliff looked at him. 'Vienna?' he asked, Jack nodded. 'The Soviets will have the airport in Budapest covered, looking for us moving personnel in or out. My face is probably known well enough to be recognised by certain people on the other side. They're certainly staking out the embassy. So, we'll get the

Vienna embassy to arrange a hire car from Swechat airport, and it's only about a hundred and fifty miles to Budapest. Hopefully I'll pass over the border in an Austrian plated car at Hegyeshalom unnoticed among the day-trippers. I'll steer clear of our embassy and get booked into one of the hotels away from the centre of town. See if you can arrange that with David Samek in Budapest; you can pass the details to Vienna.'

Cliff drummed his knuckles on the desk. 'I've got a good feeling about things now. With an old war-horse like you on the scene, it can only get better.'

Jack smiled scornfully. 'You mean that you hope I can save all our asses by pulling a rabbit out of the hat. I sure hope that your faith in my magic is justified, because I don't have anything up my sleeve.'

The phone on his desk rang. He picked up the handset and heard that he was booked on the Vienna flight from Heathrow and that a car would be ready for him in the basement garage within fifteen minutes.

'All systems are *go*, Cliff.'

He opened a large cupboard and took out a small suitcase which was always ready for last-minute occasions such as this. From his desk he took an envelope marked J. Spalding, containing a Canadian passport and driver's licence in that name, and a bundle of US dollar bills.

Jack picked up a folder and placed it in front of Cliff.

'All the information up to this morning is in this file. Vienna and Budapest will keep us in touch. I hope I see you again soon.'

'Good luck, Jack, and take things carefully. I want to see you back here safe.' They shook hands and Jack picked up his case.

The sun was bright at eight that morning in the suburb of Vosendorf on the south side of Vienna. The cycling bobbies did a last minute check of their bikes before the next stage of their journey.

Jock Marshall whistled cheerfully as he checked his tyre pressures. This prompted some groans from the survivors of the previous night's visit to the wine cellar.

'Quiet please, Jock.' pleaded Ron Meadows, the support driver. 'Have a bit of respect for the dying. My head doesn't belong to me this morning.'

This was supported by muted muttering from some of the others.

Their motor cycle escort from the Austrian Gendarmerie arrived and quickly got them out of town and through Maria Lanzendof, Himberg and across country until they joined Route 10 at Shwadorf.

The next thirty miles to Nickelsdorf and the Hungarian border made a very pleasant ride in the sunshine. Their crossing into Hungary went smoothly and quickly and they were greeted by a group of police officers from the town of Gyor where the police were also providing overnight accommodation.

Amongst the Hungarian welcome party was a schoolgirl, Suzy, a neighbour of one of the officers, and she acted as interpreter. Her English was slow and formal, since she was still learning the language at school, but she was a great boon to both sides.

With their escort of a Lada police car and a motorcyclist, the party moved off through Hegyeshalom, then the town of Mosonmagyarovar, passing through some small villages where the poverty of the people was evident.

At the village of Otteveny, the escort guided the bobbies into the car park behind a restaurant. Here a pleasant surprise awaited them. A magnificent lunch had been prepared; a lunch of gargantuan proportions with dishes they had not encountered before.

At the start of the meal, the host poured glasses of drinks for everyone. There was a brief embarrassed silence as both sides looked to the other to make a move.

By a curious twist of fate, the Vienna taxi-drivers had taught some of the bobbies the Hungarian version of 'cheers' the previous evening. They now lifted their glasses as one and called out, '*Egeszegedre!*'

After astonished looks on the Hungarian faces, they burst out laughing and the ice was well and truly broken. Several more drinks accompanied the various courses until they reached the famous *palacsinta* pancakes. The whole scene was magnificently rounded off by the presence of a violinist who played a selection of haunting and exciting gypsy tunes.

One touching moment occurred during the lunch. It became apparent as they asked numerous questions of young Suzy, just how poor she and her family were.

Dave got up and went out to the minibus, returning with a box full of a variety of the many chocolate bars the cyclists consumed along their route each day. She was astonished. She had never seen anything like it, and she looked like one of the old media images of a refugee child, as she hugged the box close to her.

After lunch, the Hungarian police officers suggested, via Suzy, that it might be a good idea to put the bikes in the back of the bus and drive to Gyor, but the bobbies would have none of that. They were determined to ride the whole way. So, despite the overloaded waistlines, they mounted up and rode the final ten miles into Gyor.

Their accommodation for the night was in the police sports club, which was really a small pavilion with a couple of rooms and a shower. It was adequate for their needs and a lot more primitive than any of their previous overnight stops..

After such an enormous lunch, they did not feel the need for another meal, and wandered into the old part of town where they visited the cathedral. A priest showed them a holy cloth, with bloodstains, which had been acquired by one of his Irish predecessors. This started Paddy off on his tales of Irishmen civilising the world.

They found a cafe which sold Urquell beer and played rock and roll records of the fifties and sixties, and spent a relaxed hour there, amusing the hostess by singing along to Bill Haley and Elvis Presley.

29

Jack Berger's flight was on time into Vienna's Swechat airport. He found a public phone in the arrivals hall, and dialled one of the embassy's unlisted numbers. His contact, Isobel Jardine, gave him details of his hire car booking and that Budapest had booked him into the Novotel hotel, just out of the downtown area of the city. There was no further news from London.

He picked up his hire car, a mid-range Opel, and headed south. In less than half an hour he joined the queue at the Hungarian border near Nickelsdorf. As he slowly moved towards the crossing point, he viewed the scene carefully, but saw nothing to indicate that there was anything untoward in the procedure.

Having presented his passport for stamping, Jack parked the Opel by the gift shop and toilets and ostensibly answered the call of nature. He then had a quick look around the gift shop, carefully looking out through the windows. He noticed several men, dressed in suits of a Russian cut, heading towards the exit crossing point. A minute later, a number of similarly dressed men came walking from the same direction and entered one of the buildings.

'Looks like change-over time for the bloodhounds,' he mused. 'They are covering the bases.'

He returned to his car and continued his journey.

Just before Gyor, he saw a group of vehicles, including a

police car, on the road ahead of him and moving more slowly than normal traffic. As he came up behind them, the police driver waved him past. He overtook carefully and drew past a Renault minibus with the logo 'Coppers for Kids' along the side of it, then passed a group of cyclists who were headed by a police motorcyclist.

The coincidence of the meeting surprised him. 'Those crazy bobbies have nearly done it! They'll be in Budapest tomorrow. Looks like I won't be able to use them as a diversion after all, unless something turns up quick,' he said to himself.

After Gyor, the motorway took him speedily via the industrial haze of Tatabanya to the outskirts of Budapest. The road led straight into Alkotas Street and he soon spotted the Novotel where he turned in and parked.

Jack booked in and found a letter waiting for him at reception. In his room he opened the letter and found an invitation to dinner, from David Samek, at one of the small restaurants on Castle Hill.

A couple of hours later Jack stepped from a taxi near the Matthias Church, walked over to the Pierrot restaurant and joined David Samek. They exchanged greetings and ordered their food, then went over their collective knowledge of recent events slowly and quietly.

David expressed his thanks to Jack for joining him in Budapest.

'My view,' said David, 'is that the foul-up at the crossing point has put us on the back foot and essentially blindfolded us. Yes, we have all sorts of resources and facilities at our disposal, but nowhere to deploy them. We are very much in unknown waters, and I appreciate you being here to help me.'

'You summed it up,' replied Jack, 'and when - not if, but when - we get the breakthrough, we will have to move quickly because the other side won't be far behind. Our biggest problem is that we can't call any shots until we hear some good news. Have you anything at all that makes good news for us?'

'Nothing to add to our earlier info,' he responded. 'The telephone call came from somewhere in the right area, over in the north-east. The girl sounded like she had been rehearsed, and of course, she asked after his wife.'

'That makes it seem likely to be genuine,' Jack affirmed. 'Our man and his wife appear to be pretty close to each other. What have you worked out as possibilities for his likely route?'

'Well, using what you guys told me, we've estimated his departure from the truck on the Kisvarda road close to the Ukraine border. That's a farming area, so there are a lot of small to medium farms; there's also the River Tisza which is navigable and has a lot of traffic on it. If he injured himself, he could either be lying low somewhere among the farms or he could have travelled along the river. I'm not convinced about the river because that phone call indicates he hasn't travelled far. None of this really takes us much further, although we did hear about the Russians at the Kisvarda camp asking for local police to help find a deserter. It's nothing new for these Russian kids to desert in the hope of getting out to the West, so it may mean nothing.'

'We'll mark time on that one,' said Jack. 'What we must do now is minimise the risks where we can. How secure are our communications at the embassy if we get that phone call?'

'As I told you before, the majority of our telephone staff are American and most of them speak varying degrees of

Hungarian. We do have some local staff, and we've tried to ensure that they are security cleared but that isn't foolproof in this environment. There's nothing to stop anyone passing on information outside the embassy, when they go home for instance.'

'How about personal callers at the embassy?' asked Jack.

'Most callers are people looking for visas to the US,' David said. 'There's a local police presence outside, most of the time. We've noticed some additional plainclothes attention since our current situation developed. Certain ministers have been taken into the ambassador's confidence, as a courtesy to our hosts, and the unofficial message coming back is that the Hungarians don't want to be involved and will take umbrage if any 'incidents' occur. That's just covering their backs. I've been in touch with my man in the Hungarian military and he will help us all he can, behind the scenes. He's aware of the increased Russian presence watching our embassy and shadowing our personnel. I came out tonight in the back of the emergency electrician's van, and fortunately, I wasn't followed!'

'The odds are that any further contact will be via you, now that the initial call has been made, so you are our lifeline. I'll call you tomorrow from a public phone,' said Jack, 'and you can leave any messages at the Novotel for me.'

'Let's hope I've got something to tell you,' said David.

30

Alexei lay awake, watching the dawn creep into the sky. Thoughts of what the day ahead might hold had kept him awake for much of the night. Nevertheless, he felt excited now and visualised his happy reunion with Katya.

Soon he heard the sounds of the family moving about the house, and he slowly raised himself to a sitting position.

I don't feel too bad, he thought. His shoulder still ached, and his left arm did not move very much but he was aware that he felt stronger as he gently put his legs over the edge of the bed and stood up.

No dizziness, he thought, and I could eat a horse.

There was a knock on the door and Josefina came into the room with a mug of coffee and several slices of brown bread spread with honey. She smiled with surprise to see him on his feet.

'You look like you could walk to Budapest on your own,' she laughed. 'I think you must be feeling better?'

'Yes, I am, thank you,' replied Alexei. 'And I hope this improvement lasts. How soon do we leave?'

'Doctor Hasz should be here in a half-hour. You have time to eat, and to wash yourself. My father can help you if you wish.'

'No, I think I will manage that myself today.' He sipped some coffee, then asked, 'Can Doctor Hasz get us through these roadblocks? I don't want to put anyone else into danger.

I feel guilty enough.'

Josefina shook her head dismissively. 'It's not as bad as it sounds. Young Russian soldiers are regularly running away. The police put in a few roadblocks here and there, but it only seems to be a token gesture. I don't think we will meet any problems today. Now eat your breakfast and get ready to move.'

Alexei felt he was living on adrenalin as he ate his breakfast then washed and dressed himself. Getting his shirt and jacket over his injured shoulder was painful and difficult, but he felt much better when fully dressed. A look in the mirror brought him down to earth. The scratches on his face had faded somewhat though they were still visible, but the dark shadows under his eyes and his sunken cheeks made him look like a refugee from the gulags. It was not a face to put on public display in an area where there were police roadblocks. He suddenly felt apprehensive again at the danger of the KGB getting hold of him.

He pulled himself together and carefully collected up his precious notes in their sealed bags to put into his jacket pockets. This was what had prompted him and Katya to embark on this risky adventure. He sat down on the bed and thought of the series of events that had brought him to his present situation.

He suddenly smiled and thought of his Ukrainian friends and their motto: We're not dead yet.

He stood up and muttered to himself, 'And I'm not dead yet either.'

In the living room, the family greeted him with smiles and complimentary gestures about his appearance. With Josefina translating, he thanked them for their help and their kindness. He shook Zoltan's hand. Zoltan's reaction was to pat him gently on the cheek, whilst maintaining his calm smile.

When he turned to Margit, she put her arms around him and hugged him then kissed both his cheeks. Josefina translated her words.

'My mother asks for God to take care of you and bring you safely to your wife.'

Alexei was touched by their kindness.

'Tell your mother that her God will need to be very special to care for me better than she has. You and your mother have been my guardian angels.'

Josefina translated this to Margit who burst into tears and gave him another hug.

The sound of a car prevented the scene from becoming embarrassing, and they turned to see Doctor Hasz drive his old Lada into the yard. He got out and waved before walking over to the door where they had all gathered.

'Are you ready to go?' he asked. 'I saw a police car heading up the Nyiregyhaza road with three officers aboard, so it looks like they are about to start their roadblocks.'

Josefina looked concerned. 'Which road will you take, Doctor?'

He smiled at her. 'We will take the lanes over to Tokaj, bypassing Nagyhalasz, and we should be fine. If we do meet any police, the chances are it will be someone I know; but even if it's a stranger they will give an old doctor and his student,' he looked at the girl, 'an easy time. Now let us get moving.'

He led the way to the car where he directed Alexei to the back seat and gestured for him to lie down. Josefina's holdall was propped on the seat alongside him, then a rolled up travel rug and a loosely draped anorak completely covered him.

Margit and Zoltan both hugged their daughter and bade her take care. The doctor started the car and they were off.

Their journey took them along unsurfaced farm lanes, roughly parallel to the river, cutting across the main road near Nagyhalasz before continuing along tracks until they joined the major road into Tokaj.

The pleasant village, world-famous for its wine, was stirring to life with farm traffic. Doctor Hasz carried on at a steady pace, turning eventually onto Route 3 through Szerencs until they reached the city of Miskolc where he stopped near the city centre.

'I think we are in safer waters now,' he said. 'There is a good cafe in this street where I suggest we have some coffee and cake. Our friend will be glad to see daylight again, I think.' He leaned over and gently pulled the coverings from Alexei who had dozed off.

Alexei slowly raised himself on the seat and looked about him. 'Is this Budapest?' he asked.

Doctor Hasz smiled, 'Another hundred and eighty kilometres, my friend. It's time for coffee.'

They got out of the car, Alexei very stiffly, and walked the few yards to an old shop entrance. Inside, it was poorly lit but had several tables and a number of customers. They sat at a table in a corner, where the lighting was at its poorest, and positioned Alexei with his back to the room. Doctor Hasz ordered coffee and cake which soon arrived and they gratefully sipped the coffee.

'We are making good time,' the doctor said, 'another two or three hours to Budapest, perhaps.'

He turned to Josefina, 'Where are you going to in the city?

Does your friend here have a room in the university, or does he have a flat somewhere nearby?'

Josefina was thinking fast and ignored the doctor's direct question.

'Another two or three hours you say. That will make a really long day for you, Doctor Hasz. I could phone one of my friends in Budapest to come out and meet us along the road. This could cut some time out of the journey and allow you to get home at a civilised hour.'

She explained to Alexei what she was suggesting, and he nodded in agreement, pointing out that they still didn't know how they would negotiate any hurdles once they got to Budapest.

Turning again to the doctor, she said quietly, 'Dear Doctor Hasz, some day I will tell you what you have done and you will be pleased to know what you have contributed to. I feel it would be a bit too much to impose on your kindness all the way to Budapest. It would be better, I think, if I call my friend Laci. He can arrange to meet us on the road.'

Doctor Hasz smiled and bowed slightly. 'I look forward to hearing the full story, one day. You phone your friend and see what you can arrange.'

She went out to a public telephone in the street and returned after a few minutes.

Both men looked at her expectantly as she sat down.

'It's fine,' she told the doctor. 'My friend Laci is a student with me. His father is a doctor in Budapest and he is borrowing his father's car to come to us. He is leaving now and says he could meet us on the road at the Eger turn off. He drives fast and he will easily get there in time to meet us.'

Doctor Hasz spread his hands in front of him. 'What chance do I have with such an organised young lady?' he laughed. 'I'm only a man after all.'

Josefina explained to Alexei what was happening. He asked her about Laci and whether he could be trusted.

Her eyes softened as she described him as a good friend.

Alexei looked at the doctor, who was obviously following most of their conversation. The doctor repeated 'good friend' and winked. Alexei smiled in reply.

With the pressure now off, to some extent, they relaxed a little and ordered more coffee and cake. Eventually they returned to the car and started out on the next leg of the journey with Alexei sitting up in the back, but wearing the doctor's hat pulled low over his eyes.

Doctor Hasz and Josefina, between them, gave Alexei an interesting travelogue as they passed through Miskolc and the surrounding countryside. He heard of the city's importance in the wars against the Turks, and of its famous black icon, presented to the Orthodox Church by the Tsarina Catherine. He also heard of the thermal springs and Ice Age caves and gradually nodded off again.

He woke as the car slowed and ran across a stretch of gravel before stopping. He looked up and saw that they had stopped in a rough lay-by. In front of them was a black Mercedes. His immediate thought in his sleepy state was that Peter and the KGB had caught him. Then he saw a young man in jeans and a tee shirt get out of it and wave towards them.

Josefina waved back and said, 'That's Laci.'

Doctor Hasz turned round towards Alexei, winked again, and said knowingly, 'That's Laci.'

They got out of the car and were introduced to the pleasant young man who was obviously pleased to see Josefina; and she him.

Before leaving, Alexei expressed his thanks to Doctor Hasz. In his faltering Russian, the doctor said, 'I think you are doing something that is right - I hope you are doing something right. We all try to make the world a better place. Welcome to the world.'

They waved him off, then the other three got into the Mercedes. Josefina started a conversation with Laci which Alexei could not follow. Laci kept asking her questions and she appeared to answer with some hesitation. Eventually Laci looked at Alexei in some amazement. The conversation continued, with Josefina becoming more positive in her delivery. Eventually Laci shrugged his shoulders and seemed to acquiesce to her arguments.

She said to Alexei, 'I have told Laci virtually everything I know of you. He was not happy to be involved in such a thing, but now he agrees to help. His father was a doctor under the old regime, so he knows how the system used to work. He agrees that there are still some who worked with the KGB and would help their old masters.'

Laci turned to Alexei, 'We need to know what you will do in Budapest,' he asked in passable Russian.

'I need to make contact with the American embassy. The Russians probably suspect I am in Hungary - you have heard of the roadblocks?'

Laci nodded.

'They will probably be staking out the American embassy, so it would be mad to go there directly. It's likely that the telephone is tapped, and I don't have any safe numbers to phone because the original plan went wrong; so I need to think of a way to let them know where I am.'

Laci spoke to Josefina. She then launched into a lengthy explanation of something which, again, Alexei could not understand. At last the young people appeared to be in agreement, though Laci did not look too pleased.

Josefina said, 'We have decided what to do. I will go to the American embassy, pretending to be asking for a visa, and once I get inside I will ask for the man I spoke to on the telephone, Mr Samek. In the meantime, we have a good plan for hiding you.'

She looked pleased with herself.

Alexei nodded to her, 'Go on. What is your plan for me?'

'Well,' she started, 'Laci has been doing an attachment to the Peto Clinic, learning about children with cerebral palsy. He still goes there regularly as part of his course. He says it will not be difficult to smuggle you in there and keep you safe for a day or two until your friends can take you to safety.' She looked at him with a faint smile on her lips.

'Are you sure it's safe there, at the clinic? And are you sure that Laci will not get himself into trouble for this action?'

Laci waved his hand. 'Don't worry about it. One of the chaps had his girl friend in there for a week and nobody found out. It's safe.'

They started off for Budapest. The Mercedes was infinitely more comfortable than the doctor's old car, and Laci was a fast driver.

By early afternoon they entered the city. Alexei was impressed by some of the old buildings dating back to the days of its imperial grandeur. They swung along the river front, past the magnificent parliament building and the Chain Bridge then over the Elizabeth Bridge and out into the hills behind Buda.

The Peto Clinic was a modern building, totally at odds with his impression of an impoverished society. Laci drove the Mercedes along a service road and into a loading bay. Alexei was told to keep his head down. Laci slowed at the entrance where a guard looked up and waved at him. The barrier was open and he drove through.

At the far end of the loading bay they stopped and got out. Laci led the way through a warren of corridors and storage areas until they were sidling down a narrow space behind a stack of pallets and boxed stores. A door in the wall let them into a small room which looked like some sort of workshop or maintenance room.

'This room has not been used for some time since the maintenance area at the other side of the building was enlarged and modernised,' said Laci. 'There is a fold-out bed here and a toilet, so you will be safe for a short stay.'

Alexei looked round the gloomy little cell. It was not very attractive, but if it kept him safe until the next move it would have to do.

'Thank you, Laci,' he said to the young man, 'and I'm sorry that you have become involved in my problems.'

Laci shrugged his shoulders and looked pointedly at Josefina, 'She is my problem.'

Alexei patted the young man's shoulder and said, 'You are a very lucky man. Most men would give their right arm for a problem like her. Take care of her.'

Josefina pouted and scoffed, 'You are being smooth again. But it's right that you should tell him what a great prize I am.'

She laughed as Laci grimaced.

They went over how Josefina should handle her visit to the American embassy, and how much she needed to remember if she made contact with the military attaché. Between the three of them they came up with sufficient English to make a credible presentation.

Josefina gave Alexei the food her mother had given her before she and Laci left him in his spartan quarters.

That morning, the bobbies took to the road for the last leg of their journey; eighty miles to Budapest. Their hosts of the Gyor police escorted them through the town and out onto the Budapest road. They followed the Danube through villages, fields and small towns until they came to Komarom, which is a fair-sized town.

In the town centre, Ron Meadows spotted a supermarket and they pulled up there to restock their larder. Ron and Jock did the shopping as usual and were amazed at the limited range of goods. Fresh fruit and vegetables were in very short supply. Many of the shelves were nearly empty. They were able to get bread and some tasty cheese, both of which would keep the legs spinning to Budapest.

A lunch halt was called near the Danube, just before the road heads away from the river into some low hills. They had just finished their snacks and were changing into their Union Jack shirts when two police motor cyclists appeared. They spoke no English, but their welcome was obviously warm and genuine, and they made it clear that they would escort the team on their run into town.

The next stop was at Pilisvorosvar where the bobbies had

agreed to lay a poppy wreath on behalf of the Royal British Legion at the Commonwealth War Cemetery there. As they drew up at the cemetery, they were greeted by a party of Hungarian police officers and photographers.

One of the police officers, another Suzy who was a lieutenant, was the interpreter, and her English was perfect. She made all the introductions. The Hungarian party was under the command of Colonel Laszlo Vary, who was to become a good friend and a marvellous host to them over the next two days.

The Hungarians had brought their own wreath, and a simple but touching ceremony took place as the bobbies, who had cycled thirteen hundred miles, laid their wreath to honour the dead with their colleagues from Budapest.

The subsequent press photographs of Colonel Vary in uniform alongside Ron in his bobby's uniform both saluting the memorial, with the cyclists in Union Jack shirts standing alongside them became treasured souvenirs to them all.

The final ride into Budapest was fairly short from there. They were escorted to the Parliament building and welcomed by some members of the newly-democratic government. From there, they were escorted up the Castle Hill with its uncomfortable cobbles to the Pierrot restaurant where they met some of the British families with their children who were receiving treatment for cerebral palsy at the Peto Clinic.

They found it very sobering, hearing of the trials and worries these people had endured to help their children. It made their own efforts to raise money for an expanded facility in Britain seem worthwhile. A representative of the Hungarian Cycling Federation presented them with badges and congratulated them on a record-breaking ride.

With the cycling journey over, the bikes were loaded into the minibus and they all piled inside. Their Hungarian colleagues escorted them to the Novotel which was hosting them for two nights.

Jack Bergen had his breakfast and checked at the desk for any messages - with negative result - before taking a cab into the city centre. He did the tourist trail, using his professional skills to establish that he was not being followed. He was happy that he had not been spotted by the other side - yet.

He enjoyed Heroes Square and its art galleries. He liked the river front, the Margit Island; the Parliament Building was magnificent in its position on the river.

Putting on his sunglasses and his straw hat, he wandered in the midday sunshine away from the river and drifted across Szabadsag Square where the US embassy is sited.

There certainly was a uniformed police presence near the embassy entrance. He sat on a bench in the gardens near the National Bank and pretended to study his street map. A quick look over his glasses showed there to be a sprinkling of suited KGB clones scattered around the entrance to the embassy.

He walked on until he found a public phone and called David Samek. 'Hi. This is Jack. Has my wife left me any messages?'

'No, I'm sorry Jack. We haven't heard from your wife. Please feel free to ring us later.'

Jack hung up and walked on. David still had nothing new for him. He found a decent restaurant near St Stephen's Basilica and had a good lunch.

He was having initial doubts about the value of his presence here. At least in London he had all the lines of communication at his fingertips. In his present situation he had only covert communication and he had to try to keep his presence secret for as long as possible. At the moment, neither of these burdens was helping him, he felt.

On the other hand, nothing he had been doing in London was speeding things up. He would just have to be more patient. He would go and visit the Castle, the Fisherman's Bastion and the Matthias Church then try David Samek again.

31

Josefina and Laci drove cautiously towards the exit of the loading area where the barrier was now down. He waved to the guard in his booth who recognised him and waved back, then walked out to them.

The guard bent down to look into the car.

'Hello Laci, haven't you finished with the clinic yet?', his eyes on Josefina as he spoke. 'I thought you were back at university.'

Laci smiled, 'Later this week we start again,' he nodded towards Josefina. 'This is my friend who is on the same course as me. She is helping me finish my notes.'

'Very nice,' leered the guard.

Laci engaged gear. 'We will probably be back later, or maybe tomorrow morning, to finish off the last of my work. See you then.'

The guard raised the barrier and they drove out.

'I did not like him,' said Josefina. 'He made my skin creep.'

'He's not too bad,' Laci replied. 'He's just a dirty old man who likes pretty girls.'

He looked at his watch.

'We will have to get moving. Look at the time, it's after three o'clock. When does the visa section at the American embassy close?' he asked.

'I don't have a clue,' the girl replied. 'I guess it would stay open until five, like the shops.'

'I think that it closes earlier than that. I seem to recall that it's around four or four-thirty. So we had better get back into town quick,' he said accelerating through the tree-lined streets of the Buda Hills.

Josefina looked concerned. 'I wanted to go back to Semmelweiss University to pick up my passport, then I would look like a genuine visa applicant. Will we have time?' she asked Laci.

He shook his head. 'Traffic will be growing now. We will be lucky to make it to the embassy in time. If we go out to the university, that means using Ulloi Street, the airport road, and you know how busy it gets. If anybody asks for your passport, you could say you were just making a general inquiry, or looking for an application form.'

The girl brightened and said, 'Yes; that should sound perfectly normal. I can always smile at them, that usually works.'

He glanced across at her. 'Your smile softens most hearts,' he said.

She prodded his arm gently. 'You are trying the smooth treatment now.' Then looking straight ahead she said quietly, 'I hope this works.'

He slowed the car as they turned into one of the larger avenues leading into the city, then said, 'You don't have to do any of this. There are real dangers in playing this game. After all, this man you are helping is a Russian. What do we owe any Russian? My father often talks of the Russian brutality in 1956. They treated the Hungarians like the Tsars treated the serfs. If you want to call the game off, I will support you.'

'It's not right to think like that, Laci,' she said gently. 'I know that you are concerned for my safety, and I thank you for that.'

She placed her hand lightly on his arm. 'This man we are helping is not some Cossack with a sabre or a Soviet tank driver. He is a doctor, which you and I will be when our time at Semmelweiss is completed. He seems to have been involved in some nasty research programmes, but his basic decency has given him back his conscience and now he wants to help his fellow human beings. Not so different from us, I think.'

She looked at the young man, 'He has really suffered to get this far; you didn't see him when I found him in an old boat. It would be inhuman for me to turn against him after all the help my family has given. I could not live with myself if I did that.'

Laci nodded and smiled. 'I guessed you would say something like that. You have enough conscience for both of us. But I am still worried for you.'

She patted his arm then smiled, 'Don't worry too much. What could be more innocent than calling into an embassy to ask about visas? After all, we don't live in a soviet-style police state anymore.'

'You are right up to a point,' Laci returned, 'but I don't think all the leopards have changed their spots. Some of them might still be in the pay of their old bosses.'

'Do I look like some kind of a spy?' She fluttered her eyes at him innocently.

He laughed at her play-acting and kept the Mercedes up to speed, heading back towards the tunnel under Castle Hill. Over the Chain Bridge and following the one-way system brought them close to Szabadsag Square. Josefina kissed Laci briefly and hopped out of the car.

'Where will I meet you?' he called to her.

'Don't hang around,' she said. 'The police might wonder

228

what you are doing. I'll catch the metro back to Nagyvarad Square, and I'll see you at the university.'

He nodded and drove off.

The girl crossed the square to the embassy. She could see a few uniformed police near the entrance, but none of them stopped her as she entered the building.

An immaculately-uniformed marine guard stopped her at a barrier in the foyer.

'Can I help you ma'am?' he said.

'Yes please,' Josefina replied. 'I must speak to David Samek. You know him?'

Expressionless, the marine asked, 'What is your business with Mr Samek, ma'am?'

'Please you tell him, I am girl on telephone. I help his friend.'

The marine turned towards a desk and lifted the telephone. He spoke quietly for a few moments then replaced the receiver.

He pointed towards a number of chairs. 'Please sit over there, ma'am. Someone is coming to speak to you.'

She sat as directed and looked around her. Besides the marine who stopped her, another marine stood in an elevated booth, overseeing the entrance area. Between her position and the rest of the building was a wide desk with two clerks seated at it, and beyond them another uniformed marine stood at the foot of a staircase facing into the foyer area.

She saw a man come from the staircase and walk towards her. David Samek was in his early forties, a career soldier who had slotted quite smoothly from uniform duty into the diplomatic role of military attaché.

'Hallo. I'm David Samek. What can I do for you?' he said to Josefina.

'Hallo,' she said hesitantly. 'I telephone you on Friday. I help your friend, Alexei, after he has accident. You remember me?'

He smiled at her. 'Would you like to come with me Miss?' Not so much a question as a direction.

They walked upstairs and he led the way into a large office. He pointed to a chair, then sat on the other side of a broad desk facing her.

'Who are you and where are you from?' David asked her.

'Please,' said Josefina, 'I must know that we keep secret.'

David raised his hands in a placating gesture. 'You have no worries on that score ma'am. Everything you tell me is a secret. I assure you.' He smiled.

'You talk too quickly,' the girl replied. He repeated his assurances slowly.

She nodded, 'Thank you. I am Josefina Maria Huba. I am from Tiszavany, near Kisvarda. I find your friend in old boat in river Tisza. He has accident.'

She gestured towards her shoulder, 'And he is sick; high temperature; fever.' She grasped for the words.

'Where is he now?' David asked.

'He is in Budapest,' the girl replied calmly.

Controlling his excitement, David Samek produced an envelope from which he produced five photographs. Each showed a different man's face. He gestured towards the photographs.

'Do you see anyone here that you recognise?' he asked.

Puzzled, the girl leaned forwards and looked at the photographs. She leaned back into her chair.

'You not trust me?' she asked.

David Samek smiled reassuringly. 'I want to believe you, and I must make certain. This is a very delicate situation; we have

230

to keep everyone safe. You understand?'

'I think so,' the girl replied doubtfully.

'Did you see any faces you recognised?' David asked again. 'I see Alexei,' she said.

David took a deep breath. 'Can you point to him, please.'

Josefina leaned forward again and touched one of the photographs. 'Thank you, Josefina. That's the right one.'

'I know it is right one.' Josefina felt offended. 'You think I spend all day in car from Tiszavany to tell you lie? Alexei is good man. He want to help world. You want to help him, or you just ask me questions? If only questions, I go. I tell Alexei you not interested.' She started to rise from her chair.

David Samek jumped up and rushed round the desk.

'Please Miss Huba, Josefina; I promise you that I want to help Alexei. He is very important. But you must understand that we have to be very careful. The Russians are also looking for him, and they will try all sorts of tricks to find him or to embarrass the Americans. We have to be certain of our sources.'

Josefina shook her head, 'Not understand everything. You will help Alexei?'

'You bet,' said David. 'Where is he?'

'We hide him in Peto Clinic. My friend is medical student - me too - and he does work sometimes at Peto Clinic. He knows place to hide Alexei. We take him there today. He is safe for one or two days.'

David was scribbling quickly on a pad in front of him. 'Is it easy to get him out of your hiding place?' he asked.

The girl shook her head. 'You must know where to go. In store, behind boxes.' She shook her head. 'I don't know the words. You need me and Laci to show you where he is.'

David glanced up at the clock. 'Josefina, I don't want to keep you late in the embassy. That might bring attention on you when you leave. Can I get you on the telephone? Where are you staying?'

'I am student at Semmelweiss University. No telephone in room. Only one telephone for all students.' She said.

David looked at her, 'Are you staying there tonight?' She nodded.

'Give me your room number and I will get someone to call there and speak to you in person. His name is Jack Spalding, and you can trust him.'

Again she looked dubious. 'He will call tonight? Is he American?'

'He will call tonight, and he is American. He is a professional and will do everything to help Alexei. You can explain the hiding place at the clinic to him.'

Josefina gave the details he asked for and they agreed a time between eight and nine for 'Jack Spalding' to call.

David Samek escorted her back to the visa entrance area where they collected a visa application form which she carried with her when she left the building. He hurried back to his office and was soon busy on the telephone to various people within the embassy.

A young woman knocked at his door and he waved her in. He put down the phone.

'You wanted me to do something, David?' she said.

'Debbie, the hot potato our guys have been looking for has landed in our lap. We have to move fast. I'll give you all the details, which I want you to take out to the Novotel on Alkotas Street. Ask for Jack Spalding, who is registered there. He is

232

the man who organised the operation and he'll take over from us. Introduce yourself at the hotel as Mrs Spalding. You can accompany him to the university to speak to the Hungarian girl, Josefina. Your presence adds to his cover. You okay with that?' He asked.

'Sure. I haven't any commitments tonight. But I'd better change and look like a wife meeting her husband. How am I going to recognise him?' she asked.

David went to his safe and took out a folder. He leafed through the contents then produced a sheet of paper with a passport style photograph attached. He passed it to Debbie who looked at it and said, 'Not bad. I quite like the older types.'

David laughed. 'I promise not to tell him that.'

32

At the Novotel, the bobbies had got themselves sorted out. They had enjoyed refreshing baths, scribbled out their postcards for their wives and friends and were preparing for a get-together with the British families and helpers from the Peto Clinic, plus some of the British embassy staff who had helped in their many arrangements.

The hotel had agreed to them using the cocktail bar and they were looking forward to meeting everyone about six-thirty.

On his way to the same hotel, Jack Bergen used a public phone to call David Samek. 'Hi, it's Jack Spalding here. Has my wife been in touch with you?' said Jack.

David Samek tried to keep the excitement from his voice. 'Yes Jack, your wife Debbie contacted us a short time ago. We gave her your address and she will meet you at the hotel about six-thirty. How's that for service?'

Jack replied, 'Thank you so much. That's good news. Some guys might be happy to lose their wife in Budapest, but I'm delighted with your service.'

'No problem,' said David. 'Only too glad to be of service.'

Jack felt the old familiar butterflies in his stomach. Every operation, where he had been on the ground like this, had such moments. He thrived on them.

So, Debbie would be bringing him the information. David

had sounded upbeat on the phone. It was now - he checked his watch - ten minutes to five. He had better get back to the hotel quickly; the traffic looked busy.

He caught a cab near the Castle and was back at the hotel by five-fifteen. He had a shower and slowly dressed, watching the satellite news as he did so.

Around six-fifteen he went down to the ground floor and ambled over to the cocktail bar to get himself a drink. He was aware of six men in blazers and flannels gathered at the bar. As he approached he was surprised to hear that they were speaking English.

He leaned on the bar as he waited to be served and looked sideways at the group of men. He heard one being addressed as 'Jock' and suddenly recognised Jock Marshall, the bobby he had given sponsorship money to for his cycle ride.

'What the hell is he doing here?' Jack thought, just as Jock looked in his direction.

'Hello,' said Jock, 'Haven't we met, somewhere?'

Jack put out his hand, 'Jack Spalding. I think we met at the American embassy in London.'

Jock shook his hand. 'Hallo; I thought you looked familiar. What are you doing in Budapest?'

'It's a long story. But how has your trip gone? Any hiccups on the way?'

'Nothing serious,' Jock replied. 'We hit all our target times. We got soaked a few times and we got marginally lost a few times. But we made it. Let me introduce you to the rest of the lads. You remember Paddy, of course.'

Jack gripped his arm. 'Just a moment, Jock. I'd appreciate it if you don't mention the US Embassy. I'm on business, and as far as you know, I'm Jack Spalding from Canada. You can say we met at a social event at the US Embassy, if you like.'

'No problem,' said Jock. 'I can only hazard a guess at what you're here for. Now meet the lads.'

Jack was introduced as an old associate of Jock and was warmly welcomed by the team. He asked all the appropriate questions about the cycling, and got into a detailed conversation with Paddy about gears and cog numbers. He asked what their plans were for the evening and they told him about the parents and helpers from the Peto Clinic meeting for a drink, and also the British Embassy staff coming for a drink too.

Soon, a number of people started arriving and were welcomed by the bobbies. Jack sidled off to the lounge area by the reception desk. He had only sat down when a voice said, 'Jack, there you are at last.'

He looked up and saw a pretty young woman looking down at him. He stood up and she embraced him. As he put his cheek to hers he whispered, 'Debbie?'

She whispered, 'Yes. Hey, I like your after-shave.'

Jack took her back up to his room where he switched on the television again, to mask their voices. Old habits die hard. Debbie had some notes from David Samek covering all the points Josefina had contributed, and directions how to get to the Semmelweiss University to see the girl.

Jack read the information quickly. Debbie looked at Jack. 'Is it good news?'

Jack looked slightly bemused. 'I can't believe what I'm reading here. We've been hunting over a large part of Eastern Europe for this man; he's found by a stroppy student, and she hides him in a hospital.'

He looked at Debbie. 'Three weeks ago, in London, I gave some money towards sponsoring a bunch of London bobbies cycling across Europe. Those bobbies are standing at the bar downstairs; they're staying at this hotel, and they are visiting the Peto Clinic tomorrow morning at ten. How weird is that?'

Debbie looked at him in amazement.

Jack memorised the information he needed then burned the notes in the bathroom sink, flushing away the ashes.

'We'll have a quick drink with the bobbies,' he told Debbie, 'then I think we had better get moving. How far to the metro station?'

'It's a good ten minute walk to the end of the main street here, and we have to change trains, as David pointed out.'

'Let's go,' said Jack.

The hotel cocktail bar was busy when they went back downstairs, with the bobbies acting the friendly hosts. Jack and Debbie walked over to where Jock and Paddy were talking to some embassy staff. He introduced Debbie, who took over the conversation whilst Jack gently pulled Jock and Paddy aside.

'I'll be back here sometime around ten tonight,' said Jack. 'I'd very much like to have a talk with you about something important. Where are you likely to be at that time?'

'A question I can't answer, I'm afraid,' said Jock. He nodded towards a group of people and said, 'Those are some of the British helpers at the clinic, and they have suggested going out for a meal shortly at a restaurant where the food is good and the prices are low. If the beer prices are low, we could be some time.'

'Understood,' said Nick. 'After the ride you guys have done, you deserve to have a bit of a celebration. I'll find you later.'

Jock and Paddy returned to their guests while Jack and Debbie headed out into the night.

It was a mild evening and they enjoyed their walk to the terminus station at *Deli Palyaudvar*. Four stops later they got off at Deak Square and joined the south-eastern line to Nagyvarad Square.

Semmelweiss University comprises of the old, original buildings fronting on Ulloi Street, and the modern building behind them which dominates the area. They followed David Samek's directions to the halls of residence and at the office, asked for Josefina Huba. Debbie's Hungarian was passable and she did the talking. She introduced them as Canadian cousins and that they were expected. They followed the directions the office girl gave them and found Josefina's room.

She answered the door when they knocked. Debbie did the introductions and Josefina invited them in.

After she was satisfied with their identities, Josefina sat down and listened to their questions. Debbie was able to help clarify the difficult points of language.

Jack was impressed by the young girl. She seemed to wear her principles on her sleeve, but then she tempered this illusion with a pinch of street-wise thinking. She and her family certainly had guts to do what they had done, especially after learning that their patient was a Russian escapee.

Jack felt slightly hamstrung. The way the youngsters had hidden Alexei meant that nothing could be done without their involvement. He was unsure how sick the Russian might be and wanted to get him moved as soon as he possibly could. It would take a day to get his preferred extraction team drawn in from Czechoslovakia and north-eastern Hungary. He would have to go and see Alexei and try to assess his condition. If he could be moved, he would do it.

He arranged to meet Josefina and Laci next morning near the clinic and they would take him in to see Alexei. He and Debbie reassured Josefina that after that, she would no longer have any worries as they would take over Alexei's care.

Josefina accompanied them to the entrance then used the public telephone to call Laci. Keeping the conversation short, she told him to pick her up the next morning and she would tell him all her news then.

Jack and Debbie made their way back to the metro station where they also used a public telephone to call David Samek. His news was not good.

'The opposition appear to have got a whiff of the deal we are negotiating, and their bankers are putting more funds into a counter-bid,' David told them.

Jack knew this meant that the Russians were on the scent, and might be getting close enough to pose a threat. He knew it was only a matter of time. The other side was as professional as his team. He and Debbie parted back at Deak Square, she to her apartment, and he back to the hotel.

It all seemed quiet in the hotel reception after the earlier friendly gathering. He ordered a coffee and sat with an English language newspaper reading the local news.

Around ten-thirty, the bobbies arrived back at the hotel. Jack waved a welcome and they all joined him.

There was some talk about the restaurant where the Bobbies had enjoyed a rather large meal at a very small price. They were obviously impressed by the experience.

Jack was looking for an opening to talk to Dave and Jock,

who sensed what he was doing and asked who was buying the next round; the bar still being open. The majority moved over to the bar, leaving Jock and Dave Hastings with Jack. 'So, my friend,' said Jock. 'What's on your mind? Can Dave and I help you?'

Jack looked at them and said, 'I'll keep this brief. You are going to the Peto Clinic tomorrow morning. I'm going to the same place about the same time. I'd like to bring a certain article out of the clinic as unobtrusively as possible. If you guys are around, you could be helpful to me.'

The police officers looked at each other.

Dave said, 'What do you mean by article? We won't get involved in anything illegal. We can't embarrass Colonel Laszlo and our Hungarian hosts.'

Jack replied, 'I understand your concerns. There is only so much I can tell you. I am on business for my country, and probably for the good of humanity if truth be known. I'm trying to save a guy's life. This guy's not a criminal. He has committed no crimes in this country, but he sure is as important as hell to your country and mine. His progress has been held up and I need to expedite matters.'

Jock shook his head, 'Look, don't talk gobbledegook. We hear enough of that in Westminster. Whatever you tell Dave and I, we will keep confidential. So, lay the cards on the table and if we can help, we will. If we don't go along with it, we'll tell you.'

Jack considered for a moment then told the officers the briefest details of his task.

Jock looked questioningly at Dave, who shrugged his shoulders and nodded. 'Right,' said Jock. 'We are up for it, but we'll have to put it to the other four.'

'What do you mean? How can we keep this confidential when you are going to bring another four guys into the game?' objected Jack.

'Stay calm,' said Dave. 'We are a team, and everyone can be trusted. The lads will keep your secret, and if they agree to go along with it, it will work all the better.'

Jack threw his hands up in despair, with visions of his professional career disappearing rapidly down the drain.

The other bobbies joined the table with a tray of drinks. After toasting each other, Dave and Jock gently broached the subject of Jack's suggestion. There was a shocked silence for a few moments before Paddy chimed in.

'Well now, did I ever tell you when I was out in the desert with the SAS? Those were hard times I tell you.' He turned to his colleague. 'What do you think, Tommy? We can do this, no bother. But I'm not wearing the false moustache,' he laughed.

'Never mind a false moustache,' said Tommy, 'It's your turn to wear the wig tonight.'

As the laughter died down, Roy Kitchen asked, 'What dangers are there for us?'

Jack replied, 'My cover hasn't been blown, as yet, so there is no immediate danger that I can see. None of the other side is on to me yet; I just need a bit of help in a hurry to pull this guy out.'

Ron Meadows chimed in, cheerfully, 'I suppose that means I'll be driving him out.'

Jack agreed, 'Yes, that would be the ideal method, but we'll have to get your vehicle close to the building somehow.'

Ron said, 'That's no problem. We have a load of medicines,

chocolate and other goodies for the children, and we arranged with the helpers tonight that we would back the bus into their loading bay and get the stuff off there.'

Jack smiled, 'I salute you guys. Somebody up above must have sent you to save my day.'

Jock winked across to Paddy who said, 'That's settled. Now we've just got to agree the price.'

Jack's expression froze. He slowly looked around the table and saw a sea of smiling and expectant faces. 'Price?' he asked.

Jock began, 'Yes, this whole enterprise has been made with the intention of raising money for sick children. A lot of individuals and commercial companies are supporting us. Princess Diana is supporting us, for example. However, we are struggling to get the sponsorship up to the ten thousand pound mark. It wouldn't take a lot to get us up there.' He looked towards Paddy.

'We all know how rich you Americans are,' said Paddy. 'Now it would only take about a week's wages for an American to make the difference to our target. You could arrange it. You don't have to send a cheque with Uncle Sam's name on it, because I'm sure you've got the right kind of bank accounts for this sort of thing,' he winked to Jack.

'OK,' said Jack. 'You got it. Just give me the figure and I'll see if I can arrange it.' Jock scribbled a figure on a piece of paper and slid it over to Jack. He looked at it and said, 'I might have gone higher.'

'Wait and see the results,' said Jock. 'You might want to add a bonus.'

'Right,' said Dave, 'That's it for me. I think I've had enough to drink tonight.

242

I can't see me absorbing any more details, I'll see you in the morning.'

'Bright and early,' agreed Jack.

Alexei sat on the fold-down bed and looked around him. He was in a dingy, depressing little room with no windows and a feeble electric light doing little to lighten his mood or his surroundings. He felt very tired. The elation of getting on the move from Tiszavany to Budapest had died away and his body cried out for rest. He looked in the bag of food which Josefina had left him and found a bottle of water. With this, he washed down the last of the pills Doctor Hasz had given him.

He consoled himself with the thought that his body was getting better, and that his current state of exhaustion did not indicate that he was relapsing into his fever of a few days ago. He just needed a sleep.

He ate some of the bread and cheese from Josefina's bag, then sank back onto the bed. As the welcome waves of sleep started to wash over him, his last thought was for Katya. How he missed her.

Perhaps tomorrow...

33

Jack Bergen was shaken from a deep sleep by the sound of a telephone ringing. He sat up abruptly, remembered where he was, and reached for the phone.

The hotel receptionist's voice said, 'Mr Spalding, your wife is here and wants to see you urgently.'

'I'll be right down,' said Jack.

He threw on a sweat shirt and trousers then hurried down to reception.

Debbie was waiting for him. As he walked towards her, she came to meet him and threw her arms around him, whispering in his ear, 'They're on to you.'

He drew her aside to sit a safe distance from the reception desk. 'What have you got?' he asked.

'I got a call from the duty officer at the embassy just over an hour ago, at four o'clock. He told me to get in, and that he had called David.'

She looked at him steadily. 'A signal has come in from London. Our insiders there say the Soviets have twigged that you are not in your usual place. They started a trawl and found that you had flown to Vienna. They haven't got your trail from there yet, but they have beefed up their teams in Bratislava, Prague and,' she paused, 'in Budapest.'

Jack nodded. 'It was predictable. We would have monitored the opposition in the same way. So, we'll have to think how

244

we play the game today.'

They went upstairs to Jack's room where he made them cups of instant hotel coffee, then they sat and quietly went over his plans for that day, with the television turned on to low volume in the background. They both accepted that he could be a liability if he continued with the game plan. One fortuitous sighting of him by the opposition and they could lose Alexei; and anyone with him.

'Can I make a suggestion?' asked Debbie.

'Feel free,' said Jack. 'But keep your voice low.'

'You are only a liability if you are spotted while we are dealing with our man. If you are not with him, your presence could be a great distraction and leave the field a bit clearer for others to pull him out.'

'Agreed,' said Jack. 'But my extraction team won't be here in time to take over this morning's proceedings.'

She shook her head. 'Not to worry. If you are seen going openly into the embassy about ten this morning, your presence could draw the hounds in that direction. Meanwhile, I can be meeting Josefina and her friend and teaming up with your mad bobbies to get him back to the hotel here. Then your team might be able to come into play. What do you think?'

'I think you have struck gold, Debbie.'

He stood up and paced back and forth slowly for few minutes, then stopped beside the woman. He squeezed her shoulder and said, 'It's the best idea in this situation. I can't think of anything better, given the pressure we are under to get this guy out. We'll have an early breakfast and I have to talk to these London cops anyway, so it should be easy to explain that you are playing my role.'

'Are you totally happy about using these cops?' she asked. 'We don't really know much about them, to be completely honest.'

'I hear you, Debbie, and I follow your line of thought,' Jack replied. 'But I've talked to these guys; they are professionals in their own right. Granted they don't tend to play in exactly the same games as us, but there are parallels and I think they are going to be our trump card.'

'Okay, Jack. I'll go along with your judgement,' she said. 'I really hope you have judged them correctly.'

'So do I, girl; so do I,' Jack agreed.

Katya woke early again; the central heating in the apartment made her feel hot and uncomfortable. She lay and wondered for the millionth time what might be happening to her Alexei.

The previous day had been very trying for her, and consequently even more trying for her hosts. She had given Jean and Freda a hard time from their first meeting at breakfast, and had later stormed into Fred Delaney's office demanding news.

Fred had maintained his calm composure, but had done little to calm the storm.

Her sour mood had continued all day.

Finally, just as she was about to prepare for bed, Freda had called at the apartment with Jim Bakker. Jim had kept his tone very low-key, but told her that things were expected to get off the ground the following morning. Despite her myriad questions, he did not divulge any details to her of the intended operation to collect Alexei. This did not satisfy Katya who resumed her attack, accusing him and all Americans of duplicity.

Jim's unruffled rejoinders failed to pour oil on the stormy sea he confronted. He repeated his assurances that she could be confident that they were doing everything possible to reunite her with her husband.

Katya went to bed in tears after ordering the Americans out of the apartment.

She thought over the events of the previous day and her anger started to return.

How can I go on like this? she asked herself. Only promises - 'wait till tomorrow'- 'we are doing our best'. Well tomorrow has arrived, and I want answers, she decided.

When Jack and Debbie entered the hotel restaurant that morning, it was a mass of people. He spotted the bobbies, dressed casually, grouped around a table and tucking into their food.

As he and Debbie joined them, he gestured towards the crowd of people and asked, 'What happened here? Where did the mob come from?'

Roy Kitchen spoke up. 'They're all Italian tourists. Two coach-loads of them arrived last night. Ron and I were chatting to some of the ladies.' His colleagues raised their eyes at that. 'And we found out where they came from.'

Tommy Evans piped up, 'What sort of a line were you rascals spinning them? If you do strike lucky, it's a long walk home from Italy.'

Debbie was slightly bemused by the light-hearted banter, especially with her mind attuned to the problems facing her.

Jack, speaking directly across the table, explained that he would be unable to see them at the clinic, but that Debbie would go in his place. She would liaise with the contacts and get their man to the bobbies' bus, then she would return to the hotel ahead of them and collect their passenger from them.

Pat O'Malley put down his coffee cup and said, 'I think we can manage that. It's not rocket science, is it?'

Jock turned to Ron. 'You're driving the bus, but you'll need a bit of help to cover any little problems, I'm sure.'

Ron laughed. 'After all our experiences on this trip, unloading some bits and pieces in the clinic basement should not be too difficult. But I want Roy and Paddy with me when I take the bus in there.'

Paddy rubbed his hands. 'The old three-card-trick team is in business again. Tell me Debbie,' he turned towards the young woman, 'have you ever been kissed by an Irishman?'

Debbie looked puzzled, but a smile drifted across her face as Pat planted a smacker on her cheek.

'There you go,' said Pat. 'Now you have something to boast about.'

'Jack,' she said. 'Are these guys for real?'

'I can't begin to guess what you are thinking,' replied Jack. 'But I think they are crazy enough to pull this off. I feel good on this one.'

Dave stood up. 'We are going to get changed into our uniforms now,' he announced. 'We'll see you later, Debbie.'

As the team got up from the table, Jock shook Jack's hand. 'We'll be looking for that cheque arriving at the charity's office, Jack. Will we see you before we go?'

Jack shook his head. 'Probably not. Change of plans; happens a lot in my business. But we might meet up at Grosvenor Square for lunch after you get back. And that cheque is assured.

Good luck.'

Jack and Debbie went back to his room where he packed up his case and telephoned reception to make up his bill. He explained to Debbie that he would phone the embassy from a public phone and inform them that he would be driving into the building at ten. If the lines were tapped, that would ensure coverage of his arrival and keep the bloodhounds away from her, he hoped.

She slipped out to make her way to the meeting point, and Jack made his way downstairs to settle his bill. Using the public pay phone in reception, he called the embassy to say he was on his way. He went out to his hire-car in the hotel car park and sat there for a while, killing time and watching developments.

A Hungarian police car and two motorcyclists arrived about nine-thirty and pulled up at the hotel entrance. Shortly after that, the London bobbies came out in their uniforms and greeted their Hungarian colleagues, then climbed aboard their minibus and the convoy moved off.

34

J ack started the car and consulted the street map one last
time before he too drove out of the hotel and towards the
city centre. He knew that vehicle access to the embassy was via
a back street behind Szabadsag Square and he made his way
there at a steady speed.

When he turned into the small street, he saw the expected
police officer on duty and also a black saloon car with three
well-built and thuggish looking men standing beside it. They
all looked in his direction as he turned into the street.

KGB are on form and on time, he smiled to himself.

The police officer signalled him to stop when he drew near
the entrance, which was standing open with a marine guard
just inside the gate.

Jack slowed down and the goons slowly started to walk
towards the policeman. When he was nearly up to the officer,
Jack flashed his headlights and accelerated around him and
into the embassy compound.

The initial reaction of the KGB men was to move towards
the gate, but the uniformed marine moved to the centre of the
entrance and stood smartly at ease looking out at them. Reality
took control of the situation and they all backed off, except the
policeman who walked over to remonstrate with the marine.

The police officer pointed out that his standing instructions
were to stop motor traffic and ensure that only genuine visitors

or tradesmen were admitted. It was an offence to ignore the signal of a policeman in the street.

There was a language problem between them, but the marine guard pointed out that there was nothing unlawful about an American citizen entering his own embassy.

'The United States Embassy is grateful to the Hungarian government for taking so much care of us, but you can rest easy that the person in that car is expected. Thank you, sir.' The marine saluted smartly and walked away to close the gate.

The KGB men were busy with a radio set in their car.

Meanwhile, Jack was being greeted by David Samek and walked up to his office with him.

The bobbies' trip into the Buda Hills was short, and their Hungarian friends stopped the convoy at the top of one of the avenues above a winding hill. They unloaded their bicycles, and still in uniform, rode down the hill with the motorcyclists leading them. The road surface was very rough with loose gravel, so they kept their speed down.

On one of the bends, one of the motorcyclists, a man-mountain named Stefan, had his motor-cycle slip from under him. They all watched in amazement as the bike slipped down, he landed on his feet and astride the bike, then pulled the huge BMW back onto its wheels one-handed. It was an impressive display of strength.

The group carried on a few hundred yards and saw a small crowd, including some of the children, waiting for them outside the Peto Clinic. Jock led them to a stop in front of the entrance and called out 'Good morning,' which evoked a titter of laughter and broke the ice.

The bobbies were soon surrounded by the British people and their children who had travelled there with great hopes for improvement in the children's condition. It seemed that all of them had found their faith in the clinic justified.

They trooped inside to meet the staff and children, all the time being photographed by the local press.

Ron and Roy had cast an eye around for signs of Debbie but spotted nothing.

The minibus was left, locked, outside the entrance.

Laci had made sure he was early that morning when he drove his dad's Mercedes to the Semmelweiss University to meet Josefina. There was no sign of her when he arrived, so he waited and watched for a few minutes before pulling into the parking area. He parked the car and walked slowly to the front door, where he asked the clerk if she had seen Josefina. The lady clerk responded by telling him that Josefina had warned her that he would be calling, so she was expecting him. He felt relieved, and reassured by Josefina's cool-headed thinking.

Josefina eventually appeared, after he had looked at his watch several times and wondered if they could make it. He looked at her and told himself that she would always be worth waiting for. That smile could melt the hardest heart.

She kissed his cheek and walked towards the door, calling to him, 'Come on lazybones. Time to get moving.'

Laci shook his head, speechless, and followed the girl out of the building. Once on their way, both of the young people felt the onset of nerves. Laci was unusually inconsiderate to other drivers, driving arrogantly around the slow-moving Trabants and Ladas which could not compete with his Mercedes.

Josefina had been very quiet for some minutes before realising what was happening. She patted Laci's arm and said gently, 'Take it easy, Laci, you could get the police chasing you for driving like this and that would not help us. I am worried too, but I gave my word last night that I would see this thing through. If you feel that you don't want to go ahead with it then I will carry on by myself.' She was looking at him earnestly.

'When have I ever let you down?' he sounded hurt. 'I just don't want you to be in danger. If you are going ahead with it, then I will be right there with you. Anyway,' he added with some satisfaction, 'how would you get into the basement of the clinic without me?'

'I never doubted you,' she smiled.

When they reached the meeting place, a quiet avenue of widely-spaced houses, they could see only a solitary woman standing in the distance. As they drew nearer, the girl recognised Debbie from the previous night. Looking puzzled, Josefina told Laci to stop alongside Debbie.

Debbie waved cheerfully and climbed into the back seat. In her passable Hungarian she greeted them both and launched into a sanitised explanation for Jack's absence. She assured them that she had been briefed by Jack and that the plan would go ahead. All she needed was for them to get her into the hideout and she would explain everything to Alexei.

Laci drove on and within a few minutes they were nearing the clinic. As they approached, they could see quite a lot of people going in the main entrance, and a British registered minibus parked outside.

'Everything's in place,' commented Debbie, then ducked

down on the back seat as Laci slowed and turned towards the loading bay entrance.

The Mercedes slowed at the entrance and Laci smiled and waved to the security guard who winked and looked towards Josefina before saying, 'Enjoy yourself, Laci.'

'What did he mean by that?' asked Josefina.

'Forget it,' the young man replied. 'He's just a dirty old man who thinks we are here for some mischief.'

She laughed. 'If he only knew what kind of mischief is going on here, he would have a fit.'

Laci tucked the Mercedes neatly between stacks of pallets and nudged Debbie, who sat up. They all got out and followed Laci, threading their way amongst stacked stores.

Debbie was keeping a mental note of the route through the stacks until Laci stopped in front of the door in the wall. He tapped gently and went in, closely followed by Josefina.

Alexei had been lying on the narrow bed, and was slowly raising himself to a sitting position when Debbie entered the room. He looked at her in alarm, then towards Josefina.

The girl smiled and said, 'It's all right. This is Debbie from the American embassy. She is going to take you to safety.'

Speaking fluent Russian, Debbie greeted Alexei and held out her hand. He slowly raised his hand which she shook gently. She sat down beside him and asked how he was feeling.

'I'm not too bad, but I don't think I can do any serious running and hiding,' he said.

'Don't worry about that Alexei,' Debbie said. 'No more running for the time being, though there will be a bit of hiding before we are out of Hungary. But the worst is behind you.'

Alexei sat quietly, absorbing the news, then asked, 'Katya?

254

Is she safe?' He looked drawn and worried.

'Yes Alexei, she is safe. When this young lady, 'she indicated Josefina,' telephoned the embassy and asked about your wife, we guessed the call was genuine. Your wife's exit from Russia went like clockwork. She is safe on a US base in Germany, and we hear that she is very worried about you. You should meet up very soon.'

Alexei closed his eyes and smiled. His body appeared to relax.

Debbie then told him about the next stage of his journey. When she explained his journey out of the clinic would be with a minibus of London bobbies, he looked at her in disbelief.

He turned to Josefina and Laci and looked at them questioningly. Josefina came over and knelt down in front of him.

Nodding and smiling she told him, 'It sounds crazy, and nobody will ever believe it, but it's true. We are waiting for their bus to come into the basement and then we will hide you on the bus and collect you back at the hotel. It's true my friend.' She took his face gently in her hands. 'You are going to meet your wife, and we will probably not meet again. It has been exciting meeting you and I hope that your dreams will come true.' She kissed his cheek.

Alexei took the girl's hand. 'You have saved my life. When the great plans of the mighty USA fell to pieces, it took a lovely Hungarian student girl to put the pieces together again and save me. I will never forget what you and your family, and your Doctor Hasz, have done. For Hungarians to help a citizen of the Soviet Union as you did was a miracle.'

He looked at her kindly. 'You can be sure that we will meet again. Katya must meet you and see what an angel looks like.'

He inclined his head towards Debbie, adding, 'I don't know when that meeting will be. It will depend on my new American friends.'

35

O n the floor above Alexei's hiding place, the bobbies were welcomed to the clinic by the deputy director, Doctor Barbarics. He congratulated them on being the first group to have cycled from London to Budapest, and the first uniformed bobbies to be seen at the clinic. With police lieutenant Suzy as their interpreter, they toured part of the building, meeting again many of the parents and children who had turned out to greet them.

Since the bobbies were all parents themselves, they were soon on the floor joining in the different games and exercises with the children, and enjoying it immensely.

The time eventually came to move on, and they went outside for another photo-call. They were joined by some of the British helpers who had arranged for the minibus to be off-loaded in the basement.

Ron got into the driving seat and started up the bus while Roy and Pat walked over to the loading bay entrance with the helpers. Ron reversed the bus down the ramp and into the basement area, waving cheerily to the guard who looked completely bemused to see a London bobby driving a minibus into his basement. The others arrived and started to empty the packages from the minibus and carry them into a secure, caged area.

Laci was by the door and heard a vehicle drive into the

basement. He went out and returned within seconds, answering the expectant faces with a vigorous nod. They got Alexei to his feet and led him out into the main basement area where they could see the activity around the back of the minibus. Debbie went forward a little and was spotted by Pat who gave her a discreet 'thumbs-up'.

She watched as the party finished their unloading and Roy and Pat started to drift towards the entrance, talking happily to the helpers and drawing them along with them, away from the back of the van.

'Now,' said Debbie and waved the others forward.

Alexei shuffled as quickly as he could, supported by Josefina and Laci.

He was amazed to see Ron, in his bobby's uniform and with a big smile on his face, waving him on, saying, 'Come on, me old mate. All aboard the number 12 for Regent Street and Oxford Circus.'

He climbed in the minibus and lay down as he was directed between the line of bicycles stacked in the back. Ron drew a couple of sleeping bags over him and closed the doors.

'See you later, Debbie,' said Ron. 'Don't be late. We are behind schedule and our Hungarian friends are taking us to lunch, so we will be doing a very quick change at the hotel.'

'I'll be there before you,' said Debbie.

Ron drove the minibus out and round to the front where goodbyes were still being said.

Debbie got back into the Mercedes with Laci and Josefina. Once again she crouched down in the back as they passed the guard, who had not yet lowered the barrier, and who proudly showed them a police badge he had been given by the bobbies.

Laci waved to him and drove on. He saw the bobbies getting into their bus, as he left the driveway, and the escorting Hungarian police starting up their motorcycles. He accelerated up the hill.

Descending from the Buda Hills towards the city, they suddenly came into heavy traffic which was crawling at a very slow rate.

'What can this be?' asked Debbie. 'Do you normally get this kind of traffic here?'

'No. This is totally unusual,' Laci replied. He leaned out of the window and called to a youth on a bicycle, who waved his arm pointing downhill and replied.

'He says there has been a car accident and one of the cars caught fire. It's right in the middle of a major junction, so the traffic must be like this in all directions,' said Laci.

'Do you know any shortcuts?' asked Josefina.

'Not if that junction is fouled up.' Laci looked glum. 'It hasn't long happened, according to that boy on the bike, so it could take a while to get moving. We could turn around and go back the way we came and over the other side of the hills. That would bring us in from the motorway, but could take some time.'

Josefina, being philosophical about their problem, concluded, 'Well the minibus with Alexei will be held up too, so we should still be at the hotel ages before them.'

Just then, they heard the sound of police sirens and saw the convoy of motorcyclists, police cars and the bobbies' minibus go speeding past them on the wrong side of the road and disappear into the distance.

Laci looked round at Debbie who just put her hands up

and said, 'Shit!'

Katya was in a fighting mood. She joined Jean and Freda for breakfast in their usual dining area, but did not respond to their pleasantries. The American women looked at each other and shared a feeling of impending trouble.

When she had finished her coffee, Katya stood up. 'Now I go to see Mr Fred Delaney, and he must tell me the truth,' she declared.

Jean rose hurriedly. 'I don't think that's a very good idea, honey. Mr Delaney has a lot of work and responsibilities. We just can't go interrupting him whenever we feel like it. We don't want to get him too upset, do we?'

'Upset? Is his problem if he is upset. You look at me,' she thundered, 'You see what upset is.'

She strode away from the table as Freda and Jean grabbed their coats and chased after her.

Walking across the parade ground towards the office block, Katya would not be dissuaded from her resolve by any of their arguments or entreaties.

Outside Fred Delaney's office, a secretary smiled at Katya as she arrived and asked if she could help.

'I see Mr Fred Delaney,' announced Katya.

The secretary was well aware of who Katya was, and of the delicate situation. She continued to smile benignly. 'Mr Delaney is busy right now; can I make an appointment for you later today? How about three o'clock?'

Katya ignored her, and rounded the desk, grasping the door to Delaney's office and was in the room before the girl could gain her feet.

Fred Delaney looked up in surprise, then smiled at Katya and invited her to sit down.

'Good morning ma'am. How are you today?' he smiled. 'I did not expect you this early, but that doesn't matter.' He waved his concerned secretary back to her desk.

'Mr Delaney,' she began.

'Call me Fred, please,' he interrupted.

'Mr Delaney,' she continued. 'You promise me news tomorrow; well it is now the tomorrow. What is the news?'

'Katya,' he began, 'There is some news. Alexei is in a safe place and is being collected from that place this morning. I don't know how long it will take, but we are hopeful that he will be here tonight.'

As she opened her mouth to bombard him with questions, he held up his hand and said, 'I have no more news at the moment. You must understand that this kind of operation is carried out in secret. It's not part of the television news, constantly being updated, so there is nothing more to tell you. I have already told you that there were problems, and that everything did not go according to plan. I don't know the whole story, but I have been told that he is in good shape. That's it.' He looked across the desk at her.

'Why should I believe you?' she asked. 'I want to believe you. I want to believe that Alexei will be here soon. All you give me is make-believe.'

'Katya,' he softened his voice and smiled, 'Do you really think I want you storming into my office and shouting at me? It looks like things are back on course, I assure you. And by the way,' he added, 'Your English is improving. That 'make-believe' attack was pretty good.'

She glared at him. 'You think yourself lucky I don't use all the new words I have learned here.' She stood up and left.

Fred Delaney took out his handkerchief and mopped his brow.

36

The police convoy arrived at the Novotel with little time lost. The bobbies had seen the traffic situation and deduced that Debbie would be seriously delayed.

Ron was chuckling, as usual, weaving the minibus around obstacles as he followed the motorcyclists.

'What are we going to do with our mate in the back? We can't just leave the poor bugger in there while we go and have lunch,' he said.

'There's nothing else for it but to take him into the hotel and stick him in one of our rooms,' suggested Tommy.

'He'll stand out a bit among us, dressed as we are, if he walks into the hotel with us,' put in Roy.

'What gear have we got in the back?' Roy asked Pat.

'Yes; good thinking,' said Pat. 'We've got some tracksuit tops in the back.'

'Leave the uniform jackets and the helmets in the bus,' said Roy. 'Some of us put on tracksuit tops, including chummy in the back. Get him over here beside us. Ron will draw up at the door. Pat and Tommy can whizz our man in while we mill about a bit and it might work.'

Pat, who was coaxing Alexei over the back of the seat, added, 'It's all done by mirrors, you know. Did I ever tell you that the Shannon is the only river that flows uphill?'

'Shut up, you daft tart,' said Tommy, 'And get that lad sat down.'

Alexei hunched himself down between Tommy and Roy while Pat retrieved tracksuit tops and tossed them to the others. Alexei found himself in a bright blue top and baseball cap, and Pat asking him, 'Do you understand English, old son?'

'I speak a little, and I understand if you speak slowly,' Alexei nodded.

'Champion,' said Pat and introduced him to them all.

As they approached the hotel, Jock told Alexei to stay with Pat and Tommy who would take care of him.

He nodded his understanding, and muttered, 'Thank you.' though he looked worried.

The police outriders came to a halt just past the hotel entrance, leaving space for Ron to stop immediately in front of the door.

'Go,' hissed Jock, as he got out of the front, leaving the door wide as a partial shield.

Pat and Tommy were out like scalded cats while Ron got out on the far side and walked away from the bus towards the police officers, ostensibly asking when they were due to leave. Roy and Dave came round from the other side, adding to the shielding of the fugitive.

Pat and Tommy were quickly inside with Alexei between them. He had managed their fast pace as far as the front door, but had to slow down once inside. They reached the lift and went up to their room without incident.

The bobbies invited Alexei to relax on one of the beds whilst they quickly changed into blazers and flannels.

Tommy pointed out the bathroom and said, 'Make yourself at home, mate. Take a bath if you feel like it.'

Pat produced a tee shirt and clean underwear from his

luggage and gave it to Alexei. 'There you go, old son. A good bath and some clean drawers and you'll feel a new man,' he said.

Tommy switched on the kettle to make a drink, when they heard a knock at the door, and Dave calling, 'Open up, it's a raid.'

He and Jock came into the room with a carton from the minibus containing several of the high-energy food bars and drinks which they used when cycling.

Alexei recognised their value to him and started tucking into the contents. He had kept a piece of Josefina's bread until that morning, but it had been so dry and hard when he came to eat it that he felt little good came from it. This cyclists' food would give him a boost, he decided.

Dave explained to Alexei, in very slow English, that they would have to leave him in the room. They would put the 'Do not disturb' sign on the door, but as the rooms had already been serviced that morning, it was unlikely that anyone would call. Since the bobbies had to keep to their schedule, he explained, they didn't know when they could liaise with Debbie or Jack but it would have to be later that afternoon when they had completed the programme their hosts had organised.

'Please don't worry,' said Alexei. 'My situation is my problem and I will try to solve it myself.'

'No!' Dave was emphatic. 'We will sort things out for you. You must rest and stay out of sight. You don't look well enough to organise much at the moment. No doubt Debbie will make contact with us and we can help you on your way. We're not dead yet.'

'That's the Ukrainian anthem again. I surrender to the London bobbies,' Alexei smiled. 'Thank you for helping me.'

They left him in the room, but waited outside until they

heard him slot the safety chain in place. Back at the main entrance the bobbies found that the Budapest police had supplied a police minibus to take them on their next outing. First stop was the magnificent Parliament building where they were introduced to their counterparts, the police who guarded the building. There followed a tour of the building, which was beautiful and had some similarities to the Palace of Westminster.

Their visit concluded with an interview by the parliamentary television station, when Jock was the spokesman and Suzy the interpreter. The session was going very well until the interviewer threw in a stinker of a question suggesting that the history of the communist-era Hungarian police could never measure up to the high standards of the British police.

Jock heard a muttered, 'Bloody hell,' from one of his colleagues behind him. Thinking on his feet and laying on the bullshit with a trowel, he managed to come out of it without maligning his Hungarian hosts and was patted on the back by their interpreter.

All the officers were presented with the Freedom Medal by the Speaker of the parliament. A short trip followed to the Margaret Island where a lunch was laid on for them at the Thermal Hotel, which they found to be a splendid setting. They enjoyed the walk across the park there and the Japanese Garden which Colonel Laszlo was very proud of.

The traffic jam in the Buda Hills was slowly cleared and Laci continued the drive to the Novotel. As they turned into the entrance, they spotted the bobbies' minibus and Debbie's spirits soared.

'They're still here,' she burst out, and jumped out of the car as soon as Laci stopped.

She hurried to the reception desk and asked the clerk to call Jock Marshall or Dave Hastings. The clerk tried the telephone then was interrupted by a colleague.

'I am sorry, but my friend here says that the British policemen have gone,' the girl said. 'You can leave a message for them if you wish.'

Debbie went to a table and quickly penned a message on the hotel's stationery, and sealed it in an envelope. She addressed it to Jock Marshall and left it with the reception staff.

On the way out, she spoke to the uniformed doorman who told her that the group had left in a Budapest police bus about twenty minutes before.

Debbie returned to the Mercedes and joined Josefina and Laci. She explained the situation, but was upbeat that it could all be retrieved when the policemen got her message and rang her at home. She asked if the young couple would drop her in the town centre and she would make her way from there.

Before saying goodbye to Debbie, Josefina pleaded with her to be told how the story ended, as soon as Alexei was safe. Debbie promised to tell the girl and thanked them both for their help. She told Josefina that her parents would be thanked too.

At the first public phone she found, Debbie telephoned David Samek's unlisted number. The phone was answered instantly.

'Hi, this is the lady from Milwaukee,' she began, using her coded cover. 'Yes ma'am,' said David, playing to the rules, 'How can we help you.'

'I collected my traveller's cheques, as you arranged for me, but they've gone missing. I hope they turn up soon. Should I call in at the embassy or go to the bank?'

David cursed under his breath. 'You had best go to the bank and see what can be done, ma'am,' he said.

'Thank you,' replied Debbie, knowing that he had agreed she should go to her flat.

David turned to Jack, 'Debbie has lost the cops, and our man. She doesn't sound suicidal, so I guess that we can recover things. She's on her way home now, which was her suggestion, so I suppose she must be expecting a phone call or someone to contact her there.'

Jack was on his feet. 'How far away does she live? I'll have to see her and get the full story. I'll need some of your equipment to disguise myself.'

David called in one of his staff who soon transformed Jack's thin greying hair into a black Central European thatch. Colouring the eyebrows and adding an authentic moustache and an old pair of bifocal spectacles made a Magyar of him. Local clothing and shoes completed the metamorphosis.

Jack was taken through the building and was slipped into the visa section from where he walked out amongst a group of applicants and made his way to the metro station. His experienced eye told him that he was not being followed.

Debbie's flat was a few hundred yards from the Moszkva Square metro station, and he made a circuitous journey there to ensure, again, that he was not followed.

Debbie told Jack how everything had gone smoothly until the traffic snarl-up had delayed her, and she now had no idea where their prize escapee was hidden. She expected a call later that afternoon in answer to her message left at the hotel reception.

Jack shrugged his shoulders. 'This affair has been one hurdle after another, and we seem to be tripping on most of them. How did Alexei appear to you?' he asked.

Debbie pursed her lips. 'He looks like he's had a tough time. There are some scratches on his face which are healing. He doesn't walk too fast. Overall, he looks like he needs a couple of weeks of tender, loving care,' she concluded.

'Poor guy,' said Jack. 'This was meant to be a copybook operation, but it's been one glitch after another, and he's been dropped in the mire each time. His wife's arrangements ran like a Swiss watch. I hope he manages to keep focused and stay on the team. We can't have him giving up at this stage.'

Debbie smiled slightly, 'Those mad cops are not so mad as I first thought. They organised his transfer into their bus so smoothly, getting the locals out of the way without them realising what was happening. I'm sure they are looking after him, wherever he is.'

Jack looked at Debbie and said, 'Tell me, since you have the advantage of actually being there, do you think we could have got him out of that clinic without using the cops' bus?'

'Difficult to say, Jack,' replied the girl. 'As it turned out, having the cops there was the ideal distraction, and they kept the attention of the security guard and the civilians away from us while we got Alexei into the police bus. If they hadn't been there, the guard might have started patrolling, or come over to speak to Laci, like Josefina told us he did before, or dropped the barrier and we could have been stuck. Had we known the layout exactly, and had we been able to orchestrate the cops' actions in fine detail, it's possible that we might have got him out in Laci's car, but that would have needed one of us in the car in addition to Alexei and it could have been more difficult to conceal two people in a saloon car. Also, we didn't know the layout exactly, there wasn't any time for rehearsals and the cops played their role brilliantly.'

She spread her hands, 'It was a great success, they even had a police escort with sirens to get them through the traffic jam. Unfortunately we had to sit it out in the traffic jam. I still think it will work out.'

'We'll have to be patient,' Jack agreed. 'Those guys will surely phone us before it gets too late.'

After their excellent lunch in splendid surroundings, and a walk through the gardens of Margit Island, the Hungarians took the bobbies for a quick spin around the city, visiting Heroes Square, a market area and a street cafe where they sat outside and enjoyed a beer.

They called at the main police station where Tommy achieved an ambition when he was allowed to drive a Trabant which was owned by one of the officers. There were clouds of smoke and a good deal of leg-pulling by his colleagues.

It was nearly five when they returned to the hotel and Jock found that a message was waiting for him at reception. He showed the note to Dave. It read, 'Missed you earlier, give me a ring and we'll arrange a meal. Debbie.' Her telephone number was added at the bottom of the note.

Using the pay-phone in the lounge, Jock dialled Debbie's number. She answered with a non-committal, 'Hello.'

'Hallo there,' said Jock. 'Got your message. Sorry we missed you, we've had a very busy day.'

'I guessed that would happen,' said Debbie. 'Maybe I can meet up with you later?'

'We've arranged to meet some of the British people from the Peto Clinic again tonight at a restaurant just round the corner from here in Kiraly Hago Square.' Jock replied. 'We meet at seven, and if you and your husband are free we'd be very happy to see you.'

'That's a great idea,' Debbie said. 'My husband might be able to make it, if he is back from Szentendre in time.' She looked across at Jack who nodded in agreement.

She went on, 'Maybe I can pick up that souvenir you promised me.'

'But of course,' said Jock with mock gallantry, 'I have it here in the hotel. Anything to please a lady. Why don't you call here first, and we can all walk round together?'

Debbie laughed, 'Thank you, kind sir. I'll see you around seven.' She gave Jack the full content of the message.

He consulted her street map then went out to the nearest public phone where he dialled a number.

A guttural voice answered, 'Hallo.'

Slipping into fairly good German, Jack said, 'I wondered if you were free for dinner tonight?'

The voice answered, 'Of course I am. Where do you fancy eating?'

'I'll meet you outside the Deli Palyaudvar, the Southern Station, about quarter to seven,' said Jack. 'I've been told about a decent restaurant near there.'

'Fine,' came the reply, 'I'll see you there.'

He returned to Debbie's flat and gave her the run-down on

271

his arrangements. She should go to the hotel in good time. He would be picked up by his exit team and they would make their way to the lower-level service entrance. He had worked out during his stay at the hotel that the fire escape staircase came out at that level. That would be the best point to pick up Alexei, provided they didn't bring him down to the bar to wait for her. He raised his eyebrows in mock disbelief.

'You surely don't think they'll bring him out openly to the bar?' she interjected.

'We're in unknown territory here,' said Jack. 'We don't know how they got him into the hotel, but they did it somehow. If they do bring him downstairs, we'll have to hope he's not easily recognised.'

'Like you, you mean,' Debbie laughed. 'You look like an escapee from an Italian television game show.'

Jack smiled. 'I know, but the disguise worked.'

272

37

Pat knocked on his room door, saying, 'Is that yourself in there? Come on and open the door, me old mate.'

The door opened a crack and Alexei's face appeared. He took off the chain and stepped back. Pat and Tommy entered and closed the door.

Alexei looked better. He had soaked in the bath, then borrowed one of their razors and cleaned up his face. The fresh tee shirt completed his transformation.

'How are you?' asked Tommy. 'Did you enjoy the bath?'

'Very good,' said Alexei. 'I feel clean. Nice shirt.' He patted his chest.

'It looks better on you than on this old goat,' Tommy pointed at Pat.

Alexei looked at them both and asked, 'What is happening now? Do I go?'

'Just you hang on a wee minute,' said Pat. 'Things are being arranged. Jock will give us the news when he comes up.' He mimed a gesture, 'He is on telephone.'

'I understand,' said Alexei quietly, and sat down.

A knock at the door and Jock's voice again calling, 'Penny for the guy!'

He came into the room and smiled to Alexei. 'Things are moving,' he said, walking over to sit beside him. 'I've just spoken to Debbie on the telephone. She will be here before we go out for dinner. I should think she will probably wait until it's dark, and then you will be on your way, old chum. Did you understand all of that?'

Alexei had a slight frown on his face as he had concentrated on what was said.

He replied, 'I think so. Debbie comes here to take me away in the night. Yes?'

'That's it,' said Jock. 'Once it starts to get dark, we'll help you get ready.'

Alexei smiled at them. 'You are all from England, but you all speak different,' he observed.

'Now just a wee minute,' Pat cut in. 'We may live and work in England, but there are no Englishmen in this room.'

Alexei was confused.

'I'm a good Dublin boy from old Ireland,' continued Pat. 'Tommy's a Welsh boy from the valleys, and Jock is one of those mad kilted heathens from Scotland.'

Alexei appeared even more confused. 'Just call us British,' declared Tommy.

'I think I understand,' said Alexei doubtfully.

They got the kettle going as the others joined them, and cups of tea and cans of beer were distributed according to tastes.

Pat and Jock started an exchange of pleasantries with Alexei, telling him about their journey across Europe. He became more involved in the conversation, asking about their home lives. They in turn gradually drew out some of his history, though he was unwilling to reveal every detail of his more recent working life. Policemen being policemen, they all worked out a fair assessment of what he had been up to.

It was Roy who posed the question, 'So, we can guess that

you have been a scientist of some description, right?'

Alexei hesitated, then nodded.

'And you have been making nuclear weapons or nerve gas or something equally dangerous?' He looked at Alexei who shrugged in silent acquiescence.

'We'll take that as a 'Yes', and now you have some information to sell to the Americans. Is that right?'

Alexei shook his head vigorously. 'No, not sell. You must have very bad idea of me. All Russians are not like KGB. I see what my work can do. It is bad. I want world to be a better place, then I can be like you. My wife can have children in safety. I know what I am talking about.' His face had gone white with emotion.

Dave patted his shoulder. 'It's all right, my friend. We are not judging you. It's just that policemen are always curious, and we all wondered what your story might be. Believe me; if you are trying to make the world a safer place, we are all with you.'

There was a chorus of agreement, and Alexei started to relax.

Ron went out of the room and returned with a cardboard box containing a large selection of potato crisps, chocolate and high-energy bars, and their old favourite, tins of creamed rice.

'Just need to take the edge off my appetite,' he said. 'Anyone else hungry?'

They all helped themselves, encouraging Alexei to join in. The television was switched on to catch the English-language news, then a card game started.

Dave and Jock left the cards to the others, continuing to chat to Alexei who opened up quite a bit. He told them of Katya and how he was looking forward to seeing her. After some prompting, he told them that she had escaped via Leningrad, though he did not know how it had gone.

He told them of Josefina and her family and the help they had given him, and how he hoped to be able to show his thanks to them one day, and generally unburdened himself of his escape nightmares.

Darkness was starting to fall and they agreed it was time they got Alexei ready.

Ron produced the travel iron, and they soon had his suit looking reasonable. One of Tommy's white police shirts fitted Alexei and they gave him a presentation tie, decorated with the Scotland Yard crest, to make him look the businessman.

Around six-thirty, leaving Pat and Tommy with Alexei, the party went down to the bar to await developments.

Debbie left Jack at the metro station. He stood back in the shadows whilst she carried on towards the hotel.

A few minutes later, a large Citroen saloon stopped opposite Jack. Without hesitation he walked over and climbed into the back seat.

'Are the others on way? he asked.

The front passenger turned. 'They are right behind us now,' he pointed.

Jack looked round and saw a Volkswagen camper van closing up behind them.

They reached the service entrance beside the hotel, pulled in and both vehicles had their lights extinguished.

The driver of the Citroen got out and looked around, then returned to the car. 'No problems.' He pointed, 'That's the fire escape exit there, and next to it is the bowling alley fire exit. It's up to your lady now.'

Debbie walked into the hotel and saw the bobbies at the

bar. They welcomed her and offered her a drink. She accepted a mineral water before stepping back from the bar to talk.

'Where is he? In one of your rooms?' she asked.

'On the fourth floor,' Jock pointed out. 'How do you want this done?'

'Quite simple,' she said, 'We just want him down the fire escape. Jack is waiting in the service area at the foot of the stairs with our transport team.'

'Right,' said Jock. 'We'll go and bring him down that way.'

'I'll come with you,' said Debbie.

'Not a good idea,' said Dave. 'Two of the lads are up there looking after him. The less activity we make the better. Ron and I will drift over to the ground floor emergency exit and make sure the foot of the staircase is clear. You join us in a minute or so; we'll want you there to identify your team.'

'OK,' said Debbie. 'I'll go along with that. I didn't mean to imply that you couldn't manage it. It's just that the responsibility for this end is mine.'

'That's understood, but you're not wearing the right shoes for running down fire-escapes.'

They both laughed.

Pat opened the door when Jock knocked. Alexei was sitting nervously in an armchair, looking towards them.

'Righto, Alexei. Your carriage awaits,' Jock announced. 'We are going down the fire escape and the welcome party is at the bottom. Let's go.'

Pat went out first and walked the few yards to the fire escape door, listening for any signs of life from the rooms he passed. He opened the fire escape door and looked into the stairwell then waved the all-clear.

Jock went out with Alexei between him and Tommy with Roy behind them. They quickly reached the door and all of them went down the stairs in an extended line, their pace dictated by Alexei's limited speed.

At the last landing before the bottom of the stair well, Pat and Tommy stayed back with Alexei whilst Jock and Roy went down to the door. Debbie and the others were waiting by the partly-opened door.

They heard a car door open, and a figure approached them through the gloom. As they stood ready to close the door, they recognised Jack's voice calling gently,

'Debbie, it's me.'

Jack came into view. He had removed the false moustache in the car, but still had the black hairpiece. He held his hands up, 'I know, I'm in a bit of disguise, but we play silly games. Where is our boy?'

Jock waved up the stairs to Pat, and he and Tommy came down with Alexei. Jack held out his hand to Alexei and said, 'I am so glad to meet you at last, and I'm sorry for all the troubles you have suffered because the plan went wrong. Tonight you should be back with your wife. This way.' He stepped aside and indicated the camper van.

Alexei turned to thank the bobbies, who wished him luck. Jack added his thanks and was gone.

The police officers went back up one flight of stairs and entered the reception area adjacent to the bar.

Debbie looked at them quizzically.

Pat called to her, 'Would you like a real drink now?'

'You bet,' she replied, and taking hold of Pat's arm, swung him round and planted a kiss on his cheek.

'Now you can boast too,' she laughed.

It goes without saying that a very convivial evening followed, and they all made it to the restaurant and had a good meal. As they were finishing their meal, they were surprised to see Colonel Laszlo walk into the restaurant. With a big smile, he walked over to their table, pulled up a chair and joined them.

As they looked at him in some bemusement, he said, 'Well done, all of you. My men have confirmed that your friend is safely on his way, without any interference from the bad guys.'

As one, they said, 'You knew?'

Still smiling, he said, 'Your friend is not a problem once he has left Hungary. It was in our interests to help a little.'

More drinks were ordered, and the story emerged of how they had all been, directly and indirectly, helping each other to a satisfactory result. The drinking went on late into the night.

38

Alexei was helped into the camper van by Jack, who climbed aboard to sit opposite him. The Citroen moved out into light traffic, closely followed by the van and they headed off at a steady speed around the northern flank of Castle Hill.

Jack produced a vacuum flask of coffee, and sandwiches and offered them to Alexei, who took a cup of coffee but declined the sandwiches, saying, 'Bobbies feed me too much chocolate.'

'Well, good for them,' said Jack. He went on to explain what was going to happen that night.

Because of the increased attention by the KGB around the border crossings, the Americans intended taking no chances with his safety. He would be transferred across the Danube into Czechoslovakia where a part of the original plan would be revived and a helicopter would take him up to the German border. From there, another chopper would carry him into the US base at Frankfurt.

'Thank you very much,' Alexei replied. 'But I will wait and see.'

'Ouch.' said Jack. 'That hurt, but it was a fair comment, I suppose. You have the papers with you, about the *Biopreparat* programme?' Alexei looked him straight in the eye. 'When I see my wife, you see papers.'

'Understood,' Jack acknowledged that he had fences to mend. Jack spent the greater part of their journey quizzing Alexei about his escape route and what had gone wrong. He became only too aware of how close the whole exercise had come to disaster. The contribution of Josefina and her family had proved to be priceless.

As they skirted the small town of Labatlan, a Hungarian police car overtook the camper van and drove alongside the Citroen, the passenger appearing to call across to the Citroen crew. The police car went in front and the others followed, turning off on a side road beyond the town.

Alexei could see the lights of boats on the Danube when the police car stopped and the others drew alongside. The Citroen crew were out of their car quickly, and spread out with guns in their hands.

The driver of the camper van turned to Jack and said, 'All clear.'

Jack slid the side door open and stepped out. 'Let's go, Alexei. This is where we take the boat.'

Alexei stepped down from the van into almost total darkness. Jack took his arm and led him towards the river. Alexei was aware of people in front and behind him. He heard the gentle splashing of the river against the bank and felt the surface underfoot change to level metal. A powerful engine started and the outline of a big launch became clear to him as his eyes adjusted. He was on a jetty with the launch alongside. Hands helped him step into the launch where he was guided into a low cabin. Jack joined him and the engine growled as they moved out into the mighty river.

Five minutes later, the engine noise dwindled and the sensation of forward motion died. Muffled voices came to Alexei and the boat bumped as it came alongside another jetty.

Jack led him out of the cabin and onto the jetty where they were ushered up a track and into a waiting car. The car journey was only about a mile, and then they were out and walking towards a helicopter whose engine started to whine as they approached it.

Alexei and Jack strapped themselves into seats behind the pilot and they were quickly airborne. The pilot transmitted a brief message into his radio mike.

The lights of towns and villages sparkled below them as they gained altitude and sped off in a north-west direction.

The film on television had kept Katya's attention for some time, but, as it came to an end, her doubts and fears found their way to the front of her mind.

Sensing the mood, Jean stood up briskly and said, 'I'll make the coffee and see if we have any cookies left.'

Katya looked out of the apartment window, seeing the lights in the apartment blocks around her where she assumed families and couples were enjoying each other's conversation and in some cases just each other's presence.

She felt a dull ache of emptiness inside her, almost like that when her parents died, and a feeling of anger and frustration at her own inability to change events.

Freda came and put her arm round Katya's shoulders.

'Keep thinking positively, Katya. We all want your man to come home to you. It's going to happen, I'm sure.'

'Only words,' sighed Katya.

Jean came back into the room with a coffee pot and a cookie jar and placed them on a low table. She poured out coffee and handed a cup to Katya when the telephone rang. Freda was nearest to it and answered it. She listened for a few moments, then said, 'Thanks for that. I'll tell her.'

The others were watching her.

She smiled at Katya and said, 'That was Fred Delaney. He just got the call. Your man is on the helicopter. He should be here around midnight.'

Jean whooped and jumped up. Katya sat with a faraway smile on her face, tears coursing down her cheeks.

'Just you cry, honey. Get it out of your system,' said Jean. We got plenty of time to put your face back on before he gets here.'

Alexei was relieved that the plans were working, at last. The helicopter flew past the larger conurbations, Bratislava, Brno and Ceske Budejovice whose lights he could see in the distance, before finally landing near the border village of Strazny.

A car displaying diplomatic plates whisked them over the border into Germany where a police car of the German Border Police, the *Bundesgrenzshutz*, escorted them to their base at Grafenau. At the base, an American army helicopter was waiting for them, and once again they took to the air.

The earlier excitement had passed and tiredness took over. Alexei was soon asleep, and Jack switched off the earphones to let him rest.

Jack felt a great sense of relief that things had come right, eventually. Maybe he would seriously consider the retirement his wife was suggesting, and give himself time to go back to the world of academia, an option which was becoming ever more attractive. Harvard or Yale perhaps; or even Oxford or Cambridge. He smiled to himself.

When the helicopter started the descent towards Frankfurt,

Jack gently shook Alexei awake and told him where they were. Below them, there appeared to be street lights in every direction. The pilot banked slightly to correct his direction and then they came over an airfield with American planes lined up along one side.

The helicopter landed close to some hangars where a group of people waited, alongside several cars. Jack and Alexei climbed out and were met by Fred Delaney who ushered them into a car which carried them to a large building beyond the runway.

Alexei looked all around him for that lovely face he longed to see again. He was tired and a felt confused by all that was happening to him.

Fred Delaney led the way into the building and opened the door into a large room, comfortably furnished with armchairs and low tables.

A number of men, some in uniform others in plainclothes were waiting to welcome Alexei, and Jack.

Alexei looked around the faces then turned to Jack. 'Where is she?' he pleaded.

Fred walked to another door where he knocked and opened it. A blonde whirlwind came charging past him crying, 'Alexei.'

Alexei stood and opened his arms as Katya threw herself at him. 'At last,' they said in unison.

Jack rubbed his hand over his weary face. 'Amen to that,' he said. 'Now I need a drink.'

A hand clapped his shoulder and he looked round to see a former colleague who was now highly placed in the State Department.

'Frank! What are you doing here? I haven't seen you for years.'

'Jack, this was a really important job and we have all been

holding our breath. I knew that if anyone could do it, it was you. You obviously worked your way round the pitfalls and pulled the rabbit out of the hat.'

'Yes,' said Jack. 'Thanks to those London bobbies.'

'London bobbies? What the hell are you talking about?'

'Frank, you could not make it up. Get me a drink and I'll tell you the story. Nobody is going to believe it.'

Epilogue

Most names have been changed to avoid any embarrassment, except Colonel Laszlo Vary. He completed his police service and was co-opted into the Hungarian Home Office as a special adviser. Laszlo proved to be a good friend, and my wife and I met up with him several times in Budapest. With his wife and his sister, he spent a holiday with us and enjoyed sightseeing in the West Country. Sadly, he died of pancreatic cancer in 2008. He is missed.

Jack Bergen did retire a couple of years later and enjoyed a return to the academic world. When I last spoke to him, he and his wife were very content with their new life.

The London bobbies made the return journey in their minibus, spending a day with the Bratislava police, and had a convivial evening with them. They travelled on to Bonn, where the Nordrhein Westfalia police were great hosts.

When they got back to London, they found that their charity sponsorship had taken a leap beyond the ten thousand pounds mark.

Princess Diana donated £500. They were the most successful fund-raisers in 1991 for the Foundation for Conductive Education.

They did some more charity rides, including a marathon ride from London to Rome two years later, when they met Pope John Paul II.

That is another story.

THE END